I've met your soul

AYESHA MUSHTAQ

INDIA · SINGAPORE · MALAYSIA

ISBN 979-8-88591-603-5

In the name of Allah, the most Gracious, the most Merciful.

All praise is for Allah, the lord of the worlds. Without his guidance and the constant support of Mamma, Daddy, my Brothers, Arqam and Rumaisa, I wouldn't have completed this. Dedicating this to you all, I couldn't thank you enough for always being by my side.

Contents

Contents

Preface

One of the primarily things I believe in a completion of task or achievement is mindset. Until the phase of formal operational stage of cognitive development, I've been privileged to be a part of growth mindset and a supportive family in a culture different to native. Carting back to native place, I could figure out the ambience being affected to a maximum extent, in short a 180° twist to the life. Nevertheless, sparking the extinguishing fire, keeping the zest alive, I knew I belonged to somewhere else. And this journey of identifying myself led to completion of debut in writing, which I started at the age of nineteen. The process consumed whole two years but it was a labour of love. Simultaneous to pursuing bachelor's, this has been possible because of my affection towards reading and writing. The phrases, poems and beautiful scripts always fancied me. Persisting the urge to give a try on it being an debutant though. Besides the desire to pen down , I learnt that If one's blessed with a talent, then he/she must render it's right to the creator and that the precise way of fulfilling the right is to spread his message. This book henceforth is an attempt to do the same. Olivia is an educated and sensible protagonist, that every young girl relates to as an ideal. There's no black and white in the story, every character is a protagonist in their life, and fate is the antagonist. This ubiquitous concept is the least presence of impracticality although being a fiction genre. The significance behind is to make the content relatable and applicable to all my readers.

Philosophies, perception and pen, that's all I carry on the way,

To the edge of dawn from the strike of midnight, On a delusion I might stop, Until my conscience reminds, My soul craves to write, My soul yearns to write.

CHAPTER ONE

'She passed away the last evening' A feeble whispering voice played as Olivia checked a voice message left by Clara an hour ago.

Olivia played it twice, over and over again to make sure that she's mistaken. Sadly, she heard it right. Tears rolled down her cheeks and something hard hit her heart every time she reminisced it moment after moment. It was beyond endurance to believe that her mother breathed her last. She sat in despair on the chair, pushing the plate away, as the alarming news announced loss of appetite in her body. Covering her hand with another, she leaned by the chair as her head turned numb, with the mix of emotions. She had just begun to eat, soon after returning from work and it was not what she had expected after a dog-tiring long day.

Olly! Will you take some more fries? Ryan called from kitchen. She remained silent until the third time he asked repeatedly and bought some for her. Screeching the chair opposite to her, he began to gobble. He bunged up his lunch noticing her in a bizarre quite. 'What's up Olly?'

He inquired. Olivia could not help prevent sobbing; realising the intensity Ryan held her hand and asked afresh; 'what's wrong Olly?' Ryan hadn't known a bit, but his tone was consoling. She burst into tears and face-palmed crying on his question, Resting her elbows over the table and scraping fingers through her brown hair, making a true attempt to gulp down her pain, she walked upstairs to the bed. Olivia didn't speak a word but till now Ryan was aware of the cause behind her grief. He let her cry her heart out. She tried speaking but ended up, stammering and fell asleep covering her face with the pillow.

****

Sitting beside the silently weeping Olivia, Ryan considered suggesting a visit to Whitakers; giving it a second thought he concluded the idea was vain. Mrs Victoria Whitaker was in her late seventies. She had battled many hard knocks in life to make the ends meet after Alfred had abandoned her along their four children. Olivia underwent a tough childhood. Being the eldest child of family, compelled her to take over the burden on shoulders. From distributing newspapers to selling flower bouquets on roadside, working as a salesgirl in shops or a waitress in the coffee cafe, Olivia didn't realise when her childhood fled. Responsibilities weren't only bounded to straying outside, it demanded many other traits; may it be starving all night, because leaving over the food for younger siblings or taking care of Isabella while Billy and James completed schooling and Victoria did the lawns and the gardens. She was accustomed to find contentment in concern of siblings and mother, from preparing their meals or playing with them, massaging exhausted mother making sure that they are fulfilled. It was certain, Olivia forever longed for the love and peace of a happy family.

Walking down the memory lane she remembers marrying Ryan Wilson was the first decision she took for her own, it was the first time ever in the years spent that she happened to be selfish. However this didn't go down well with Victoria. She could justify it in her own terms and perspective. Alfred had fled Cardiff to marry Laura, Albert Wilson's only sister or more specifically Ryan's aunt. She was fearful for her daughter, that the fortune might play the same game with Olivia.

Victoria was diagnosed kidney failure a couple of years ago. Her health became critical at the heart attack she suffered four months ago. It never recovered and deteriorated day after day. Olivia geared up the courage to visit her mother last Sunday, but she failed to recognise them as well. It wasn't the millionth time she was visiting her ill mother at the death door. Alas, she had successfully visited her almost after half a decade.

****

Olivia woke at midnight. Her stomach was growling, but more than that she felt a twinge in her heart reminding about the catastrophe occurred. She didn't want to mourn anymore. 'Let's have dinner Olly' Ryan spoke, please take care of your health; you're starving since morning.' He sat by her side all the time.

There was an eerie silence at the table, Olivia sat leaning on the table not wanting to eat anything, Ryan passed the plate to her and put two large slices of cheesy pizza, it was Olly's favourite. ' ketchup?...Uhm...chilli flakes?' he offered. But she refused.

She was perplexed, overwhelmed by a mix of emotions, she felt guilty but didn't want to know why, she felt broken for losing her biggest support, she felt unfortunate for being years apart from her mother, she felt hurt, for her mother didn't understand her, she felt cursed because she couldn't even witness the corpse. felt annoyed cause she didn't want to mourn over it, but she could not help.

Breaking the long silence once more Ryan interrupted her thoughts 'you've got a check up appointment on

Thursday, remember?'

It appeared as though Olivia spoke after an eternity, 'oh yeah I almost forgot it, I think I must take a leave, as you return from office we'll drive to the hospital.

'That's brilliant 'Ryan replied gratefully, as she surprisingly spoke.

'This had to happen someday Olly, I understand what you're going through, and I sincerely wish if I could help, but you can't meet the expense of spoiling your health over it. Negativities mustn't surround you. Next week, you'll step into seventh month of gestation period.' Ryan mentioned at the bed time conversation. Followed by a long exhausting day, he fell asleep.

Olivia knew Ryan was dying inside for her. He wasn't responsible for Victoria's death but he was partly responsible for the broken ties between the mother daughter duos. He never admitted it but Olly always knew Ryan felt guilty about it. Olly never blamed Ryan for any of the consequences; she knew he was worth it. He is a man of golden heart, Olivia thought.

****

After the strong criticism and strict denial from orthodox Victoria, and her sons, Olivia was left with the last choice to plump for court marriage, with the assistance of Ryan she executed the idea only hoping that her mother would accept their relation since it would have become officially authorized by the time. To her, misfortune Victoria remained adamant.

CHAPTER TWO

Four months ago, after a prolonged debate and series of discussions, Olivia resolved to pay a visit to Whitakers and burst the bubble besides. She woke up early in the morning, dressed up well-heeled, and her wedding ring of course, with an intention to convince her mother that Ryan wasn't among the deceivers; bought a sorry card, flower bouquet, a tray full of sweets as a treat for Isabella, also her scan reports to share with them and what not she wished to take along her except Ryan.

He was a significant other but a man of policies too. Olivia was certain that he would never refuse if ever she would ask him to throw a visit to accompany her at Whitakers, but she minded his self respect. He would never do that happily. After all, years ago their last meeting didn't end on a good note, in fact matters turned worse that time. Considering the grudges grown over the time Olivia just informed him rather than offering an invitation to a house, where even her membership was at stake. She prepared his breakfast and left to the office prior to Ryan, which had never happened in the years. Not because Olivia was a couch potato, instead Ryan was a methodical gentleman. Winding up the office work speedily, she made the final touch in the washroom and started to her home.

'Home?' she thought to herself, it wasn't her home now, it was just a house where her previous family resided, but she couldn't deny the good memories she made in that place either. She felt an adrenaline rush as she reached nearer to the lane, reminiscing the last time she left the way, firmly determined never to return again. how's the irony of life, she smirked and parked the car.

Sitting in the car along with the butterflies in stomach, finger nail between the teeth and thoughts creating traffic jam in her mind, she thought, 'What if an old man opens to the fiftieth knock and says this place is abandoned since years! No, no! How's that supposed to happen, what will be their response, a never ending hug? Bursting into tears, happy reunion? Or an apology from Whitakers to Ryan, plentiful possibilities surrounded her mind. Was she really expecting all that? She didn't want to think further, she was excited to see her family after five long years.

As she walked to the door, nothing displayed like before, lawn was a well maintained garden with myriad collection of flowers, the house seemed to be renovated, walls brightly painted and it seemed as though James and Billy were doing well. Not making notice of the bell switch, she knocked the door hesitatingly, with a subconscious Ahem, and a gulp of anxiety. Waiting for an answer Olivia overheard the conversation inside.

'Check the door, Billy.' A faint, subdued yet recognisable voice spoke.

'Now who's this blind guest, too lazy to ring the bell' A tepid, cold tone sounded,

Olivia's heart accelerated, upon listening to the footsteps progressing towards the door, she wished if she could escape now, or become invisible. Her heart skipped a beat, as the opening door revealed Victoria.

'MOMMY!' Olivia said. Tears filling in her eyes, she stood stunned.

'What brings you here?' Not wasting the second moment, Victoria turned her gaze and inquired. Her tone made no difference between Olivia or any stranger or even any unwanted advertiser passing by.

Isabella sneaked from the window, she was grown up now, she could still read her eyes, they were begging for her return, behind her stood a new face, whoever she was, she appeared to be pleased at her sight.

Pretending unnoticed, Olivia looked back at Victoria to find her closing the door.

She held back the bouquet, taken aback by her reaction, blank at mind and no words to speak...

'I'm pregnant' she whispered, with trembling voice, her gestures pleading forgiveness,

Victoria lifted her head and made an eye to eye contact as though astonished by the news, but to her disappointment it wasn't a matter of her concern.

'Ever met that man?'

Olivia comprehended she was alluding to Alfred

'He died years before I married Ryan' she yelled helplessly, explaining no living cause of clash preserved.

Paying no heed to prolong conversation further, Victoria ruthlessly banged the door, on her face.

Furious at the conduct, she proceeded to the car with heavy steps, flinging all the stuff she had, on the lawn; Cursing herself why the hell did she made a blunder to visit these dead hearts.

Just when she was about to leave; that same lady she saw behind Isabella, knocked at the window of the car, signalling 'stop'. Olivia thought for a moment and lowered the glass.

'Hey I m Clara, James' wife'

'Nice meeting you' she answered with a formal smile, flaring her nostrils.

Clara handed a piece of paper to her, she placed it at the dashboard, unwilling to read, and drove away devastated.

Shattered by the exhibition of brutality, she felt worthless, tears rolling down her cheeks; she went to the house and buried her face in the pillow, of guilt. But Guilty for what; for marrying Ryan, was it such a blunder, but he never proved himself to be a mistake. She was sure about never being deserted.

Olivia was a lady of peace. She always believed in maintaining relations at heart, growing nil grudges even against a pet, she loved every person in her life, because she knew the pain of being stranded. She wished to sow the seeds of love, compassion and forgiveness and believed that fortune will reap the same for her. She was a fair complexioned, incredibly thin and tall twenty-five. Her hazel shaded large eyes expressed her profound and serene soul. She had brown wavy hair, of medium length.

The next morning, Olivia unfolded the chit to find Clara's contact no. written on it. It was on her way to office, so she paid no heed in saving it into her phone contacts. 'Now, why on earth would Clara need to talk me!' she thought.

Olivia narrated the entire incident to Camilla, her co worker and a companion close to her heart. Olivia was a manager at the Johnson's bookstore, owned by Fredrick Johnson; a close friend of Ryan's. Camilla worked as a data analyst; they've been working together for almost three years now.

'You must call her, I think'. Camilla suggested

'I presume mommy battled worse in these years'

'If that's the case I insist you to call her, don no what stopping you'

'What if she tells me never to show again...?' Olivia thought, tapping fingers.

' or tells you Olly, your face looks so oily!' Camilla added jokingly, breaking into fits of laughter, while Olivia threw *a not so funny* look. Neither she commented sarcastically, nor Olivia got offended any time. The two girls always sipped coffee on a lighter note.

****

The couple took a start to see the doctor; Olivia had applied leave for a week, She felt like she couldn't manage her grief, health, domestic chores and office work all at a time.

She needed time. Time to analyse what all happened in the past months, passing away of her mommy, not a single message from her brothers, what was her fault after all, the decision to separate wasn't her, and it was her mother who insisted her to leave, where could she live then. Her last visit to Whitakers was not more than a catastrophe; she could never repeat the same.

They entered the hospital; a sense of excitement took over, every time they stepped inside...

'Mrs Olivia Whitaker'

Waiting for half an hour Olivia proceeded to the scan room.

Ryan gestured good luck to her and she gave a quick smile in response, unlike every time when she used to wink expressing positivity and gratitude.

'Good morning', Olivia greeted,

'Please be seated; let's get your blood pressure checked.'

Writing a few digits on the report slip, she added.

'Let's measure your weight'

Olivia stood on the weigh machine, and the nurse noted down the weight.

She lay straight on the bed to get her scan done.

'You may go to room no. 9; Doctor Emma smith will attend you.'

Olivia felt comfortable with her, she always wished to consult her, she spoke gently; her soft voice never failed to calm her nervousness. she entered the room, handing over the reports to doctor, she took her place followed by Ryan sitting beside her.

Dr Emma smith studied the reports, looking over the edge of rim of her glasses, 'Mrs. Olivia, are you undergoing any kind of stress, anxiety or something like that?' she asked.

'Actually my mother passed away...'. Olivia spoke dejectedly,

'Ohm I m sorry about that, but you need to take care of your health.

Your blood pressure has shoot up, you didn't put on a single ounce, since the last scan, I m worried, the condition is called preeclampsia, you need to take proper bed rest until delivery; these are the prescribed medicines you may collect it from the drug store.' Doctor Emma advised.

Ryan became tensed to hear the reports.

'You'll have to take rest Olly'. Ryan said.

Olivia nodded positively in response.

****

They entered the house and Olivia sat on the couch removing her sandals, while Ryan sat on the study table rereading the reports.' Hb 8, amniotic fluid – 9, blood pressure 140/90. 'Dr. Emma had already spoken to him, about Olivia's health, she was quite disappointed to see the reports, and so was Ryan.

'We need to talk Olly.' He sounded like a tedious professor, speaking to a student who's going to be suspended.

'I m listening' she guessed about the upcoming lecture which would obviously last more than it should be. She was rather blown by Ryan's new tolerance record, as she was expecting it to start on the way home; surprisingly he drove mute.

Ryan wasn't a calm person unlike Olivia. He loved Olly; he cared for her, which sometimes raise his temper but whenever he did it was a disguised care. More than anything he would take every effort for her health to improve.

'This is not the solution Olly, you need to grow up. You can't just take your health for granted; I know it kills you in. You need to speak up, you have to cry, just don't grow it in, it'll ruin you. Things don't work this way Olly, you must be strong. Trying not to express your pain doesn't make your fierce, the world goes on, and so must you. Your mourning has become a threat to your health, our baby's health; I would still never mind that, only if it could bring back her to life.' A vein popped out of his neck as he chided, and he tightened his jaw, controlling the urge to speak. While she listened to her, thankful of his support at the back of her mind.

'Tragedies take place, they're certain, it's not about what happens to you, it's about how you deal with the shit.' He added.

'Really? Ryan!!! Does this sound shit to you?' her breaking voice expressing the cracks formed at her heart. Her face grimaced, indicating the amount of pain greater than the physical prick.

'You're simply assuming it wrong Olly, I never meant that', Ryan walked towards her, held her shoulders tight, annoyed at the misinterpretation, Olivia struggled to get rid of his hold; she didn't need any explanations further. It wasn't about the ego; it was something that hit her sentiments. She shrugged hard to drop his arms with a heavy sigh.

'I'm worried about you, that is it Olly.' his voice turned serene, like an accused plaintiff's lawyer whose about to be defeated.

Distraught at the argument she went upstairs and locked herself into the room. Lying on the bed, looking upon their framed photograph, she thought, 'I was a fool to believe

this man, let alone condolences, at the least he must have understood my grief!' This wasn't the first fight they had in the years spent, but this was a different one indeed. She cried aloud, holding onto her bump, like a mother hugging her child, like a lost warrior, feeling so lonely at the moment, such that her heart could ache, for any person it was a random argument, but only she knew how it pricked. The thought haunted her, that she misinterpreted Ryan, he had mistakenly revealed what her mother meant to her. All their other fights comprised of misunderstandings, untold surprises, anger that was disguised love and at times pillow fights; this time it was the difference in their perception towards the loss of her mother, and that wasn't a petty issue for Olivia.

CHAPTER THREE

At mid of the night, Olivia woke up to her growling stomach. This was a very unusual scenario, lights were still turned on, blanket wasn't put upon her, and on top of everything Ryan wasn't sleeping beside her. She walked drowsily, tying her messy bun, to the door and realised she had locked the door last night. Feeling sorry about the thought that Ryan must have been sleeping out there, she walked down to discover bizarre silence and gloom. She eloped the railing, standing on the middle of staircase she called out,

'Ryan! Are you there?

The silence continued; as she headed back to the room, all of a sudden lights turned on, her heart took a leap and mind creating scenes of a typical burglar standing with a gun on her back, while she turned back to spot the cause,

'HAPPY BIRTHDAY OLLY!'

The crowd chorused, and she took a breath of peace that leaped into a rush in adrenaline, it was evidently a surprise from Ryan, she chortled with delight and walked down carrying a palpable smile on her face, Camilla had come along Richard, Hannah, a friend of Olivia, Neil and Alex too were a part of event. Olivia was startled by the surprise, the décor appeared elegant, the stack of packed gifts also elevated her smile, she quickly slid her gaze to pretend unnoticed. Apart from the guests Ryan was dressed up too and looked graceful. He was a well built, tall guy, black hair styled upturned, almond shaped brown eyes and a sharp jawline. His olive skinned cheeks pulled inwards as he smiled, forming a shallow dimple and revealing uniform beaming teeth. He wore ritzy clothes, his style always remained undisputed. The icing on the cake was the cake, fondant layers of chocolate, surrounded with crispy wafers, white note read 'mom to be soon'; the phrase which accelerated her heart and brought an unpreventable curve to her lips.

'Hey, when did you all come?' Olivia asked delighted

'Well, Ryan has been planning this since last week, and we are here!' Camilla shrugged, heartily happy for surprising her friend.

'Camilla approached me day before yesterday and I thought it wasn't a bad idea to throw a surprise visit to you,' Hannah popped up.

'And honestly speaking we never mind having birthday treats 'Neil joked

' Especially when it costs you nothing 'Alex looked at Richard, pulling his leg, tauntingly.

'Oh please, my honourable presence was cordially invited, unlike other wanderers who run to the smell of feasts' Richard teased back.

'Who's a wanderer here; I am a sincere well wisher of my friend Olly' Neil answered. Olivia rolled her eyes at the cheesy dialogue and smirked.

They were friends and shared keen bond, the cascade of their jokes was never ending, not too close and not too far; in short they were simply a family.

'Oh let's cut the cake Olly' , Camilla said

'Just love it' Olivia exclaimed.

'I know why you adore it because the number twenty six isn't written over there, its hiding your age Olly! 'Hannah teased again,

'Who said twenty six, its thirty two' Camilla winked.

'I don't really tag on these age concealing tactics, in any case, I'm still so young', Olivia trailed off, a sense of embarrassment took over as she realised she was wearing a tank top and a mismatch pyjamas. Reconsidering the thought she decided not to dress up now, as it would get more awkward to take everyone's time for nothing but to get ready.

She stood beside Ryan, clenched her palm tight in his fingers and the other hand on her belly, she closed her eyes to wish for her dreams, with the belief that they shall be accomplished, not because of her faith on creator, but because of the simplicity in her prayers, She wished not a pin more than the well being and togetherness of her family, which shall soon be shared by a little soul too,; being abandoned, was a nightmare for her.

Everybody took suitable positions and Richard took his phone out for a wide selfie, after all preserving memories was also as vital as making memories.

Cake cutting was followed by late night dinner and of course it's never too late for gossips, Camilla had presented a baby boy essentials set, Hannah gifted a large sized photo frame which was supposed to be hung on the wall after their baby's first photo shoot, Neil and Alex together bought them couple's watch set, and the most awaited and special present from Ryan was a book '50 guidelines for would be moms'! Ryan has always been daft at the ideas of gift, let alone this occasion, he gifted her an alarm clock on their first anniversary, ' Anti aging wrinkle free' on the second, third was comparatively a better one an electric toothbrush and the list goes on; but Olivia she wasn't materialistic, she was obsessed about Ryan, his efforts to surprise her and his concern towards her never ran short to suffice her contentment. While speaking to Hannah, Olivia reminisced about the argument she had with Ryan, and out of reflex she glanced at him. Ryan was pouring juice in the glasses to be served and caught her staring, interpreting the stare was an expression of gratitude, he winked back at her, signalling 'mention not'. Olivia decided to let go of it, his one smile was worth it, she could have forgave all his crimes if ever committed, he was a precious gem she concluded. She couldn't afford to ruin the precious moments by holding on to minor arguments. She was sincerely happy for the surprise.

Days were dragged into weeks and finally a month later Olivia decided to call Clara,

'Hello Clara, Olivia here; err James sister ... you remember,'

'Oh hi, just a second' after a while she resumed, it seemed she walked into a quiet place, or maybe moving away from the sight of Victoria,

'Finally, you showed up, Isabella had been waiting for you since ever I know her existence, just to keep in touch I thought I shouldn't miss the opportunity so gave you the contact number, I will inform her about your call'

'And where is she now? Is it college? She was a nerd since kindergarten..I know.'

'No it's actually some sort of beauty pageant '

'How's mommy?' Olivia couldn't help the quiver in her voice.

'Err...she's absolutely fine.'

'What about James, and how's Billy, my little champ?'

'They're all doing great,'

Giving a long pause Olivia continued 'They don't miss me, right?' She asked in despair.

Clara remained silent for a while as if puzzled by the question, 'they do, and yeah they keep talking about you,'

Dejected by her quietude, she deduced from their conversation

'I m expecting a call from Isabella anytime; pleasure talking you,'

'Uhm, on a serious note, don't expect a call, I mean I don't think she's ever going to call you, actually she wanted to, until you last visited here,'

'And what sin have I committed after that?' Olivia's voice turned brusque at the discourse,

'The fact is that Mrs. Victoria is a dialysis patient, her kidneys gave up almost two years ago, she's been fighting hard to keep up her well being, in fact it was a joint effort; everyone in the house preserved a composed and unruffled atmosphere and at long last she gained a state of stability by mid November.

Matters became shoddier post your visit, followed by a compliant of severe chest pain, an hour later she suddenly collapsed, upon regaining conscious she was undergoing shortness of breath, James had called the ambulance and they rushed to the hospital, a week later she was discharged.

Contrary to the fact that it was a coincidence or a consequence of your meeting; everybody assumes that you're an offender.

Isabella was the only person who awaited you since I've known them all, after this mishap, she compelled her conscience to agree with everyone else,

This is the reason most probably she s not going to contact you,'

Olivia became distressed upon being informed of the callous truth,

'You believe the same about me right?' Her trembling voice uttered

'Well, to be frank; your side of the story is still a mystery to me, and until that's exposed ill have to believe what they do.' Clara sounded bold and just.

'Pleasure talking you INDEED' Olivia said sarcastically and ended the call.

Olivia was entirely shattered; those words pierced her heart beyond tolerance, struck her emotions across crying. Letting go off the previous experience, she was regretting to make a futile attempt to mend the broken ties. 'Why on earth did I choose to call her? How heartless have they grown to me? Anyway what's Clara's fault, who's she to me, she doesn't know me either.

No matter whatever turns up, I'm not going to change my mind' she decided, and her determination was nothing less than an oath, let alone exceptions. Disheartened at the series of trip over, this moment a firm verdict, the hopes of reunion were brought to a halt, and she was resolute.

CHAPTER FOUR

'Olly! You ready? Were getting late' this was the third time Ryan called her; he's been sitting in the car for past twenty minutes.

'No honey it's still quarter past one, max a five minute drive to the hospital and the appointment is at three, don't you think that you are hurrying for no reason,' Olivia explained slothfully.

'May I know what are you doing right now?'

'Am actually fetching that pink tunic with yellow strips which had turtle neck design...bought last winter from the red lady shop... think I wore it last at the dinner we had at Johnsons, remember?'

'Oh!! The night we bought along the huge teddy bear for his daughter as a present? Amazing'

'And where's that amazing tunic?' she asked gratefully,

'No idea, I was just talking about the amazing dinner we had,'

No doubt that Ryan was an organised person, aware of every hook and corner of the house but as they say, 'exceptions prove the rule'; Olivia's belongings were excluded from the list.

She disconnected the call and flung away the phone on the bed then began searching the possible places she could find. At ten past two, she finally managed to get down putting on a blue top with beige pants carrying a bag for antenatal card, her scan reports etc., and a scarf rolled over her neck with neatly tied high pony, a few light brown strands falling on her shoulders, highlighting her jaw line. She wore a nude shade lipstick, complimenting her dark, long eyelashes. He silently adored her, walking from the door into the car, no matter they knew each other since years, but some people deserved eternal admiration and Olivia was one of them, beautiful in and out. She hustled to sit in the car, placing the bag on the back seat, adjusting her seat, pretending to be busy, so as to avoid Ryan's heated stare. Only if she knew the stare was a disguised contentment. Admiring the beauty of his wife; the appealing actions she does to avoid his anger, and of course the excitement of junior Ryan. Nevertheless, these minor wrangles were a proof of the resilient bond they shared.

It was a month now, since Olivia had been taking bed rest. This was a dreadful period spent for her, no office, no parties, no junk food and no night outs with friends. Well the latter wasn't prescribed by the doctor but fortune had prescribed though. Camilla had been busy with her office work, and Hannah was on a holiday trip to Malaysia. And Olivia wasn't in a mental state to make friends with the newly shifted neighbours. However she managed to drag it by watching movies, at times silently weeping thinking about her family, receiving well wishes from friends and ordering the food cravings she had, consoling herself to remain happy for her child, online shopping for the baby, and planning about the after birth event celebrations etc. Awaiting the marked date on the calendar, she counted days and hours to be free. She wanted to re-join her office, get rid of the bed rest; she was tired of the boredom. Undoubtedly, Ryan was with her; but obviously not always.

****

'Please be seated Mrs. Olivia,' Dr Emma smith said,

Checking the scan reports and her card, she spoke

'I must say you're health reports are quite impressive, good going girl! Besides reports I must appreciate your punctuality,'

Looking at the clock she sniffed, at dot three she was present opposite to her.

Checking the calendar, she marked a date and asked her to consult 15 days

'No more bed rest please, Doctor,' Olivia requested

'Sure, do these prescribed exercises, and go for walk once a day, but remember be calm and slow, no jogging, running or heavy steps. And try to rest as much as possible.'

Olivia collected her files and left the cabin, with a beaming smile and thank you. Sitting in the car, she discussed the reports with Ryan. Together they were in high spirits, hearing the good news Ryan decided to go for a long drive and celebrate their happiness. Olivia was ecstatic, enjoying such petite moments with Ryan was life for her, she would miss these drives after delivering the baby she thought to herself. But who would have time to miss these rides, she would be busy enjoying with her baby. She rubbed her hand on her bump and felt vigorous movements of the baby, adding more excitement to her happiness; she couldn't help but hoorayed out loud with laughter, waving her scarf in the air, leaving Ryan amused.

'I am so grateful to life, for finally blessing me' she confessed as they neared their home.

'Yeah, so am I' he shrugged, parking the car.

'There's still an incomplete dream of us' she enunciated. His brows crawled, questioning why.

'You had a dream of becoming a journalist. Right?' She announced tucking her hair behind the ear.

'Oh! My happiness and peace lies in yours and our babies, I am not a career obsessed guy, for god's sake!' he chortled.

She gazed at him, disagreeing.

****

As The phone beeped, Olivia checked the message it was from Clara,

Texted 'Mrs. Victoria's health is worsening day by day, she's admitted since last week, and I fear she might not do any better, you must show here asap. Visiting hours are from 5 to 7 PM'

An attached file of the hospital's location was sent.

Reading the message she bent her head over the desk, then sat straight running her fingers hard on her cheeks, just before she could make a call to Camilla, She caught her sight at the library door. Pushing the chair backwards, she checked for sir Benjamin on the sides of the corridor as she neared Camilla. After a non verbal greeting they exchanged through eyes and smile, she displayed her the text message received from Clara.

'To err is human; to forgive is divine Olly, turn blind eye to others, go and see your mom, maybe she needs you.'

'Thank you but I am good as a human have no wishes of being divine'

'Olly! Camilla rolled her eyes, 'you know very well, how critical is this decision'

'No she doesn't need me, why will she even want to see me? Neither does she wants me nor her children. You very well know that too.'

'Right Olivia, I too suppose you mustn't waste your time.' Camilla agreed expressing sarcasm.

She stood baffled, scribbling in her notepad, just as Camilla was about to walk away, she called her, 'listen'

'Hmm'

'You know what, actually this Clara has kept me on hook, and it's not that easy to let it go,

As always the obstacle in their conversation had entered the corridor,

Supervisor of the branch, Mr. Benjamin, was on rounds, wearing chequered under his uniform dungaree, lifting his stomach, as of a sack tightly stuffed, he carried a signature style of notepad in his hand, with grumpy wicked and wrinkled face his round glasses resting on the nose, below apparently shrunk eyes, whose presumed vision might be 7/6, and his lips glued reasoning his obvious silence. In short a 'BOSS' for every office.

Olivia and Camilla hustled to find a desk in the library, unluckily all the seats were occupied except two; one at the computer and another at the study both the chairs were poles apart and they took their places before he could enter the library. Standing at the threshold, Mr. Benjamin supposedly gave a stare at Camilla for almost one whole minute, she was scrolling on the computer, pretending to note something on the pad. Next was Olivia's turn, and he moved limping unsteady towards her with his flat stare over the rim of his glasses.

'What is it you do?' he asked in a gruff voice.

'Uhm, well, I was here... making a list of the bestselling books of the past month...sir.'

Olivia spoke the last words confident and loud, a smile crept on her lips, grateful to herself that she made up the excuse very well.

'And where are you studying from?' Again a gruff voice questioned.

'Here it...............' Olivia took a pause gesturing to her notepad, which had turned invisible at the moment! Her desk was clean, hands were empty, no desktop, her eyes widened and lips parted in shock, leaving her stunned and ultimately embarrassed. She turned back at Benjamin with an expressionless face.

'I see you working, very dedicated' Benjamin taunted, noting down something in his book, probably related to Olivia.

To avoid his direct stare she pretended to search the book under below the desk screeching her chair back that got bumps on Benjamin's skin; hoping that he would leave anytime. But he stood firm taking a notice of the play. She got up from below the table with no reply to see that Benjamin had turned around to walk out meanwhile all other faces looked fixedly at her, making her feel sheepish to walk out.

****

'Two cappuccino please' Camilla placed an order at the cafe.

'Damn it! just stop' Olivia got cranky at Camilla for her nonstop laughter.

'Good for you, this was hysterical Olly!' she replied 'anyways I just can't believe that you don't remember you handed me your notepad and phone spotting that Coffin dodger and you tell him that you're making a list of bestselling..'

'This will be a memorable one for all the staff members' Camilla added after a pause.

'Can we discuss that for we have come here?' Olivia asked fuming.

'There's no reconsideration or second thought to the matter Olly.' Camilla answered sincerely.

'Fine; Today's Saturday, most probably I'll see her tomorrow evening.' She marked, placing the cup on the table.

'I still can't believe Olly' Camilla helplessly broke into fits of laughter again.

'Stop it please!' Olivia chided.

****

Next evening, as decided; Olivia and Ryan reached the hospital. Olivia had inquired Clara about the room no. earlier, so they walked into the elevator and knocked at the door 404, Billy opened the door silently and gazed upon the couple, continuing the silence, he sat back at the chair, scrolling down in the phone. Mrs. Victoria lied subconscious on the bed, tied among pipes, her drowsy eyes half open, hands left loose on the sides, a miserable plight to witness.

'Olivia sat by her side, giving a gentle kiss on her fore head running her fingers through her grey hair, tears filled her eyes, blurring the vision as she placed her hand in her palm. Her throat had clogged up with emotions. How wrinkled had her skin turned, her lean spine was the strongest of all once. 'Mummy' she whispered and it seemed that she missed it. This time in a very audible voice she spoke up, 'mummy'. Mrs. Victoria looked up at Olivia with her drowsy eyes, released her hand of Olivia's hold, and tied both her hands at the chest, like a child behaving to a stranger. Ryan stood by the window placing the fruits and flowers they had brought on the table. 'It seems she has lapse of memory' Billy the royal highness finally made an effort to speak. 'Thank god you didn't' Ryan muttered. 'Sorry?' Billy questioned instantaneously frowning. 'I feel sorry too' Ryan changed the gear.

Almost an hour later, the door flung open, and a lady marched in to the room wearing high heels, handbag on her arm, a wrist watch and diamond ring wrapped her delicate finger, long nails, neatly polished; she must be probably a fashion model. A goggle rested on her forehead; going perfect with her blonde sleek ponytail. A face resembling somebody in Olivia's memory lane yet not sure of recognition. Placing her bag, she proceeded the perfectly manicured hands with heavy steps towards Olivia and yelled, holding her collar, staring into her eyes 'why are you here?, are you not done with this, that you've come here to ruin the left over. Mind it Olivia, you are only responsible for mommy's condition.' Folding into fists she took her hands back, and a step away.

'Both of you can leave.' She ordered in outstare, waiting for them to step out of the room. Ryan held Olivia's hand furiously to leave while she was standing speechless yet again.

****

At bedtime, Olivia was moisturizing her hands and applying nail paint, still in a daze about the appalling incident. This time she was upset though, but then she wasn't expecting something better. It was her conscience, Ryan's and Camilla's compulsion at which she decided to visit her mother at the death door. She kept pondering over the incident, just then the word lady used ' mommy' strikes into her head, and she sat upright neglecting the bun in her oven. After all there was a perfectly rational explanation to her blow.

The familiar face was none other than Isabella Whitaker.

CHAPTER FIVE

Now, Soon to be parents' excitement knew no bounds, from dinner table discussions to bedtime conversations; baby was the only subject they talked on. Ryan stood by the balustrade scrolling his phone, and Olivia sat in the bubble swing sipping their late night coffee admiring the full moon amidst the dark clouds, the glittery stars bright but not more than their lives, this phase was beautiful and it just felt complete. 'Have you thought about the name Olly?' Ryan initiated another baby related conversation.

'We'll name him something resembling with yours, like R initials, something kind of ROWAN' Olivia thought aloud.

'No cliché names Olly, we'll think of something newer you know' Ryan suggested. 'Listen here's a list of names' Ryan started reading out loud.

'Edmond...Amon...Dustin...Nah...nah...Uhm...hmm...Nah, no...I m not gonna name my pet even this one 'Ryan started to eliminate the names scrolling down his phone, and ended up quiet, maybe those were not of his choice.

Taking a sip of coffee, Olivia thought aloud 'I must probably join the office day after tomorrow'.

'What's wrong Olivia? you are supposed to rest, complete bed rest.'

Ryan instructed, placing his coffee mug at the table and sitting on the fence, still into his phone.

'Not anymore Ryan, I can work, I've inquired the doctor and even she has permitted. I very well remember the precautions to take. Moreover Camilla is gonna pick and drop me home.' she explained.

Ryan remained silent expressing disagreement.

'You okay?' Olivia questioned gazing at him awaiting a proper answer.

'Hmm' Ryan replied reluctantly keeping his phone aside.

'You know what Ryan; this bed rest was... it was a house arrest to me.

I can't live this way; I've never lived such since I woke to my conscious. Understanding the intensity of matter, however hard must have been it I tried my best to fit in and I did for the last month. But now I just can't.'

She explained further.

'Precaution is better than cure, Olly. One more month and you're safe. Our baby is gonna be safe. I cannot afford to take a risk Olly. It's not as easy as it seems to you.' he laid out his fears before Olivia.

'I was glad, you cared about me, but this care is suffocating me now Ryan, try to analyse my point as well' giving a pause she waited for Ryan to answer in agreement, and ended up sacrificing ' still if you feel so, then here am I surrendering to your command' presenting a statement of sarcasm.

'Thank you Olly, sooner or Later you'll realise, the wisdom in your decision.'

Ryan expressed gratitude, overlooking Olivia's face which had turned gloomy. Comparatively this wasn't the issue of concern for him. As every time, this time also Olivia set aside her decision for Ryan's. Olivia's personality fell into the category of those people, who could adjust with no's but definitely not ending up requesting, or pleading.

Sorry yes, please no . Amidst her practice she made sure that ego remained a stranger to their love. She could sacrifice anything for his charming smile, compromising on her decision every time, she was sure deep inside that someday Ryan's conscience will prove himself guilty rather than she herself concluding him to be a offender, ending up to embarrass him. The other side of the story was that no doubt he was a great partner who loved Olivia beyond measures, respected her desire of being self made and made no stone unturned to keep her face bloomed with gratitude. As a matter of fact Olivia's childhood lesson was to make every effort to keep up the family bonding by staying loyal; in short, being devoted to your partner. This habit of her had grown over the years and Ryan's nature had become subconsciously dominating to which she had never objected either.

'Poor battery backup' Ryan murmured and walked out of the gallery just when a battery low notification popped up on his screen or perhaps it was something else.

****

Next morning, Olivia sat at the bed, drowsy and still yawning as Ryan awakened her forcefully to have breakfast.

'Hello beautiful, am I the privileged one whom you had agreed to have your breakfast with, this blessed morning?' Ryan asked dramatically placing the tray on the bed.

Olivia remained tight lipped and stared at Ryan with sleepy eyes while her lips involuntarily spread into a smile looking at his comical expression.

'Presenting you the a glass of milk, eggs rich with proteins, delicious Welsh rarebit, promising to melt in your mouth with every bite you take, paired up with a considerable looking chef Ryan Wilson.'

'You're included in the menu, but out of the tray?' Olivia questioned sarcastically.

'No we're going to have it together.'

'Olly, I need to say you something' Ryan soberly putting a pause to the fun conversation they were having previously.

'You are hooked up with that red-haired early woman at your office?' Olivia guessed to tease him.

'Olly, I m serious,' he chided.

'Of course honey I know you are serious with her,' she was enjoying the snubbed expressions he kept throwing. He silently enjoyed the moments she laughed heartily.

'Ok! Come on, tell me this time I am serious', Olivia was all ears.

'Next week I have annual staff meeting in London; I'll have to stay there for a couple of days. Would you live at Camilla's until then?"

Olivia thought for a while and asked, 'London? What happened to Cardiff?'

They're planning the Inauguration ceremony of the new branch.

'Am I not supposed to accompany you?' Olivia inquired batting her long eyelashes.

'I would surely but you're not supposed to travel Olly'. Ryan explicated brushing her chin.

'I'll ask Camilla if she's not busy..., but there's a condition to this agreement!'

Olivia popped out with something. Mind it, this wasn't a request it was a condition that had to be fulfilled.

'I'll join the office right away tomorrow and continue till you return,

After a moment of thinking, Ryan looked into her eyes that were not less than that of a warrior at the war zone ready to fire, and then he gestured tick mark with his index finger indicating yes.

Olivia was full of appreciation for the treaty of peace, between the couple.

****

Post evening chores, Olivia dialled to Camilla

'Hey Olly, was sup,'

'Great and how are you doing?'

'I am doing well;'

'Hmm, just we were talking about you'

'Oh did I disturb at the gossip hour?'

'No actually I and John were planning a dinner outside' givinga pause she added 'you can join us either, if you're not tied up, double date you know,'

'That's so sweet, you people carry on, maybe some other time, and Ryan is not home yet'; giving a pause she continued 'next week, Ryan's got a meeting in London, I wanted to know.. If you're not occupied so'

'Sure, in fact it's a great idea; you are most welcomed gal pal'

'Thanks a million; I'll hang the phone before John hits me from over the phone for stealing your time.'

'See ya, take care Bubye'

Camilla was so much into PDAs, and John, in the past ten months he was probably the sixth reason of her existence she discovered, well the other five reasons were Xavier, Chris, David etc. It seemed this time it was a true and final love. Though Olivia didn't bother to believe her this time as well. Swiping away the Camilla tab from the task manager of her mind, Olivia was still happy and content with the deal they made. She thought of making a diary entry, her writings were usually philosophical one-liners or two-three pages written for a day and the size of entries were made for a delighted and sad incident respectively.

'I find your love, calming my soul like the fresh water waves embracing my feet, a satisfying scene to witness, and an urge to still until forever, like a bud just bloomed, like an enticing rose, every petal of which is vibrant, fragrance of its wafts along all the ups and downs' Just as she completed the sentence, the door bell rang; she closed her diary and placed it safely in the last drawer of desk.

****

On Monday evening, while Ryan was packing his bag, Olivia returned back home from the office, placing her bag on the table, she lie down tired.

Ryan bought her a glass of water and sat beside with a heavy sigh and superficial smile on face, preventing the emotions to takeover he added 'I've packed the bags, remind me if I am missing anything, your clothes, brush, towel, toothbrush, charger, wallet, medicines, file, socks, night dress.'

Olivia's eyes were filled with tears upon the realisation of the fact, that he would apart from her, may it be for two days, but separation was a hard pill to swallow. She gulped the clogged throat, hugged him, glanced at the clock and announced, 'promise me! Three days later at the same time 19:20, you will be seated right here with us.' The word us indicated Olivia and her unborn baby.

'Is that the deal? Then, pinkie swear!' he held her hand, folding the fingers and interlocked their little fingers, closing his fist hard until Olivia called out 'you are hurting me!' she took her phone out of the bag, stretching her arm in the opposite direction of light, the couple clicked a selfie.

He smiled adoring her for almost two minutes, his brown eyes began to get teary and the silence continued until she broke it, 'let's hurry it up you're getting late, no big deal Ryan; I've survived six lonnnnng years by you, I owe the right to get at least a three-day treat man!' she joked making the moment lighter.

****

Camilla had already come to pick her, Olivia locked the door, and Ryan headed towards his car, only after wrapping her arm around her giving a peck on forehead, and wishing each other to have great time. As both the friends sat in the car, Ryan walked out of his car, Camilla lowered the glass and he forewarned 'I m just a call away Olly, anytime you need; just text me up and god forbid if any emergency arises, rush to the nearest hospital.'

'The professor spirit has taken over on him' Camilla murmured, looking out, upon the display of unnecessary teachings.

'He assumes you a little one. Doesn't he?' Camilla asked as he walked away.

'Every individual has a different way of loving, that is his, and I am grateful to life's bounties. At times I get annoyed but then you've got to know that human nature never changes, whatever may be the circumstances, human is bound to do what he is and this is the rule of nature.' Olivia explicated.

'And what is your habit that you think you'd never leave?' Camilla questioned.

'Ahan... Let me think...' Olivia took a pause,

'Well, I believe I would never stop annoying Ryan the way I do' Olivia answered dreamily.

'Aww that's so sweet.' she replied. 'Any dinner plans tonight?'

'Passing by the dumballs road, we can't miss The Caribbean way' Olivia gave a voice to her cravings.

'Done!' the two agreed on the sea food dinner.

****

Camilla's apartment was a brew of memories and showpieces, it seemed like there were more photo frames than the bricks wall had. She had visited there several times but never to stay. On the right corner of the living room she had a ceramic crafted Mérida statue, reasonably because she believed she resembled her. And below it on the shelf were the souvenir she got from parts of the world she visited. Olivia concluded that the excuse she serves every weekend is not an excuse actually, it's a fact instead, obviously one would have to spend a day to tidy this up. And to be honest every hook and corner was spotless.

Camilla decided to sleep at the couch and Olivia would sleep at the bed, there was an extra room too, but Camilla was freaking out if her water breaks tonight.

At midnight Olivia lied adoring their selfie, how complete her life seemed with Ryan. Camilla rushed to the mirror tying her curls, applying a gloss on her lips and adjusting herself, switched off the light and put her lamp on, sat on the couch to answer the incoming video chat from John.

Olivia took her diary out made an entry in the flashlight of her phone,

'Neither am I a sixteen year old nor you are an eighteen, still I am reminiscing the days when our journey started and till date how have we grown up. Six years is no less time and we've covered it like a moment of celebration. The day when we first met at the Johnson's annual awards ceremony at the Broadway boulevard...the only year when I won the employee of the year award........."

After a while she paused writing and hurried to washroom, she frequently did as it was the last term of pregnancy, meanwhile Camilla sneaked into the diary as she kept bragging about the infinite talents she had, turning around the pages she confessed one more overloaded cheesy dialogue

'J, I have written something for you,...'

John spoke from the other side ' What is it?'

'you remember the other day I said you I hold a good grip at pen too,

'oh yeah, but when did you write?'

'...uhm...a couple of days ago...probably' she answered puzzled at the question

'I was just finding it hard to speak in front of you, anyway

My stealthy glance
met his intense gaze
A sparkle of smile,
and worlds set ablaze!',

'That's amazing Camilla, you're indeed full of surprises!'

'Oh thank-you it was just an attempt' she kept bragging and turned around to see Olivia fuming at her with eyes open wide in shock and she disconnected the phone at the moment while Olivia yelled 'you cheater! You're such a liar Camilla, I couldn't just believe you touched my diary without permission and even stole my poem!'

'No big deal Olly' Camilla tried normalizing the not less than a crime act.

Olivia hurried to close the diary and put in her bag, safe and secure in the millionth zip of her huge bag.

'You're right it won't be a bigger deal either when I will call John and reveal your offence.' Olivia warned giving a sigh.

'Do you want me to publish a mea culpa statement in tomorrows newspaper?' Camilla asked at rejection of apology. 'whatever' Olivia sniffed.

CHAPTER SIX

The following day Olivia woke not to the alarm instead to the alarming news by Camilla that they'll be leaving for London asap, 'get up Olly, gulp this down, and get ready we're going London' she brought her breakfast at bed, two toasted slice of brown bread with butter, glass of orange juice, fingerbowl, a knife, fork and neatly placed napkins, now Olivia realised the obvious reason of her jam-packed apartment,

'But why?' Olivia questioned.

'John has been waiting for this since a long time, he needs to visit his mother at the deathbed, and set about some property affairs as well..' Camilla explained.

'Waiting since a long time ...but for what?' Olivia was puzzled by the inadequate information.

'He had applied for a leave last week ago but luckily got granted today, and he said he wants me to meet her mom, as she won't be able to see us walk down the aisle' she turned crimson while spelling out.

'If I am not mistaken, you're checking him since last month, and within this time span have you sealed your dating list?'

'I find it hard to swallow' she taunted taking a sip of juice.

'He's worth settling for..' Camilla grinned broadly.

'Okay, let's see the doctor and get to know if you could accompany us.'

'And you want me to play gooseberry?'

'Oh come on! It's a matter of day and we will be right back, get ready we'll go to the doctor' Camilla reminded and left the room.

'I suppose I better call her rather than..' Olivia looked around for the phone, and dialled to Dr Emma.

****

'Have you informed Ryan that we're coming there?'

'I tried but I think there's some network issue, he's phone is not reachable.

Moreover I m not sure about how will he react upon this decision of travelling.'

'You've consulted the doctor. haven't you?"

'Oh, yeah I did and she showed me a green signal too' Olivia huffed.

'No worries bae, have this ' Camilla twisted from her seat and passed the snacks to her while John drove silently. He was apparently a decent man, and her heart was satisfied that her friends made a good choice.

They started towards London, this journey wasn't of the usual ones, this time everything was very unusual, Olivia was traveling without Ryan's consent, and she couldn't connect him either. On one hand she wasn't willing to travel and on the other she didn't have anywhere to live. There were other friends too but then she wasn't comfortable with them the way she was with Camilla. Camilla had however convinced her telling it is just a matter of one day. Olivia leaned over the headrest, staring at the passing street lights and dozed off along the setting sun and woke up to find herself surrounded with skyscrapers.

****

By 9:30PM they had reached the hotel, it was a two-bedroom apartment.

They placed their baggage on the table and were waiting for dinner. Olivia moved to the window and lifted the curtains up, meanwhile

'Ohoo! Gallery!' Camilla exclaimed, and rushed to open the glass door,

'Woohoo, that's the real blower bae!' she enjoyed the breath taking view.

It was twenty-seventh floor and the platform displayed the heavenly porch, with the largest swimming pools of the hotel. Taking her phone out she stood beside Olivia and captured a wide selfie with a background dazzling enough to brag for next few months. This typical scene would have been still incomplete without the flaunting selfie updated on Instagram with a caption

#bffsdontneedareasontocelebrate.

As decided, John stayed at his house and the girls preferred a hotel room.

Following the dinner, Olivia wore her night suit and walked frazzled in the corridor. Still in a brown study, was it a right decision to travel all the way without Ryan's consent, while Camilla peeked from the door at her.

'I swear, that's annoying like hell Camilla!' Olivia chided.

'Hush! Get in Olly, I heard that RJ Drake has booked the room next door'

'Why on earth is he important to you now?' Olivia exclaimed entering the room.

Camilla hurried to close the door and turned to Olivia,

'Ryan isn't taking your call. Right?' she said in undertone, on all fours before Olivia. A tear rolled down her cheek and she nodded signalling yes.

'No biggie bae! He must be wrapped up at work, anyway what's bothering you Olly?'

'I suppose anxiety attack, breathlessness and what not? Its not every time that I take a decision to travel and haven't informed him yet. I understand...he must be tied up with some stuff, but I am used to share even my sneeze count with him ...am also worried about him, his colleague Richard isn't taking the calls either '

'To be honest Olly, one must be able to differentiate between loving and idolizing...hope you understand.' She said while searching in the bag and pulled out a grey night suit. 'how's this?' she asked cheekily to digress the subject.

'Mystifying' Olivia remarked sardonically, realizing her deviation.

'This or me?' Camilla questioned hanging the shirt in the air.

'Grey colour, neither black, nor white. Amidst the extremes it finds a way to exist, just like life' Olivia replied.

'its hurting me, that you couldn't spell me out.'

'Seems your teaching is way more important' Camilla put forward tongue-in-cheek.

'Not really maybe. But it would break me if life starts teaching you these lessons.' Replying she moved out of the room.

****

At quarter past three, the phone announced its existence amidst the pillows, cushions, comforter, Camilla and plump Olivia. She pulled out the phone from the mess and put it on vibration mode, long pressing the side button. The device buzzed again loud enough to break her sleep once more. Olivia sat up still dozing, and focused on the screen. She cleared her heavy eyes and wide opened on realizing, it was Ryan's missed call!

Olivia pushed off a load from heart after receiving the voice recording of Ryan's well being and an explanation that he couldn't connect because of the tight schedule and a reminding of the promise that he'll return in two days.'

No doubt it would have been a better situation if she could have put a word of her whereabouts, but suffice it to say she was contented. She squinted at Camilla to make sure she's asleep and picked up her diary to make a new entry.

'Let us walk till the end of world
Sit on a cliff and have a word,
In the middle of night, gazing at glittering stars,
Turn by turn, let's reveal our scars,
Let the falling rain hide all the tears,
Shake by the thunder, disclose pettiest fears.
Relive in a while, all past memories,
Forget the guilt, and forgive guilty
Loudest we laugh, once more and more
Till we burst into tears like never before!
Keeping thoughts aside, and pour out hearts out,
Beneath guilt and complaints, a wish falls on ground.
It begins to whisper and ends reading loud,
'...you and me..., together and throughout!'

****

'Put a sock in it!' Olivia muttered frustrating from the bed pressing cushions against her ears. It was half past noon and Camilla lay down with a face mask put on and headsets on, she didn't have any idea how her hoarse voice had turned wobbly on an attempt to sing. ' itzz a love stooory, baeby just sayyyyyy yeasssz'

'One more word and am gonna bang your head into the gallery, so that straight away you collapse into the pool and never think of singing ever!' Olivia threatened hitting the a/c remote at her, luckily which flipped over and failed to reach the target. Camilla split into her sides and the wobbly voice had then turned into nasal and high pitched shrieks, which was far worse than the earlier one and caused Olivia to sit up straight.

****

In the early hours of evening, Camilla was ready to visit her would be in laws and had again succeeded in persuading Olivia to accompany her, as this meeting wouldn't take more than half an hour to end and that Camilla had promised Ryan to take care of her and she thought it was unsafe for her to leave her alone in the room. Camilla had temporarily straightened her blonde curls and tied them neatly in to a high pony tail, and put on an off shoulder denim dress, matching it with black heels. Her glossy lips completed the look. 'Touchwood! You look graceful Camilla! Thank heavens you stepped out of that Mérida persona.' Olivia announced to the room and she wore a floral maxi dress to keep it comfy. The two friends hired a taxi to reach the address, whereas John kept waiting for them at the other end. The taxi halted after moving through half a dozen traffic signals, after getting through a board 'West London Residential'.

Camilla had bought a flower bouquet and 'Get well soon' Card on the way and sat back sniffing, as she was upset with the high-priced bills in London. They walked into the large brown gate, stepping at the second stair Olivia turned around and gazed at the lawn while Camilla rang the doorbell. While she checked herself on the screen of her phone, John opened the door.

'Good evening, John' Camilla hugged him and gave a forehead peck. Olivia immediately looked below her feet to confirm the presence of six inches heels which only made her reach by his side, and then looked down with an expression of self-disgust for such thoughts. A grey haired plump old lady dozing at the chair wearing a green muumuu, was snoring like bum. Olivia made her way through the sitting and took a chair facing opposite to her. Camilla sat at the chair beside her after placing the bouquet on the centre piece.

'Mommy!' John murmured, stroking his hand over her shoulder and she opened her eyes alarmed to his hush.

'This is Camilla and her friend Olivia'

Both the girls greeted 'hello'

'Hello children 'A warbling sound took over as she chose to speak.

'How's your health now, aunty?' Camilla debriefed. John had bought them a tray of snacks and juice. The silted conversation continued to be meal and discrete whereas Olivia maintained her reticent trait. This lady kept throwing snobbish looks at Olivia. Beside the wall clock there hung a family photograph of John's convocation ceremony. He wore a graduation cap standing in between his parents. The old man's smile appeared familiar to her. Her thoughts were interrupted by the lady's cough attack. Her rattling chest described the uneasiness of her health. 'How helpless is a person before the judgements of creator. Or had this lady been wicked all age, and its all about the karma play' Olivia thought . She wasn't an assuming aunty but she could create a hypothetical situation and case study it. Sitting for long hours in the book store, she had developed this not-so-useful talent. Now she could even picturise her with red devilish horns and a cursed ring above her head. The bell rang and once again popped into her thoughts. John who's been sitting beside Camilla got up to check the door. The door opened with a screech and the stepping in sound continued. Olivia was a lady of ethics, she would never sneak and poke into others matters and knew how to behave like a well behaved guest.

'Where's dad?' John questioned to the person just entered.

'He is on phone with the lawyer' A man with an adenoidal voice spoke that made Olivia skip a beat,

Hearing this answer, Olivia and Camilla turned spontaneously to see the man behind. And why wouldn't they if the voice of his resembled with Ryan . Or was he Ryan himself?

CHAPTER SEVEN

Yes, It was Ryan indeed!

'Ryan?' her eyes fell down the step where he stood, Olivia paused in perplexity, scrunching her nose and with raised eyebrows, she tread towards him. Responding to her voice Ryan raised his bowed head at knee Jerk from the phone to confirm the countdown to his misfortune.

'You were supposed to be at the new branch?' she asked stupefied at the unjustified coincidence.

'Yeah I had just come here to pick my colleague.' he completed, stammering thrice and scratching his neck with his index finger after rubbing his nose. Meanwhile John stared at the duo in confusion. Without completing the statement he turned back at the door to leave,

'Bye Olly I m in a hurry, meet you tonight' he again faced towards Olivia, looking in the air, gave a forehead kiss and headed towards the door. As he pulled in the door, there stepped in an elderly person on the threshold and Ryan moved aside to free his way. He was a heavily bodied gentle man, with an unsteady walk.

Camilla stood beside the chair trying to figure out the mess. This man was senior John. To add up on the confusion rate, looking at John's fathers face, clicked something blurred in Olivia's mind. 'Ryan, my son!' He exclaimed gratefully. 'without you it wouldn't have been completed way easily.'

'Look at this good-for-nothing son' he continued pointing at John

'We're blessed to have a nephew like you boy!' He gave a bunny hug to panic-stricken Ryan. Olivia interrupted the man, 'Can anyone explain me what is going on here, before I start believing in parallel universe postulates!'

'Who is this?' Daddy John asked John looking at Olivia.

Now John pointed towards Camilla and got her introduced first, 'I had mentioned earlier to you about Camilla, Dad, this is Camilla Jonas and she is her friend, Olivia.' he seemed daring enough to hint about girlfriend before a hulk.

Turning at Olivia he asked with heavy and mysterious voice, ' Olivia...'

'Olivia Whitaker'. She put forward rolling her eyes, noticing the wrinkles on his face and the blood flecked eyes.

On listening the reply, his lowered eyebrows relaxed and spread miles apart, widening his shrunk eyes, the curiosity faded from his face, his eye balls dilated in shock and the squinted eyes widened, eventually dropping his jaw.

Ignoring the needless drama, she snatched the file from muted Ryan, turned over the pages and continued reading. 'now I get it!' She closed the file after going through the pages and slapped the file over the stunned Ryan which fell on the floor, with the papers scattered all over. Still not more than her heart, which shattered into infinite pieces.

'You are such a cheat, Ryan!' Olivia exclaimed, holding Ryan by his collar, and pushed him away of anger, this time the fragrance of his vintage perfume also couldn't suppress her wrath, while tears filled in her eyes, her face had turned red. Camilla interrupted to wrap up the situation after all it was about her impression on in laws, 'what's wrong Olly, we can sort it out at home.'

'No Camilla, I'm not so fond of creating nuisance in front of the guests...' she continued with a pause 'but only if they would have been guests, this Ryan is a liar' she sounded shattered pointing at him and continued ' he has deceived me. Neither he is here with the office shit nor..' she paused taking a deep breath while her tears rolled down the cheeks, 'nor that Whitaker has died!' she buried her hands into her open brown hair. Her upper lashes pressed against the lower eyelids dropping tears all along.

'I can explain it to you Olivia' Ryan spoke timidly raising his head, and placing his arms on her sides.

'No more fallacies, Ryan. Please! I don't need any explanations' she spoke with a quavering voice and passed on a concluding statement.

'How could you judge, without even listening to me.' Ryan pleaded before her, guilty and helpless.

'I had lied to my mother all these time, that this man has died several years ago!' pushing his arms aside, she screamed loudly pointing at Mr Alfred Whitaker, who was none other than Olivia's father.

Camilla walked towards Olivia, wiped her tears, and tried consoling her, 'it's ok Olly, your blood pressure will shoot up, we can sort out the matter calmly, Its no big deal.' Yet Her consoling seemed worthless.

'Not a problem for you Camilla, because you hadn't spent homeless nights at the roadside, because you didn't have to become a breadwinner of the family turning into school dropout, because you didn't live like how orphans live!' she cried noisily and was in no mood to calm down, and anyone would not expect anything less than this.

'Now you are exaggerating this Olly' he replied. It seemed as Ryan was trying a counteraction strategy.

'Really? You know what Ryan, you couldn't fall beneath this, I've trusted you, more than myself, all these years and you turned out to be a traitor.' Her screams knew no bounds, her eyes could explain the pain in her heart and her face expressed rage as a vein popped out her neck.

'Is this your trust that you followed me all the way to London! Spying me? No Olly, this is not how trust works!' Ryan threw a fierce look, as never before, staring into her eyes. His voice lacked guiltiness now. he misinterpreted the situation and answered sarcastically.

'I don't find it necessary to justify my actions before you any more, I know under what circumstances I have been here.

'Wow!' she continued clapping her hands' I swear I m taken aback by your talent Ryan! Honestly this was a masterpiece.'

'I agree, I've lied to you Olly, but here I am now, apologising you, I am telling, I accept and I am sorry, what more do you want?' the heated argument continued as Ryan's volume turned higher as well. Just like the way Olivia had turned unpredictable, Ryan made no stone unturned to shock as well. This phase of his was never witnessed by her. No doubt, he was a dominant partner, yet this was surely not expected.

'No clarifications will suffice, none will justify your act. Now I realise my mother was right, her fears turned out to be true, but now it's too late!' she defended. Her lips started trembling, and pain took over the anger on her face. She sat at the chair, amused at the fortunes play.

Taking a pause of a minute or two, Ryan walked towards her, stood on his knees, tucking strand of hair behind her ear, he wiped her tears with a napkin as usual as gentle as a breeze but not enough to win Olivia again, not enough to warm up smile, not enough to melt her heart. he held her face by his palms and appealed, 'I am sorry Olly, can't we make the things right again, I am sorry for all my mistakes, let's get untangled from the mess of misconceptions, I'll forget your spying and you forgive me, deal? He persuaded with a promising smile.

'There's a condition to this ' Olivia spoke not so kindly as Ryan.

'Let's go home, right now!' she ordered.

'Its not possible Olly' he tried explaining.

'Then forget me Ryan, the reality is that you never deserved me, you carry a deceiving habit in your bloodline, how could I expect that you'll get rid of that!' She chided.

'How can I ignore my aunt on the deathbed?' Ryan's calmness had expired. His wide open, glaring eyes had begun to frighten her, he was not that Ryan which always wiped of her tiredness. Agreeing the fact that the professor spirit had been a bit irritating but it was far better than this, behaviour of his which had left her stunned. Every breath had become restless to her. Not compromising on her self respect and morals, she chose to fight. And this was no less than an army fighting at border for her, forsaking their lives and families. 'just like you ignored your heavily pregnant wife for being the heir of her property! Now this bitch will die in piece! First she ruined my mother's life and now mine. I don't care Ryan if you choose to live or die with this woman, just go to hell from my side!' she sobbed.

'I said I am sorry, once, twice, thrice, and what more do you expect? I doubt you overheard the wealth distributing conversations between us, by the way tactic was amazing' he blamed tired of constantly wooing.

A vibe of worthlessness ran through her heart, her chest was paining of agony, she gulped down the clogged throat, took a deep breath, her lips started to tremble and she closed her eyes tight realising her helplessness and to keep a line of self respect, she wailed 'let's go Camilla, let's just leave.' her words expressed throbbing of her soul. She stared with tearful eyes at Ryan, who didn't bother to pay attention.

Stepping down the first stair as she walked out, she felt an stimulation of pain below the abdomen, ignoring it she took a step further, now the intensity of pain had increased. It had turned beyond tolerance, she yelled out for help ' Camilla it's paining', and sat on the chair in the lawn 'Ryan help me please! I need you' Camilla rushed to hire a taxi and succeeded in agreeing to pay the double amount. She helped her sit at the back seat, while Olivia kept crying of the pain. Not wasting a moment awaiting Ryan, Camilla banged in the doors of the car and ordered him to head over to any nearby hospital. A few moments later the taxi halted at the knock on the drivers window. It was Alfred (Olivia's father), signalling to open the door.

****

Next evening in the hospital room Olivia broke her sleep, still with the closed eyes, her conscious correlated with the memories within a moment which revolved around the unanticipated yesterday. Her life had driven her through a roller coaster within the past few hours, this analysis was interrupted by a crying sound of a baby beside her in a cradle. Yes, this morning she had delivered a baby boy after being admitted into the nearby maternity. Her water broke last night after excessive stress and shouting. She was immediately admitted in the hospital, and the birth pangs ended after eight long hours. Camilla had been by her side all through this.

'How are you feeling now?' Camilla asked.

'I m good ' she replied with a persuading expression and a heavy heart as the other day hadn't been less than a trauma to her. Camilla left the room to get some medicines.

She lifted the head of the bed and took her baby from the cradle as he stopped crying, she ran her fingers across his head whilst he gazed around with his large brown eyes. An epitome of innocence and what could the words express. Tears rolled down her cheeks as she kissed his forehead, and held him close to her chest, brushing her lips against his head. Staring at his brown eyes, a memory clicked into her about the days they used to spend hours discussing their sons eye colour and every detailed feature; 'You won Ryan, you won! He has brown eyes and evidently I've lost!' she thought to herself. Just then her phone buzzed and she picked up to check, it was an alarm, that she had set three days ago. Ryan had promised her that three of them will be together that time.it was 19:20, little did she knew, that a hurricane would boom into her life and blow away all the roses of her dream garden. That a harsh wave of sea would erase her the footprints of promises and scatter everything beyond repair.

The door whistled opening and Alfred Whitaker walked in the room with a basket of fruits and fresh juices.

CHAPTER EIGHT

Gazing up at her father, she blinked and stepped down from the bed after placing the baby in the cradle and hurled the food, that he had placed in the refrigerator. Taking a breath full of anguish, she bawled pointing at the door, and stood covering her son, 'Go away! please, go away from me and my son, I am no more the Olly, who stood by the doorstep for your return. Just leave!' This caused an alarming situation as the nurses rushed into the room followed by Camilla, frightened of the howls the baby began to cry. Camilla shook her in an attempt to drown her shrieks and made her forcibly sit on the bed.

'Stop it Olivia you aren't allowed to scream, please be gentle, isn't the last nights show enough that you scared us by falling unconscious!, Set aside all the previous grudges, all thanks to him that, we reached the hospital on time, he assisted us throughout the time' Camilla chided.

Alfred stood overhearing the conversation at the door and left. The nurses left after instructing cum warning about her delicate health conditions and injecting sedation.

****

It was quarter past one at the midnight. Olivia put a blanket on the sleeping baby in the cradle, and lied down putting a blanket upon herself, 'can you get some painkillers from the drug store. My temples are throbbing and I need to sleep so badly.' Olivia pleaded, while Camilla agreed to her and walked out closing the door slowly. 'Call me if you need anything else too' At which Olivia gestured thumbs-up. After a minute or two she flung over the blanket, stood out to and put over slippers, grabbed Camilla's purse from the table, took her phone along and tip toed down the dark stairs, figuring a way out the hospital. Not a proper hospital, a small scale maternity centre it was. Some how she reached the parking and opened her clutch, to take the keys. She pressed the remote button and her car buzzed among the approximately thirty cars in there. Olivia sat in the car. Her raw sutures and unhealed wound made it a pathetic condition to sit causing her to grimace and jump out of the car in reflex. Breathing out the anguish, she adjusted the seat. Ignoring the worsening of wounds she drove out of the parking. It was the third day of Asher's birth, and Ryan didn't show up until now. Neither did her answer any of the calls nor did he replied to the messages. Olivia had now mentally accepted that she was wrong, and it's high time she must apologise.

Olivia never loved him, she was devoted to him. She considered Ryan over all, over her family, over her mom and even over her child. For Olivia there could be a possibility of her life without food or even maybe without water, but Ryan! No she could not even imagine surviving without him. She could never gear up the courage to picturize the consequences. She drove with a goal to fetch him out from wherever on earth he was. London wasn't an easier place to drive. The mess was driving her insane. Lowering the glass of the car, she yelled at every one out, asking for the address. A moment later the thoughts of tourist safety casted into her mind and she opened the GPS navigation. She was prepared about the apology speech she was going to utter. Swallowing the agony she was also ready to break into tears in his clasped arms. Following the address and chewing over, she managed to reach his house. The door check squeaked, placing her foot on the ground, She stepped out frowning of the pain and reached limping to the door. The lights were turned off and there was an eerie silence. Olivia banged at the door furiously. Receiving no response she pulled out her phone to call Ryan but it was vain. She glanced herself in the screen under the street light. She had turned brown, a green patient gown, hanging on her shoulders, her filthy open hair, and her huge dark circles, she looked mentally ill. This reflection scared her for a second. Hobbling back to the door she knocked several times, hard enough to hurt her palm and knuckles. Tired of the courtesy she started to scream his name ' Ryan! Ryaaaan!!!! Open the door man! I am sorry' ' I am sorry ' she added. The wriggling in her voice increased as it began to drizzle.

This was the breakdown. Till now she was keeping it all in a hope to break herself before Ryan. But where was he? She couldn't take it anymore. She allowed herself to break into tears, standing in front of his house, and cried ' Ryan! Come to me please, I beg you, I'll die!' the falling rain had soaked her already, and the cold breeze with the pitter-patter and hooting of an invisible owl in the dark night had now started to freak her. She took a breath in, a pinch of grit, clapped upon her cheeks, pursed her lips repeatedly, adjusted her strands on the face and decided to sit on the his door step, till he opens the door. As she bent down to sit, a pressure created and her wounds worsened causing an intense pain leading her to jump up back to standing position. She clenched her fist into her hair, pressing her head in confusion, taking deeper breaths but nothing worked. She could not assemble the broken self. All she could do was cry louder and loudest. Unable to find Ryan, she hobbled back into the car, and searched for a nearby police station in her GPS navigation. Just then the fuel gauge beeped indicating low diesel. She tracked the station. Reaching the pump, she lowered the glass and chucked a hundred pound through the glass. Now she was feeling dizzy, and the roads seemed to merge into another, the Voice directions was spearing into her ears, the wet clothes were peeving, she jerked off her soaked hair and Camilla's calls were exasperating on the other side but she couldn't just switch off the phone because Ryan could also call her back. It wasn't easy for her breath any more, dizziness had turned intense and she was completely drained in this throes; She felt her energy was vacuumed out of the head and it was getting harder for her to breath in. Her palms and feet were sweating, whereas her body was freezing, she gripped the steering firm, her jaw had started to shiver. Pins and needles ran through her body. Her drowsy eyes seemed to end the cooperation from mind, creating hallucinations, her brows knitted into a frown exhausted of concentrating, she was completely in a torpid state and BOOM!

****

'Good luck, Olly' Camilla wished as Olly walked into her cabin, and Camilla headed towards her. Olivia responded with an involuntary and nervous smile. It was her first day at office after the maternity leave. Asher had turned six months old, they dropped him at the nursery. Olivia was staying at Camilla's. Skimming through the pages of Olivia's calendar, her fate made sure every tick of clock pricked deep into her heart driving her nothing but insane. They had travelled back to Wales, after Olivia's surgery. i.e. She had crashed car into the pillar and cracked her head. Till now Olivia had concluded that neither life was fair nor it was a fairy tale. Separated lovers do not meet accidentally at the roadside in real life. A broken heart doesn't find an apology letter at the doorstep from her lover. Gathering courage never announced victory is of the victim. This is life and She couldn't escape her life time by overdosing sedations. Things only started to normalize after Olivia started taking counselling sessions from Dr Adler. Until then she had isolated Asher almost for a month in her depressed times. Later she was taught that hiring a baby sitter doesn't complete a mother's responsibility, and she realised that she herself was an isolated child and she could never want her child to feel the same. Her mind took a diversion from depression when she developed interest in him. It as a crystal clear display of example that for one's happiness he needs to consider others emotions. But when was she selfish, since her conscious, she always lived for others for their happiness may it be her mother, family or Ryan. Oh Ryan, he never showed up since then

She was tied up with Asher's responsibilities on her shoulders. Feeding the baby, stinky diapers, massages and baths, changing his clothes, awaiting burps, his nasty vomits and the mama son play time. Amidst these new duties, now she also found time to silently weep sitting at the corner of her room. Motherhood is a bliss indeed. She would have willingly forgive Ryan for the past, if at all he would have come to see his son. It doesn't means it doesn't hurt. It kills inside. Every promise of his Strikes her every time she looks at Asher. She hadn't asked much from the destiny, more than agony she was into trauma that her fear came out to true without leaving even a hint before. Her heart took a leap when she had stepped out of the car, she could picturise the millionth replay in her mind about the imaginary scene of Ryan pleading on her door for apology and the way she'll bash him out. She tried to side track herself, understanding the certainty of this seemed something next to impossible.

A span of eight years wasn't short enough to slip off her memory whenever she wished. Every now and then his broken vows choked her. She felt incomplete, a part of her was lost. The history had repeated before her eyes, first it was her dad who betrayed her mom and now Ryan had shattered her. Her mom deserved a salute, she thought, or why not a standing ovation, for she had warned almost a decade earlier. No second thought in Concluding 'experience over everything.' But it was too late, she had gone far away from her, may be somewhere between the moon and stars she was looking her defeated daughter. But does that really happen, do mothers sneak from the sky?, they say so. And now why would she trust the peoples saying, when the assumed trustworthy had ruined her into uncountable pieces.

Looking into Asher's eyes she felt sorry for him for not having a Dad, though he had one but that didn't even make difference of a penny. It was a dreadful perception from a mother's side than the child's. (She had witnessed both) They had a long list of mutual friends, but none ever hinted about his whereabouts. Some had visited her with gifts and greeting cum sorry statements. Others narrated a pitiful silence. Amidst these hard times Camilla had been her backbone. She was a queen at heart. She left no stone unturned to make her feel that she wasn't alone. It had been six longest months and she felt it was time that she must move back to her house. It didn't just cost them an arm and a leg instead their fortune too. It was their 'home sweet home'. Ryan never arrived to the house since then. Olivia was determined to file a missing compliant for Ryan, but

Camilla had prevented her from this folly.

****

In the evening the two sat in the sitting room sipping hot coffee, and Asher was lying in the bouncer. Camilla was scrolling down the phone and as the new usual, Olivia was lost in to her thoughts.

'Listen this seems an exciting offer' Camilla displayed the advertisement on her phone, interrupting into her silence, which had become the new usual as well.

Olivia threw an 'oh just shut up' look through her eyes. Not precisely but this was almost the tenth time she proposed the same idea since last week. It was a 15 day trip to Dublin.

'I am booking three tickets!' Camilla insisted.

'No way Camilla, am not in any mood ' she expressed reluctance.

'Get a chance to meet your favourite Catherine from the Irish TV series 'grá mo. chroí' Camilla briefed. 'listen this girl appears your doppelgänger.' She teased.

'Oops you caught! That's me actually.' She glared in condescending manner.

'You are impossible' she sighed.

'What was Benjamin blabbering in the library?' she continued.

'He is completely a different creature ... although for the first time I saw his relaxed brows,'...She paused.

'Umm' Camilla responded paying not much heed, scrolling down the phone.

'Camilla, I am so grateful for all What you have done for me, for Asher in our hardest times, when I didn't have any shadow, you held my hand and lifted us along, I cannot thank you in words. But I think it's time I must move back to my house.' Although she was very vocal, this time her voice quavered and eyes became moist, out of emotions.

'Olly I can't propose fake statements, I would just like to tell you that, I feel good when you're here, and honestly I think it's too early. I won't stop you from taking your decision, that's what I longed since ever, make your own plans, be a lady.' She continued after taking a pause to swallow. ' but I would suggest you to take some more time, today was your first day at office, along with Asher it will be a hectic. Find a suitable babysitter, get your house tidy up and get the lawn done in the coming weekends, after a few months, when Asher learns to crawl, you can move. You've taken a six month break, you'll need some weeks to get habituated. Earlier the routine was different, now with Asher, it isn't an easy task.'

'I understand your concern Camilla, but sometime or the other I will have to shift back right? Why not now. I also know it's not gonna be easy, but I am ready for the mess. In the recent past I encountered the worst, now I don't fear anymore. Let me follow my heart, I'll depart, and if God forbid, the consequences aren't manageable, your doors are open for me. Aren't they?'

'Anytime, my brave gal pal.' Camilla gestured thumbs-up, admiring her courage, wiping a tear with her thumb.

CHAPTER NINE

'Sun rays left untouched,
And wind has parted ways,
Nothings glittery in the moon
And stars shine in vain;
Guilt of your parting,
Has wrapped me enough,
Such as I could never
feel wet in the rain,
I call you once,
And again and again,
Come back love,
I can explain,
I can explain..!'

Olivia closed her diary after making a new entry on the date of their seventh wedding anniversary. Last week she had shifted to her house. It was tiring as expected and hurting unexpectedly. Every hook and corner of the house reminded her of Ryan. Letting go of wasn't in her control anymore. Her conscience was reluctant to conclude he was a cheater. The undone dishes and misplaced laundry reminded her of how organized he was. His systematic approach towards every work. Olivia missed it all. Doing the grocery, cleaning up the house, maintaining the lawn, Asher's needs and what not. Regardless of the fact that they were one of the most excited parents to welcome their baby, it was a fact now that she was a single parent. She missed how she would sleep for a couple of hours soon after gulping down hot and yummy lunch returning from the office. Forget the naps, now she finds it hard to sleep even after taking pills. It was like life had said her 'happy realization'.

****

Just when Asher was about to wake, Olivia remembered that she had to take a shower, as he had thrown up on her dress. She grabbed her beige bath gown and turned the tap on. Looking at herself in the mirror while shampooing hair she looked carefully at her eyes, she thought ' he said he loved them the most, her thick lashes, ...her sharp collar bone...he loved everything about her right?' rubbing her hand on her shoulders she missed how he used to lie his head there and confessed the wish to make his last breath in her lap.'

She wasn't the same now, that zest wasn't alive any more. She was tired of shedding tears, because no one was there to console her. Her conscience never declared that Ryan was a cheater. Though he had betrayed her, but ...! But she loved him. She missed how he handled everything at home. Asher's cry put a full stop on her thoughts. She opened the door, and struggled to find clothes to wear. She realised her laundry was undone. Asher kept screaming non stop, It was time for his lunch, she rushed to the kitchen in the bath gown and switched on the kettle, for heating the water, grabbed the baby Food jar from the shelf, put the last three scoops in the bowl and took the kettle to pour the water. Just then her phone ringed at which she spilled the hot water at her fingers!

Frustrated Olivia picked up the phone, wiping it with a her gown of course. it was Brett. Dr Brett Adler. 'good afternoon, am I speaking to Mrs Olivia?' the familiar voice greeted, and reminded her of something uneasy at which she silently face palmed. 'hello?' he questioned again.

'Good afternoon, yea this is Olivia.'

'If I am not wrong, today we had a session at your residence.'

'Err my apologies, I am not at home right now, could we post pone this meeting'

'I am sure I need to consult a psychiatrist, as I've seen you a minute ago through your kitchen window. I am standing in the lawn. Any ways we will resume the sessions only when I examine my mental health' he caught her lying red handed sarcastically.

After an awkward silence Olivia hesitatingly Excused ' great! You are outside my house, actually I was just about to leave to do the grocery and thought it would tie me in for an hour or two but no problem, we will get this done first'

This was one of the finest psychiatrist known. She had been attending counselling sessions, after the tragedy hit her. He had his ways of treating and this was that he will be visiting the house of the patient and make necessary changes to the indoor and outdoor as well.

'I'll join you in a couple of minutes' she said.

After making him sit in the drawing room, she tippy toed in embarrassment about her lie being caught. It was evident from her bath gown and wailing Asher, let alone grocery, she wasn't leaving anywhere, not even a step out.

She walked into her room to feed Asher and blow dried her hair, while her brain kept churning about the incident.

'Why was I escaping him?

Don't know I just don't like him being around.

Is he uncomfortable to be with?

No, No, he isn't that kind of guy.

Is he boring?

Yeah! No actually ...sort of.

But why don't I like him,

Because he reminds me of Ryan and my broken past. But for me to come out of it, he has to do this, that was why he's being paid for.' Olivia couldn't make it out. She was perplexed. Little did she knew that it was the way she had to narrate about how she felt every moment. And she wasn't used to it. She was habituated to share everything with Ryan. Just Ryan. Not even her mother.

He left post session which lasted about 75 long minutes, and also suggested some changes to her house setting.

She dialled to Camilla for the third time in a day and her phone was engaged. She flung away the phone on bed and let herself fall on her back at the bed. Tying a scarf round her head she travelled several dimensions of ifs and why's in her mind. It was as if Camilla was waiting for her to leave the house, ' how could she not respond to her!. Huh. And what was that Adler Chanting? Am I supposed to change the setting of the house?' She took a deep breath in and thought peacefully at the situation and the answer was, a big NO. how could she ruin the memories she had to preserve for Asher. The lounger below which he hustled on his knees to pull her nasty socks out from, this? It was impossible. Her lips turned into an involuntarily laugh and vibration at the thought of how he would do that. She walked down the stairs, the railing reminded her of a million memories which were a fallacy. Every time Ryan came home she used to climb down the stairs and jump upon him and clutch on until she felt breathless or he fell down. Once his trousers ripped off following such praxis, and they guffawed about it until months. She could clearly picturize her last birthday party, in which Ryan had surprised her, she scraped gently down, allowing herself to flow it all through her eyes. Exactly there she stood astonished, and the lights turned on... everyone wishing for a blessed year ahead...amidst the claps... where were they now! Where are their wishes now? Is that what they had wished for her, or was it that she deserved this? Why would she even question them, when her very own Ryan had deceived her.

She flumped at his dining table chair, where he used to appreciate her attempts of trying new recipes from YouTube, always ignoring the record, that they never turned out to be tasty. And the bubble swing beside their bed, which seemed to engulf her fresh morning vibes! There was no second thought for that. This was a part of her more than half of the memories. She had bought it from the balcony into the room because of the rains. But she couldn't move it anywhere out from her sight. The way they used to talk about any thing useless in the world sipping down the coffee. Appearing from the viewers side as though they were discussing on the working out ideologies of UNO or UNESCO. But they would be busy mocking each other or practicing rehearsals of speeches and presentations ending up making each other laugh at their over confidence. Basically he wanted to change everything that reminded her of Ryan. Was that even possible?

But there was the other side also, was it possible for her to live in this house, where every pin and needle reminded her of him. It just didn't remind, it pricked in her heart, like a thorn on a cushion. Wasn't it enough that she wasn't living, she was just breathing. He had already ruined everything, and now she doesn't have anything more to lose, therefore preserving his memories was all vain.

It had been eight longest month since he went missing, no one in her farthest people had heard from him. There was a sneaking suspicion in her mind, that whether was he even alive?

At this thought her heart pounded and stood up, force stopping all the brain processing and resumed thinking about the day.

According to Bret the colour of her furniture was very dark shaded, which was a factor in boosting depression. 'he's an absolute non sense, Ryan loved the colour combination of wheat and coffee. And he suggested an idiotic turquoise over white combination as though I am playing with dollars, to change the furniture.' But sub consciously was she following him? He consistently reminded her if there's no one to talk you, talk to yourself, think about it analyse! that's what she's been doing all day!

****

The door bell rang non stop and Olivia incautiously opened the door wide drowsing in sleep and the smell of freshly baked chocolate croissants lured her to her shut eyes, 'belated happy anniversary Olly!' the voice hung in her ears making her restless to see the face behind the large orchids bouquet.

Ryan curved down the bouquet and she blocked his way through the door, complaining 'But I love red roses'

'Shedding petals of rose will make you sad, and I can't hurt you anymore, Olly' his sensual voice played.

'And the wisdom behind these orchids?' she questioned sarcastically.

His long lashes raised and the magic in his eyes was still the same, 'these are artificial and promising, not to hurt you' he moved forward offering the bouquet. Opening the door she took a step further, and headed to hold but the doorbell kept on ringing. As she rubbed her eyes again he walked away along with the gifts and the vision blurred while the sound was making her uneasy, compelling her to open the eyes. She rose from bed and turned off the snoozing alarm. Tied her hair into a bun, and leaned by the bedhead and pressed in a pillow between her chest and folded knees. It was quarter past eight, she held the cushion tight against her chest and dropped of tears at the emotional dream she had.

After taking a shower she got the baby massaged, changed his diaper, prepared his bag and put on a denim jacket over. Grabbing the car keys from the key stand, holding Asher in her arms, she locked the door of the house and drove to the store. It was not a long distance to cover, but along with Asher, she found it hard to drive as he was still an infant. Walking into the glass door, she pushed the pram in, making her way, the cashier waved her a hi and threw a long time no see smile. Looking at the pram, he gestured rolling his index finger asking 'Your baby?'

She replied with a smile and took a trolley to fill in the stuff, pushing the trolley and pram simultaneously wasn't working and in a such attempt she hit the pile of cornflakes, ending up dropping boxes. Gathering all the boxes, she could feel people's eyes on her. However she tried and raised the pile back, which did not take more than two seconds to fall back again. This time thankfully there was no one around. Leaving over the mess she left the pram aside and decided to get the grocery done, just as she headed further, Asher began to shriek worse such that an announcement was made for her to reach the counter as soon as possible.

After the queue cleared at the counter, the cashier got off with a list and asked her to take a seat. It was a neatly handwritten list of items, Ryan had maintained. It was strange as well, Olivia never knew about it.

That cashier boy filled the trolley with all the items mentioned in the list and she paid the bill. Returning from the store she fed Asher and prepared a sandwich for herself. Gave a bath to Asher ironed their clothes and got dressed up, all set to leave for the office. She checked the watch, it was quarter to ten. This was the time earlier she used to struggle to wake up on. Looking in the mirror she sighed, not only this, life had taught her many more bitter lessons. Dropping Asher at the babysitter, she drove to the office.

****

Half-day had spent and Olivia kept an eye on Camilla's empty chair. She hadn't come to the office today, nor could she dial to her, Benjamin was on rounds. Sneakily she tried texting her, but no reply, this was making her worried about Camilla. No calls and messages, that too Camilla? There was something fishy, she realised.

Five minutes before five she cleared her desk and packed her bag speedily, at five dot, Benjamin walked down and she headed towards the lift. Waiting in the queue she took a place in the corner, whilst she heard greetings, gossips and goodbyes amongst crowd. And one of them were Shane and Daniel, taking the stairs, conversing loud enough

'I wonder why she didn't come today?'

'She's getting married ' A dim whisper uttered.

'How did you know about that?' he questioned not believing.

'Daisy told.'

'How does she know?''

'Camilla texted to Gladys it seems '

And the voice lowered as they climbed down, Olivia took a step back to follow their conversation, but the elevator doors opened and there was a crowd pushing her in with their eyes as she turned back. Not breaking the flow she got into the lift. She couldn't believe her ears, were they really talking about Camilla, or someone else. But she heard it right with her ears. Sitting on the car she grabbed her phone and recorded a voice note to her 'Where on earth are you Camilla? You're not taking my calls and messages! You didn't show at the office too, can you please utter out the shit, what's wrong with you!'

She picked Asher from the nursery and drove back to home. Keeping her purse on the dining table, she walked into kitchen after washing her hands. She placed the grocery she bought this morning and prepared food for Asher and herself.

After lunch, carrying sleepy Asher in her arms she ambled upstairs into her bedroom. She sang lullaby and he fell asleep, fondled him and caressed his chubby cheeks. She placed her head gently on his chest, carrying the weight of it of course, listening to his heart beat she felt peace. She kissed him on the forehead and put a blanket upon. His curly brown hair resembled Ryan's. His heartbeat reminded her of the first heartbeat they heard together, in the hospital and their happiness knew no bound. All the incidents replayed in her mind without asking her consent. Those memories which loved rent free in her head. She was now tired of reminiscing him. Rubbing her fingers in his head she laid beside him and sighed.

Stupid Adler! He thought If I change the house, I'll forget Ryan? Every breath of Asher will remind me of Ryan and nothing could be changed about it. She concluded that even if she wished she couldn't burn all the bridges from

Ryan's memories.

CHAPTER TEN

As the door bell broke her sleep she placed cushions on the two sides of Asher, wore flip flops, hoped all the way down, resisting the emerging hope that her morning dream may come true! She opened the door sneakily to see Camilla with a box of chocolates. Camilla pushed her in, making her way in to the house and sat on the lounger, keeping the box on the table.

'Cant you do a single good deed in your entire bloody life' Olivia mumbled closing the door and dragged a chair from the dining to sit.

'What did I do now ' Camilla exclaimed, and got up from the back rest.

'Anyway, it's okay that you didn't wish for my anniversary, maybe you forgot or maybe you knew that it had become awkward to wish me now, but that doesn't mean you'll escape me the entire coming week.'

'This box of choc..' Camilla spoke and was interrupted by Olivia once again.

'Oh yeah I know, for my anniversary, it's ok. What say about coffee?'

'No I m stuffed Olly,' she took a moment to clear her throat and asked' why were you calling me?'

'May I know about your whereabouts, nowadays! I m sure you found a new boyfriend, but that doesn't mean you should isolate others; what ever ' Olivia continued with a pause, 'why didn't you show today at the office? I called you, so that you could at least sign for half a day. But that Benjamin was on observation for the whole day. I wonder why he didn't enquire about you.'

Camilla sat upright at her questions and raised her head, 'listen, Olivia we need to talk...'

'That's what I've been blabbering all day, you don't know the folks, they are assuming a whole new thing...'

Camilla raised her head, placed her hands on her waist and yelled 'OLLY WILL YOU LISTEN TO ME NOW?' she took a long breath as a sense of accomplishment of finishing her sentence.

Olivia shook her head with blank expression. She took a long breath again and in a hushed tone she murmured, 'I m getting married ...'

A reply to this was the same expressionless, blinking and tight lipped statue of Olivia.

'YOU CAN SPEAK OLLY, DON'T OVER REACT' she raised her voice again and her hands in the air gesturing anger.

'Only you?' Olivia shook her head wild.

'I mean WE are getting married, Olly, WE,WE,WE, WE, WE is that clear to you now?' she pointed all unfolded fingers at her.

'Of course, nothing new, people get married, I would instead congratulate you' Olivia jumped up from the chair and threw her arms around her for expressing happiness. She ripped off the chocolate wrapper and pushed in the bar, while she struggled to push her away.

'You are not happy?' Olivia asked her.

'I am but this is gonna hurt you ...'

'Hurt me! You are getting married, and why will I feel bad about it, get some senses! By the way whose the new cow?' she asked jokingly.

Camilla was nervous, and it wasn't a usual thing, she never got nervous before mentioning her thirtieth boyfriend in row, excluding crushes. Her lips opened and closed, blocking way of the to hue and finally she uttered it all.

'He is John, I am getting married to John. We love each other, I know as a friend I shouldn't have.. I know it hurts you, but please try to stand in my shoes.' Her eyes filled, while the lips trembled, admitting almost a crime.

Olivia was awestruck, apparently. She put her hand to her mouth. 'are you kidding me ' she gasped.

Taking a pause and gulping a meaningless clogged throat, folding her arms cross, she continued ' why would you be sorry about that. It's okay. I m happy for you.' She threw her arms again around her and wished her the best. Her eyes filled though. It was becoming hard to maintain the fake smile.

'You're not mad at me?' Camilla put forward in disbelief.

'Have you lost it Camilla!' why on earth I would be mad at you, that too for marrying John..' she rolled her eyes.

Her eyes turned dewy yet again to state the fact inevitable fact, with a subtle and painful voice she spoke 'because he is Ryan's cousin and your stepbrother'

'You were already a part of my heart, now welcome to our broken family' tear rolled down her cheek and pain drooled of her lips while speaking. She widened her arms gesturing welcome.

'Is he alive?' she continued after a long pause, hopeless eyes and a begging heart beneath.

Camilla shrugged indicating 'idk'. It was an expressionless face to interpret the underlying emotion. Despite knowing her since long ago, she couldn't judge that whether she was lying, hiding or honest.

Olivia's nose turned red and she pursed her lips as though snapping down the pain in a moment. She blinked her eyes to avoid the moist and inquired with a grin ' so when are you getting married?'

'15th of June' she said excitedly.

There was again a long confused silence.

Olivia looked pleased. ' I applied leave for a month.'

'You said you broke up?' Olivia put a doubt forward.

'I was scared, of telling you all this time. But you are a girl of heart' Camilla hugged her.

How do I look?' Camilla stretched her dress at the waist,

'Not even an inch thinner!' Olivia responded bluntly, rolling her eyes.

'Exactly! This is my ideal figure into which the designer gown will fit on like tailor made love complimentary to each other' boasted Camilla.

'Like a tailor made love or a cushion cover over a king-sized pillow!' She teased.

'I can see the smoke around.. seems like someone is getting burning of jealousy '

'Lol!' Olivia rolled her eyes again.

Camilla's phone beeped ' I must leave now, John is waiting in the car.'

'Its okay you can let him in!'

'Right now in a hurry, see you soon!' she left.

She locked the door, and her phone rang. She tippy toed up the stairs in a rush, and pressed the silent button, so that Asher remains asleep. It was Asher's vaccine reminder.

****

Like the day spent, all of her days were busy, on one hand the existence of Asher reminded her of Ryan and on the other hand she was very tied up to live in her past.

Life doesn't stop teaching lessons and giving experiences, she was just trying to shape herself into the new mould. She felt blessed and complete with Asher, and she loved him beyond limits. As time passed by she had no time to mourn over the missing block of puzzle. That was the new complete. Her routine revolved around, going to office, getting back, avoiding parties, playing with him and a day before she had bought him a walker too. His new movements and actions uplifted her mood. Brett's sessions were also a part of the improvement. She hadn't tried contacting Camilla any day after she broke the news to her. Whenever she thought it pricked her in. Deep inside Olivia knew and considered she wasn't wrong. But there was something that was disturbing her, may be choosing John as a life partner. She had no personal grudges with John. But he was a part of Ryan's family. And being a true friend of hers, she couldn't do that. How could she join Ryan's side. It had began to pain. Every person she bought near to her heart and placed their worth above her, they showed their real faces. And the only person she neglected in her life; that was her mother. So right was she and her experiences. Had she listened to her earlier, she wouldn't have seen such days, but she wasn't even alive, to cry by her head and hand over a sorry note at which she would forgive and give an extra bar of chocolate as well. Time flies and had flied. The problem was that it doesn't even warn to fasten the seat belts before taking off, no parachutes and no emergency exits even if it crashes. One by one she was losing people from heart.

She had negative thoughts but never killed the voice of her conscience. It suggested that when she needed her the most, Camilla was present before her closer than her own shadow. Choosing a life partner was a different thing. She was allowed to make some decisions in her life without consulting friends.

She might have had her heart tidied for Camilla, but still she was unwilling to talk her, her busy days also supported the decision and days went by.

****

It was another random Sunday from the fortnight before Camilla's wedding day. Olivia had to leave for the expected last session of counselling. She carried Asher along her at his clinic and turned her eyes round the room for the first time. The feeling of last day had excited her, because Mr Brett didn't fall in to Olivia's category. He's table was pretty organised. The wall beside had his framed degrees. His black coat hanging over his big chair. There was a family photograph hung at the other corner. There was a lady standing beside her, on the frame, she seemed to be his girlfriend maybe Or his wife. She didn't know whether he was married or not.

'......Whenever you feel lonely or down, I m just a call away from you. Feel free to contact anytime...' Dr Brett ended the session with the words and shook hand with Olivia.

'Umm' Olivia was quiet as always and surprised by his emotional closing lines and stood up without bothering to reply. She thought that a smile could do.

'You never know you may need a friend like me' he continued still holding her hand.

She assumed that was a flirt but then kicked herself for thinking so narrow 'Why not, by the way thanks, for bearing with me, wish you luck and success ahead.' She put all the phrases at her tongue to pretend gentle.

She pulled the pram out of the room and walked happily, after all it was an achievement. Driving back to her house now she felt content and thought of dialling to Camilla.

'Knock, knock where's the bride to be?' Olivia teased.

'I live in the same old lane honey, where are you.' She replied sarcastically.

'Ohoo, I was kind of busy with the work and Asher, you know his vaccines and the counselling sessions, anyway tell me about yourselves, whose going to be the maid of honour, bridesmaids where's the bachelorette ...'

'Actually I not really impressed with competitive wedding syndrome. We'll make it an easier way, John's hunting for a better job as his company is undergoing crisis and I hardly make the bread and butter, it's all before you. We've decided to celebrate a grand reception, as soon as the things sort out. The banns were also read last Sunday and there are two more to go, at the church of Wales.'

'I'm glad you're growing, choose wisely, take decisions which help you, and not those which impresses the community,'

'There was a silence, until Olivia realised it was her turn to help.

'If at all you think, I can be of any help please let me know, am always there to help you.'

'That's so sweet of ya'

'Bye, take care.'

'See you soon'

Though the conversation seemed delighted apparently, there was a cold war between the girls. Their conversations never consisted of such formal phrases and statements. Olivia dragged it the way it was going. She had lost the courage to dig deeper and figure out the cause, somewhere she was still unhappy about something.

****

Asher! Baby! Where are you?' he came crawling back from the kitchen, excited at mother's voice. Olivia fed him the last piece of bread and he sat upright snatching the plate, licking the remaining chocolate with his sticky fingers. His face had been changing every few days, his chubby cheeks with spots of jam and chocolate spread under and over his finely shaped pink lips. All his mischiefs could be taken for granted if one had a glance on his long eyelashes falling and rising revealing the large deep hazel pupils. His two teeth sneaking from his wide smile, added on to his adorability.

****

Olivia pulled hard the bathroom door, as Asher ran in there to play with water. ' You had a shower already.' She chided. Wearing a long t shirt she came out and blow tried her and Asher's hair. Flicked her wet hair right and left, to hurry it up. She rubbed the towel against her waist and back, flung over the towel over the bed. Sliding open the cupboard and pulling out a dress, She held him in the lap and elbowed his leg into the blue striped dungaree, pushed his hand into white dotted shirt, closed the buttons and tucked in the belts. She set her hair with a brush and put on a blue hat of the suit, pulled the elastic beneath his chin, a brush of powder and he was all ready to attend Camilla's wedding ceremony.

She grabbed her previously dry cleaned dress from the cupboard, it was a white bodycon of knee length and tied her hair in a high pony tail, she wore a maroon bolero coat over it. She didn't bother to get a new dress for herself at her best friends wedding. Nothing was as expected, as exciting. She had to attend the wedding because she knew if she doesn't, then Camilla will not forgive her at least till she dies, and of course Camilla was the person who had helped her through the worst times in the recent past, she couldn't isolate her on her big day. They never planned anything such, but it was very much anticipated that how much fun they would have together at her wedding. Things went wrong with choosing the groom. It's good Camilla's settling in her life, but then considering Olivia's situation it was the worst choice made. Ryan is John's first cousin, he would be attending the ceremony, no doubt. How would she face him, rethinking on the possible scenarios, she had almost dropped the idea of visiting her, but then yester nights message of Camilla, had compelled her to face all the odds. She had never felt such anxiety even before giving a job interview. She completed her look with a natural peach shaded lipstick.

It was already 3 PM, she opened the door and Asher crawled outside in the lawn, just after putting keys in the bag, she realised Asher's forgotten shoes and socks. She unlocked the door to get the missing and started towards the church of Wales.

Parking the car outside the church, she lifted Asher in her arms. She took an empty chair on the third row, Camilla had not arrived yet. She made Asher sit on the chair beside. There were other mutual friends too, some colleagues too. She could feel some of the people pointing her out with their gazes. Asher was constantly tried to climb down the chair, Olivia had to hold him tight. There was a raise in the voices of crowd and Olivia turned her head to see, John and a few people, there was uncle Chris, Camilla's father, who escorted her down the aisle. The grudges in her heart melted at once she sighted her in the bridal look. Everybody stood up, so did Olivia. She wore an off white wrapped sleeved gown with asymmetrical hem, the deep neckline showed off her necklace distinctly. Her smoothened hair styled in a bun with a floral tiara, except a few curls ending on her blushing cheeks. A cut at the waistline, exposed her 'dream figure' belly. The large elongated train, swept along the floor as she paced gracefully. The Subtle smile amidst the birdcage veil completed her elegant look. Uncle Chris had teary eyes, feeling sentimental at the moment. John was a good guy too, she thought to herself, he wore a black suit, looking the same as she had watched him before.

There was the moment of silence reminiscing the dead ones and the minister called out the first name, Which left her stunned. Mrs. Laura Wilson. This was John's critically ill mother, the lady for whom his father had deserted them all. Her eyes searched amongst the crowd on the right side of sitting and not to her astonishment and not much to her expectations either, there was Alfred Whitaker seated in the row, wiping a tear from his right eye. At first she was shocked to hear the loss, but kicked herself for being a bogus.

'Whatever' she sniffed at the mourning husband who was an epitome of disloyalty for her. Ryan couldn't be spotted anywhere she concluded to herself. Her heart had been pounding all these minutes until she comprehended he was an utter coward. Obviously he could never muster up the courage to face her any moment in his life and it's better if he never attempts to. She thought to herself. She picked up hustling Asher from behind the chair and made him sit on her lap. There was a sermon 'love is kind...love is patient' within the time Olivia thought whether it actually is kind or fatal, but how would one lie in front of the god...where was the god but...' it was time the couple exchanged vows, among the personalized vows, Camilla made ask John 'you vow never to lie and hide anything from her' And John promising voice said ' I do.' It was quite evident that Camilla had been taking lessons from Olivia's tragedies. 'It's good' she gave an opinion in her mind.

They exchanged rings and the couple was declared married. Olivia was quite a little taken aback by Camilla's traditional wedding. She never expected her family followed customs and traditions. But they were a family right! How would Olivia know what a complete family looked like, how do they spend their day, cause she never witnessed one.

As the couple walked back, one by one all greeted and congratulated them, it was Olivia's turn. People had almost left till now, the ceremony took around seventy five minutes and more. 'Olly' Camilla called and threw her arms around her, possibly to show friendships. Olivia embraced her and involuntarily broke into tears, making others puzzled. I m sorry, do forgive me', Olivia whispered into her ears, and then Camilla's relaxed her arms and wrapped them around her, getting a firm hold and waiting for the misunderstandings to flow along their tears. Then was the real embracement.

CHAPTER ELEVEN

' *When patches were rough, you lifted my spirit,*
When waves were wild, you held me tight.
I failed it once, you taught me twice
At every new step, I am caught with fright,
On a journey way harder, you travelled with smile!
I turn hell fire at pins and needles,
On a chair of cactus, you were calm as ice,
On an easier path, I've lost every hope;
With a bunch of hurdles, the courage how you held?
Despite all troughs, you were always wise,
The heroic mommy, you were always right!

Since you left this world, nothing has remained the same, mommy. I could never gather the courage again to meet your kids. I understand that I took a wrong decision in life, but that was a mistake. I m paying for the mistake made. I wish I had listened to you earlier. I am sorry before you, I feel sorry for myself, I feel sorry for my son!

I also met your husband, he is alive. I m sorry I lied you all the time, but trust me, even I didn't know about it. Ryan had deceived me all these years. When I learnt the truth, I ended our relation. Today at Camilla's wedding, I saw your husband again, he doesn't deserve the respect to be called 'dad' As I always said. I saw him weeping at the announcement of death of his sweetheart. There marriage was quite a traditional one, unlike mine. She said it's important to start a new life in the presence of God. I don't understand this. Anyway, if there is a God then I would ask him to show me the reason of my existence. Why does the world exist if any one could wrong us and move away happily. Whatever, I await the day when I'll discover the reason of god's creations.'

Olivia closed her diary and pushed back the drawer after keeping it in. It had become more special to her, since she had lost every ear to share her feelings with. Asher had turned nine month old, he had started to stand up by the support of anything that could be reached by his hand. In such attempts he got hit several times by the tables, open drawers of the kitchen and also TV rack. Growing Asher was turning Olivia into an person. Quite a fact was hence proved, that verily not only parents teach children but also learn from them. Never mind if it were parents or a single parent.

****

'Answer me, are you in a plan to re-join ever or not?' Olivia asked wheeling the pram in the garden.

'There's no second thought to that Olly, I'll join soon after returning from our trip ' Camilla trailed off in the air.

'You are no more that Mérida!' she smiled as she nodded her head slightly.

'I've a long list of mistakes and lessons' she winked whispering 'boyfriends' At Olivia.

'Never mind if it's boyfriends or friends, the goal is to take lessons' she replied sarcastically, looking down, pushing away the stone from way by her feet.

Camilla curved her lips at the reply. This evening the two friends had joined each other at the walk in the garden. The conversation didn't strike of at first, then they busted into non stop gossips and jokes. Olivia was guilty at her behaviour, Camilla felt she was blameable for the awkward situation and hence preferred to give space. Olivia revealed what hurt her the most, that she was the last person to know the big news. And Camilla felt bad for she abandoned her at the time she needed her the most just after she supported her more than her shadow. Things sorted out one by one and ended up with mocking Daniel, as he was very interested in Camilla, but attended the wedding as Camilla asked John to call him personally and compelled to visit them.

It was time Asher felt sleepy, so Olivia bid her and drove back to the house. She carried him upstairs and made him sleep on the bed. Covering him with cushions she turned off the lights and switched on the lamp. Descending down stairs cautiously, the hunger pangs reminded her of the missed dinner. She had bought along some bread returning from the office. It would do for the dinner. The next day, probably she would get her salary paid. Such was the way she managed her expenses. And she didn't feel sorry about it. It wasn't as if she had tried every possible way to spend and save, according to her it was already too much on her, and she wished to take everything one by one. Life was so eager to teach her everything before every body around her. She took a knife and cut the corners of the bread slices.

She rubbed the toasted bread to the butter wrapper. Having the sandwich she popped up with an idea to watch a movie, but it will remind her of Ryan. No, not again! She thought of calling Camilla, but it wasn't a good idea either. She scrolled down the videos and saw Taylors new song out. She played the song, named *Mr. Perfectly fine*. After eating she closed all the lights and walked up into the room, lied beside Asher and connected the ear pods and was lip-synching along the lyrics she clicked on several suggested videos, closing that and selecting a new suggestion, she had to kill her time to drag herself into a dimension where she could enter a 'happy zone'. After one and a half hour of browsing she came over an Irish drama series. It was that one drama about Camilla had talked about her to. The protagonist had a face resembling to herself. She was awestruck looking at her. She continued to read the description and say what? It was ISABELLA WHITAKER! She Googled her name, and found out that she had acted in almost six dramas series until now, and was a rising star of Irish TV industry. She searched for her for almost an hour, her various interviews and in one of them when she was asked about siblings, she replied 'she had only two brothers and was happy about the fact that she didn't have any sister!' she chortled at the statements made. She thought ' probably she doesn't remember who managed her stinky diapers and her night stay awakes... this was the return of sacrificing literally every thing for them'

She called Camilla ignoring the fact that it was too late to talk at that time, and now that she's not alone now, her husband could mind it, but she just wanted to clear the load off her heart. She narrated the entire thing and chattered until Camilla found a good excuse to hang up the phone as she was drowsing. Olivia just longed for an ear to share her feelings with, no comments, no replies, no judgements. She was sincerely happy, for her sister and wished her lots of success ahead.

She binge watched the drama series and loved her acting Skills. She just couldn't come over the fact that how her little munchkin had grown up so fast. It was the right track that she'd chosen she thought.

****

Next day in the office, Olivia winded up her tasks to sip the hot coffee in the break time. Though in the earlier days, she felt odd to deal with loneliness, but now she was getting used to it. She missed their giggles and gossips too. She was trying to find peace in the fact that Camilla is now well settled, and she must be happy for her friends happiness for that was the mantra of a happy life.

'I desperately need a good company, and in return you get this coffee. Deal?' Shawn placed two cold coffees on the round grey table, and flumped on the chair opposite to her. It was the place where Camilla used to sit.

'Uh.. thanks, but I am stuffed.' She excused, surprised at the offer by a new face, probably an intern. He was medium heighted whitish complexioned lad.

He pulled back the mug and smirked ' oh thank you, I just couldn't find a better pick up line'

She couldn't resist and her lips pulled apart with knitted brows at the answer, she wore her sandal and raised her torso, to feel confident and grasped her phone.

'Excuse me miss,' he pointed as she was about to stand. Olivia glared in silence expressing a short green single.

'My name is Shawn, you can call me shhh' he looked into her eyes, winking with a flirting smile that revealed his crooked tooth.

'Done?' Olivia sounded cold.

'And your sweet name please...'

'What brings you here?' She asked with a high tone, gathering attention of the surrounding tables.

'Hush...okay so let me specify' he whispered, blowing out air through his plump lips.

'You resemble into an Irish actress, Isabella Whitaker.' He continued. 'I think you are her doppelgänger. By the way, many people may have already told you about that, or' ...he took a pause with eye lock, 'You look prettier..?' his black glittery eyes radiated tease, while his crooked teeth behind smile expressed childishness.

Ignoring the doubts, Olivia got super excited for at least somebody in her circle, knew her sister. 'she's my sister' her voice whispered, blushing cheeks above cheekbones broke the bubble.

He jerked back at the reply ' she doesn't have any sister, you're lying!'

She was bewildered at the scenario created, ' Yeah I am' she faked a caught smiling expression.

'I am an intern and Mr Benjamin asked me to meet the manager here, I waiting for the recess to end, and then see her. Hope the interview goes well' he crossed his fingers, sniffing in tension.

She glanced at her wrist watch and got up from the table, giving a weird expression.

****

Olivia leaned chair with her open hands, sorted all her assembled files and was awaiting the mysterious Shawn to conduct the interview.

He entered the door after knocking, and wasn't as surprised as she had expected him to get, to know that to the girl he's been talking about the his job was the manager herself. Taking a step back, as he froze staring at her and realising the irony, he proceeded concealing the shock. She compared his decent hair do, well built frame and flirtatious nature while he strode.

'Good afternoon once again' he pressed his teeth and pulled the chair only after Olivia murmured, 'have you seat' this time in a civilized manner.

He pushed forward his resume gently, and offered a confident smile. Olivia turned through the files, along with a few questions which she had learnt by heart till now.

'Tell me about yourself...'

'I've pursued my bachelor's in literature, merit student in philosophy from St Rutherford's, I've served as a senior assistant in editing department of ABC magazines for two years, an honest critic award from the same. Besides, I am also a part time content writer for designer daisies web page.'

'An introduction includes your name as well..' she pointed out.

'Name, Shawn Doyle, age twenty four years, born in Dublin and resided until five years ago.'

'Since what age you started working, I see you are too young and bagged quite a big accomplishments ...' Olivia enquired impressively.

'It's all about the situation your fortune sets and you wear the suitable glass of perception! I was exposed to certain unexpected circumstances and here it is!' he shrugged his shoulders. Olivia wondered he was deep and philosophical as green and young he seemed.

'Why do you want to was work here?'

'I have studied and always had aspired to be a part of Johnson's, I believe this is the platform my talent needs to serve and a company that recognises and appreciates efforts of its employees.'

'Why are you leaving your previous job?'

'As I mentioned earlier I always have been a subject oriented candidate, and for the a student to have a good hold on his subject, he must practice it. With some objectives I worked there and believe this is a better platform to showcase my talent and experience.'

'What makes you different from others?' Olivia asked, scribbling the pen against some questions in the form, she leaned at the chair, more focused on this answer, tossing the pen around fingers.

'Well, to be honest I am unaware of what qualities others poses, but I am a philosophical person and thinks that all others is a misused term, as everyone cannot be categorised into a group, and every individual has a set of strengths and weaknesses, furthermore I would like to say that I am a student of life, learning new lessons and finding the ultimate cause of life.' He answered every question with the same self esteem and expressed ethics.

Olivia bent forward and rested her elbows on the table' this quality of yours can deviate you from your job...'

'As far as it's about commitment, I assure you I am a responsible person, these qualities of mine won't affect the tasks that are assigned to me... if my philosophies become a barrier to my career, I will make sure I take any step only after the contract ends, but currently I am interested in the job you offer, irrespective of the wage you provide.' Shawn was full of philosophies and reasoning.

'You are not as focussed as you seem ... there's a blend in your personality or you pretending to be one, there are remarkable differences in the person I met in canteen and the one sitting opposite to me. I am sorry to say, but we've already enough of fakes and frauds. I cannot proceed your resume to the central branch. '

'You may leave,' she broke the silence.

'There must in a misunderstanding ma'am, there were differences in the two scenarios, because these are two different situations, giving a job interview and finding a friend for yourself. One of the most important lessons life has taught me is that, nothing is unconditional, everything demands it's value. An interviewer requires a set of talents and skills and therefore I expressed them, alongside my work ethics, whereas being an intern I had to make friend and creating friendship is an informal meeting, which may include casual phrases. My sincere apologies as I didn't know you're the manager itself.' Shawn explained his side. His oratory skills were influencing. He was the right candidate may be.

Olivia smiled and closed his file, 'glad meeting you Mr Shawn. Our team will contact you soon.

'Thank you' he nodded and walked out, leaving the puzzled Olivia.

CHAPTER TWELVE

'I can file a case for his custody, he is my son too!' Ryan bent to grab the sleeping Asher into his arms. His brown watch brushed against her arm as she took a step back.

'You don't deserve to touch him either, you are an absolute cheat. Had it been possible, I would have trashed out your DNA from him also. Just get out.' She snatched him back from his arms causing him to break his sleep and he started crying. She tapped on his back, making him fall asleep on her shoulder whispering a lullaby sub consciously as she was throwing heated stares. She pressed his back against her hear and kissed the fist of his hanging arm.

Climbing up the stairs she laid him down in the bed she got back to Ryan, upon returning the door left open with a note ' Asher belongs to me'

Olivia marched out of the door and tore the paper into pieces and screamed with quickest breaths as sweat collected on her forehead, 'don't show your face ever, you coward!'

She restlessly turned on the sides as her heart throbbed and jumped upright from the bed. Alas! What a nightmare it was. She bent to kiss Asher's forehead and rested by his side. Tears fell on her sides. Wiping off the sweat, She hugged him tight ignoring the possibility of his awaking. As she switched off the light after drinking water, Asher woke up to the disturbance caused, his tiny eyes with long lashes raised and he smiled looking at her. Olivia switched on the light again and Asher closed his eyes, he then opened them slowly to see Olivia beside him. He rose up from the bed and neared her, leaned by her side and threw his arms around her to continue his broken sleep.

Her happiness knew no bounds, what a moment it was, she just felt ecstatic and blessed. Every act of his surprised her, and made her overwhelmed. Unable to resume sleeping, he got off the bed and sat beside his huge white teddy bear. He had so many toys, he picked up a car and wheeled it on the table. The car fell off from his hand and he bent down to pick it up, meanwhile he made an eye contact with Olivia from behind the table. She was sitting on the bed, and whispered ' peek a boo!' he raised his head and fell into shrieks of laughter. His head upturned with rocking torso and his eyes had narrowed. This lead Oliva to giggle as she was staring him in amusement and again he bent under the table, this time not to pick up the car, but to seek her attention. ' Peek a boo!' Again he guffawed, rising from below, Olivia grinned. She wished to stop the hands of clock, it was after an eternity that the walls of the house had heard the chuckles. She dropped the toys from the bag and sat beside him on the mat. She watched him keenly, playing with the toys, and the nightmare creeped into her mind again. She could never think of losing him, Asher had become her backbone and she was nothing without him. She always thought about to raise him into a gentleman who won't cheat on any woman. She would also think about never letting him meet his father, for he never deserved that. Probably she would tell him that he died in a car accident. Her tongue wouldn't hesitate to say this lie, because it was now the same, whether he is dead or alive that didn't matter them a penny.

Asher picked up his milk bottle and walked towards her, yawning. Olivia checked the time it was 4:30 AM. She laid him in her lap and gave him an oil massage. He fell asleep only after listening to the lullaby sung by his mother.

'Lullaby and good night
Thy mother's delight
Bright angels beside
My darling abide'

****

It was 9 in the morning and Olivia turned off the alarm in her phone. She checked there was a message from Camilla, ' Call when free'. Now Olivia was in her comfort zone and she didn't want to step out from this. She felt that it needed confidence, and guts to talk her now as the situation had become awkward. She had a broken marriage, who was a devotee of relationships and Camilla, she was person who never took life too seriously, and she was living a happily married life. She wasn't jealous, but there was lack of self esteem. To add upon, john was her step brother. The inferiority complex lasted not more than 10 minutes if she would call her, she too was sure about that. But still she was resisting. There was one more message, from an unknown number.

Good morning ma'am, Shawn Doyle here,

Thanks for Shortlisting my resume and forwarding to the central branch.

Yesterday they called me for an interview, and hopefully they might select me.

Thank you once again.:)

Olivia snickered as everyone around her seemed to succeed, she was too, in terms of work, but since childhood, success for her was a happy family. She connected her phone to the charger and took her bath gown for a shower.

While taking bath, she pre-planned the days schedule, it was, Asher's diapers, packing his bag, giving him a bath, change his clothes, mama baby breakfast and start for the office, after dropping Asher at the nanny's. Camilla's absence had become a habit now, will look up to Shawn, conference meeting after lunch, library data analysis and return to house, after collecting Asher. In the wake of a sound nap, she had decided to re arrange her cupboard and do the laundry. She would treat herself with a pizza or doughnuts, that would suffice for her dinner. Playing with Asher, making his videos and feeding him. This was enough to pass her time, making her tired enough to hit the sac. She realised she was taking some good sleep, now a days, it was peaceful and complete. She wrapped herself on the gown and dried her hair, and was set for the busy day ahead.

****

It was quarter to one, Olivia stapled the observation sheets for the meeting and filled it. She unlocked her tab and checked the presentation to be submitted, it was prepared last Sunday. Things were really changing these days, she didn't have to dance at the eleventh hour, all thanks to the absence of her backbones, Ryan and Camilla. She had to learnt to stand by herself. After making a couple of background changes she settled at the maroon theme and closed the tab, she again pressed the power button to check the battery, it was 62% and that would suffice, she had had a bitter experience of getting the tab switched off during the important times. She was taking lessons and it was good. The clock had struck one by then and she felt dozy. She thought to sip some coffee and rock the meeting. Piling up the messy table, she walked into the canteen. She glanced at the Camilla's empty cabin and her heart missed her company. 'oh yeah, she texted me to call her ' her eyebrows furrowed on remembering.

Putting on an off white broad plated skirt and a pink collared shirt, She stood second in the queue and placed an order for a café latte. Scrolling down the phone's browser feed she waited for her order. Taking a good look around the canteen, she was fetching for a peaceful place to sit, because her window seat was occupied. Her eyes ran back to her place, as the seated person appeared familiar, she walked towards the table and dragged the chair in the air, to avoid attention caused due to screech. ' Good afternoon, I am almost done ma'am' Shawn stood upright, pushing the chair, and causing the same screech she wished to avoid, while everyone around looked at them, making an awkward situation. She exhaled the longest breath and said wearing a fake smile 'it's okay you can sit '

He sat down, pulling the chair nearer, and kept the coffee mug on the table,

'By the way congratulations, for the job'

'Thank you ma'am ' he replied politely raising his head. His quietude created questions in her mind.

'It's okay, you can be the earlier shhh' she smiled half heartedly.

'Actually, the other day I didn't know you were the manager, itself.'

'I know ' she replied bluntly.

Olivia thought for a while and questioned, 'Your change in behaviour represents you value job more than friends?'

He hummed for a moment and answered, 'I value ethics, I consider job ethics over befriending anyone.'

'You cannot be orthodox Shawn, diplomatically you got to deal with the circumstances' she advised.

'As I said, I am a student of life, day by day, I would like to pile up the priority hierarchy, in my own way'

'Interesting... which aspect would be on the lowest?' She commented developing interest in his philosophies, taking a long sip.

'Love life' he replied with least respect for this dimension.

'Strange' she thought he might have also have been injured with the weapon of love.

She rolled her wrist and checked the time it was quarter past one.

'Excuse me, see you again, got to go now' she got up from the chair, placing her cup. She adjusted her ruffled shirt, as she made her way to the conference hall.

****

'Some loose petals, fell off my rose,
I m blessed, for I have the stalk to hold,
And that little bud,
Is too growing old,
Who cares for the bouquet,
I'll cherish one flower,
Forget the thorns,
I m obsessed with the essence you shower,
It's almost an year,
And many more to unfold,
I'll always cherish,
the petals,
Of the rose I hold.
My footprints in the sand,
And those serene waves...

In no time, Asher would turn one year old! I can't write that time flies, it didn't initially, but the past 3-4 months, I didn't realise how fast the time passed, you learnt everything one by one, turning at back, crawling, sitting, standing by support and walking. And while learning somethings, you taught me many things more, what would I do without you my baby, lots of love and kisses to my ashhy.'

She closed her diary and looked at the sleeping Asher, within a week he would turn one and she couldn't believe it. Lying down on the bed, scrolling down the phone, she reminisced about Camilla,' she had asked to call her, I'll call her tomorrow' she thought then. Keeping the phone beside after, setting an alarm, and brushing her hair through the fingers, her thoughts travelled numerous dimensions and after seemingly endless duration, they halted at Ryan, had he been here, they would have celebrated his birthday, it was a dream. 'Its good now that I am not surrounded with fakes and frauds.' This is her sweet real life. And it had no space of any drama. She could picturize the foil balloons, 'ONE' in her lawn, with the floral décor, or may be I would be some sort of football themed party, studded with their families and friends. They would stand on the sides and cut the cake along Asher, the clicks and lights of camera would soon begin to irritate her, but no, now if it was possible to happen, it wouldn't have hurt her. The past year had taught her several lessons. It was strange that life wasn't tired of teaching her the lessons before she could even fulfil the eligibility criteria. Any way, she huffed and turned her head, trying to sleep. It was strange as well that she no more kept pondering over the possible reasons that Ryan had deceived her, or that she kept stalking him online on the various social media sites.

****

'It seems someone's busy as a bee'

'Oh not really, same old same old' she trailed off in the air.

'When are you coming back here' Olivia continued after a pause.

'I am a little mixed up actually, when ever John gets done with his pending tasks, to be honest, though I love traveling, I miss wales so badly'

'Hope you do'

'How's life?' Camilla asked expressing the guilt of abandoning her friend.

'Well to be more specific, the question would make sense if you ask me what's life instead?' Olivia sounded toneless.

'What is life?' Camilla asked mysteriously.

'Asher!' she gasped and spoke ecstatic, 'that's the meaning of life for me, I can't believe he's gonna turn one in a week'

'I am genuinely happy for you ' her voice turned brittle.

'What about that Benjamin, does he ask about me?'

'Last week he did, he doesn't bother me anymore'

'Seems like he got scared' she joked.

'Well, I wouldn't like to praise myself but that's a fact ...' Olivia boasted.

'Oh just shut up, I sent him once a no filter selfie of yours, and since then you can see, he got terrified' Camilla pulled her leg.

'Yucky! Your sense of humour got terrific in London' she tittered.

'Ok, so what are the birthday plans ...?' Camilla put a question.

'I'll apply for a leave and take him to the park in the morning, am planning to book a photographer, get the photo session done, buy him lots of toys, a big football, chocolates and his favourite jam of course, return home to play with him for the remaining time. I am sure I won't even know when the day had passed, you know what, I used to think earlier that I would be a strict parent, but now I just couldn't do that ...'

'That's great' Camilla realised her friend was overjoyed, and that was the best news she could hear in their separated time.

'I no longer get fancied by socializing, to show off, and match the fake standards of community.'

'I'm impressed'

'Cause, I am impressive' she shrugged.

'That's funny' Camilla teased,

'Hoping to see you soon'

'I think Asher is getting disturbed by me' she whispered.

'Not a problem'

'Sure, take care' she whispered again.

'Love you'

'Bye'

CHAPTER THIRTEEN

Olivia sneaked from the partly filmed glass of her cabin at the gentle knock, it was Shawn. He pushed the door in and brought along a file in his hand. She was busy in her work and had ordered him to wait. 'Have a seat please' she said her eyes glued to the screen.

Continuing to stare in the screen, she asked him 'what is it?, while her right hand pulled out the papers falling from the printer.

'It is an invitation for the annual get together at the Johnson's' he replied.

'When is it scheduled on?' she asked making a flash of eye contact and back into the screen again,

'Its on 11th of August on Friday, 8 PM.'

'Get it here' she stretched her hand to take the invite, rotated her face from left to right, reading the matter, she turned the pages, and picked up a pen from the pen stand to sign against her name, Mrs Olivia Whitaker. Viewing her classy signature, a hint of pride and satisfaction hit her as she forwarded the file to him.

'Thank you' he murmured softly and left with lowered eyes. This very formal conduct of his, had always confused Olivia. There was a huge difference between his two behaviours. The former was that he unknowingly expressed and the latter that he represented of an ideal employee.

****

At one, Olivia cleared her desk and carried her phone along to the canteen, ordered her coffee, and sat on the patent window chair. Sipping down the coffee, she realised there was some element missing, it was Shawn of course. She pressed her thumb against the fingerprint sensor of the phone, and typed a message to Shawn,

'Coffee break reminder'

She hung her thumb on the backspace option, and ran into a dilemma of whether to send or not, and ended up clicking on the send button. In his early twenties, a determined candidate sure he was she thought.

'*See you in two* minutes' her phone beeped and she checked the reply from him. Now she felt she was doing something wrong, but she didn't. Am I cheating on Ryan, a question raised from somewhere in her heart. But she put a full stop to all those questions,

What's wrong in having a healthy company?

But why is it Shawn only, it might be anybody else.

It was Camilla until now, but things have changed now and moreover she's no more present here.

But you were loving the solitude in the recent past.

That has now started to bore me now.

You are a mother of a son, you cannot afford to pay attention to any distractions.

Within the span her mind and heart were having a dirty debate, Shawn appeared before her eyes, and she shook her head wild and kicked herself for being so nasty. Meanwhile Shawn took a sip of coffee and awaited for the conversation opener from Olivia.

'Late today?'

'Just got stuck with the invitation reminders'

'Ooh I see' her phone beeped again, it was some notification. The phone lit up, displaying Asher's wallpaper.

'He's cute' Shawn commented not sneaking into.

'He is the reason I breath, the reason I am alive, he's my son' she answered proudly.

'Oh, I didn't know' he was quite taken aback by the fact, as his eyes widened brows parted, upturning the lower lip.

'Every time I get mistaken in assuming you ...' he continued with a smile.

'Really?' she asked confused.

'Indeed! at the first, I thought you were a fresher too, and you turned to be the manager here, next I thought you must be pursuing masters by now, but you are a mother. That's great' he complimented showing thumbs up.

'That's strange, one can be pursuing masters and be a mom, at a time'

'Oh yeah! Women power! One woman army?' he agreed.

'The folks here must have gossiped you about that, how should I believe it's your study? ' She felt strange for not feeling bad about being said of her unsuccessful marriage.

'I swear, none told me. Actually I don't have any friends here, I tried befriending Nick, but he's quite introvert. And Chris, every time I approach his table, Benjamin sir launches missiles with his eyes and says that he doesn't like free mixing of colleges. After all, job is more important for me than friends.'

'Where do you place friends on your priority list?'

'The list is not yet ready, but I can assure you, that it would be above the love life, of course.'

'The below your ambition' she stated,

'Exactly' he smirked.

'Do a favour to me, the day you figure out what's exactly the ranks in hierarchy of priorities, do teach me some' she spoke friendly.

'It would be a pleasure to do so, but since you are older to me and way more experienced, I believe my studies won't help you'

'As far as age is concerned, It is just a number, and experiences don't help, until one takes lessons from it. And the day you take the lesson, it teaches you the next chapter, your philosophies would be of help to me up to greater extent.'

He smiled. 'Nice meeting you, got to go now'

'Sure' she picked up the phone from the table and walked out.

****

'I find it strange that my days are now a pendulum between office and home, yet I feel content, I can swear as well that I don't even miss Ryan, Asher has not just replaced him it's even greater than that. I have made a new friend too, Shawn he's is a good boy. He would never replace Camilla, but maybe even Camilla won't get her place back. I know I am getting selfish but that is it.

The serene sound of his, that pronounces ' mommy' reaches my soul and blooms my heart. I could have never thought that I would be ever obsessed over him, he is such a an angel, a pure soul.'

On the last page of a register, with thoughts scribbled and overwritten, Olivia, sat into the room deciding the wallpaper, furniture and the colours of wall. Asher push opened the door wide and walked in curiously, sitting in the room she amassed her thoughts and feelings, after cleaning the study. She had to free one day, at least fortnightly, for maintenance of the house. Arranging the leprechaun for the lawn, dusting, cleaning and organizing her wardrobe. Doing the dishes, laundry and grocery. The study room had been of no use since the past year, and there were no signs ahead. An idea had lately emerged into her mind, of turning the it into Asher's room. Asher held the arm of computer chair and tried standing but the chair turned round, and he ended up falling, loosing the grip and balance.

Olivia tossed the pen on the sofa and ran towards him, to get him up. He got hurt at the forehead and was crying consequently. She held him and stroke his forehead, caressing his golden brown hair. 'My baby needs a haircut,' she hugged him, after saying, thence Asher cackled. 'My baby needs a haircut!' she repeated thereby he laughed again and she repeated several times. The way he guffawed, flowered her soul. This was not her habit, Olivia was a calm person at the most she would chuckle. It was Ryan's trait, and it didn't bother her, for it was the reason of her happiness. She stood up, taking the book and held his finger to help him walk out of the room. She locked the room and took along the keys, and checked the bread on the counter to prepare his lunch. After washing hands thoroughly, she took out the jam and spread on a slice and placed in a plate. She opened the fridge to grab an egg, and fried it in a pan. While she was frying, he picked up the dropped spoon and handed over to her, this again reminded her of Ryan, super organisation. She cooled the egg and placed it on the slice, washed her hands again, and walked out. Taking some steps back she switched off the light of the kitchen, just after the high bill notice, hit her memory.

****

Days passed by and there was one day for Asher's birthday, Olivia had winded up the work before time. She wished that Benjamin doesn't catch her leaving early, it was half an hour earlier. But to her misfortune as she raised her head after locking the drawers of desk, Olivia saw him passing by the filmed glass wall of her cabin. She dropped the keys into her open purse and spotted Shawn knocking at the door, before entering. She gestured an unenthusiastic nodding down, that represented the unwanted welcome. He pushed in the door and cleared his throat, understanding the intensity of his needlessness. She indicated towards the chair, 'please have a seat',

'Mr. Benjamin asked to review this file' he placed on the clean table.

She lazily took the file and turned the pages in a manner, that the sneaking Benjamin doesn't get a hint of her aggression. 'this is the list of library membership applicants!, I already checked this before noon' she rolled back the file, which fell into his lap.

'Err am sorry, actually tomorrow is my son's birthday, and I wanted to leave early for the preparations' she cleared before him taking back the file.

'I wish the best for your son; it's crystal clear that he doesn't want, you to leave early'

She tightened her lips and blankly stared at him, with the no response expression.

He sat there, quiet for almost five long minutes, and broke the silence, ' what have you planned for the birthday'

This question of his had excited her and worked as an instant stress buster, mood lifter and what not, a tropical mix of emotions. She gulped down the clog that was choking her and involuntarily a tear rolled down her cheek and she wiped it with her finger, after which a superficial smile overtook the expression. She was overwhelmed, because there was at least one person on the planet who was interested in her happiness and joy.

'I am going to get a dress for him returning from the office and a photography session and... preparation of the cake.' She was beyond delighted.

'I suggest to buy a readymade cake' he proposed confidently, leaning at the backrest.

'You won't believe, I bake wonderful cakes' she added proudly. She unlocked her phone and scrolled down infinitely to get an old picture of their fourth wedding anniversary cake, and turned the screen towards him. She later noticed passing of Benjamin by the corridor.

'Unbelievable, did you bake this?' Shawn was surprised.

'Yeah, even Ryan used to love those. ' she shrugged after pretending to talk something office related.

'Is he...' He paused hesitatingly, looking down, maybe guilty for being nosy.

'Yeah, he was my husband' her face turned expressionless, after the curved lips contracted.

'You two looked adorable' he complimented, still adoring the duo. She was wearing a red tunic and black jeans while Ryan wore a maroon checkered shirt over a denim, they had twinned that time and the cake also matched the theme, the huge red forest cake and the crowd beside them, everything had vanished in a blink.

'Seriously, in this photo you are a look alike of Isabella ' his eyebrows raised excitedly at the analysis of a fact, that he was sure, was a coincidence as his sight fell on her name plate, 'Isabella Whitaker, ...Olivia Whitaker; you must not be lying you two are sisters' he laughed at himself, thinking he was funny.

Olivia couldn't help but laughed along him, suppressing Benjamin's stares.

'Wishing your son eternal success, wisdom and prosperity.'

'Thank you,' she gave a heartily smile, it was half past four and Shawn picked up the closed file, lying on the table and bid to her. She stood up along him and grabbed the purse, put the phone in the purse, walked out of the cabin, she locked the door and dropped the keys and zipped the purse waiting for the lift.

****

The hand brake pulled back with a ratcheting sound, she raised her fastened fingers around it and pushed back the door of car. She sprinted through the stairs till the door and walked gently once she stepped in the store, while the babysitter's calls and messages popped up twice in every minute she ran her fingers through the hung dresses and selected a pilot costume from the shop while there was an increasing pressure of picking Asher in the back of her mind. It was a navy blue coat over a white shirt. She thought it was the best as he loved aeroplanes. She could already imagine his beaming white complexion against the dark colour. Stopping at the toy shop and bought a large white musical aeroplane toy, and a Mickey mouse soft toy for him. These two things formed a base for his room decorating ideas to her. After a span of six months, he would also not fall off from the bed. But how would I let him sleep away from me? It would be his playing room; she concluded. After a few years when he would go to school, I will buy him a study table.' her thoughts took a pause as she halted the car at the babysitting and opened the door to take the birthday boy in. She kept the bag at the passengers seat and adjusted him in her lap, she fastened the belt singing and swinging with her fists in the air 'Congratulations and celebrations., we are on the way to your birthday' there was no tone, rhythm and time yet this sound was soothing to ears and heart.

****

As she unlocked the door and stepped in the house, Asher was in an energetic mood, he ran towards the stairs and climbed up taking support of the railing. She locked the door, and washed her hands and face. Taking the bags she walked upstairs, Asher was busy fetching the new shoes in the shoe rack. Olivia was stunned with his powerful memory. Sitting heel down beside him She handed him the box of new lightning shoes. He struggled to open it at first but eventually succeeded and made such cute faces, she could never get over.

After having coffee and feeding Asher, she opened the bags to show him the dress she'd brought for him. He came crawling from the door and stood by the support of bedpost, jumping in excitement. He swiped his hand over the dress and silently adored it. She lifted him up on the bed, and made him sit on the lap. Placing the pilot hat on his head, she tilted from the side to look at him. 'God gracious, my baby looks so beautiful' she turned him to her side and kissed him on the cheek, chin and forehead, while he enjoyed. Love was in the air, 'Mammas boy' she called and he bend his forehead repeating 'Mommy' with his soothing voice and gave a wet peck on her forehead, this was followed with whoops of laughter. She quickly gave him the milk bottle and lied beside him. As soon as he fell asleep she woke up and dialled the grocery store, if they could home deliver the items for cake.

Within a span of twenty minutes the items were delivered. she was nervous and ecstatic and the same time, she darted in the kitchen, and started preparing the cake, for the next day she would be occupied.

Three hours later, she turned out of the fridge closing the door and screamed looking at some white faced elf behind her back.

CHAPTER FOURTEEN

Asher climbed down, with an empty bottle of face powder, calling ' Mommy'. His hair and face was completely covered with talcum powder. He walked in the kitchen, rolling the bottle of powder and scared Olivia. She screamed as she got frightened and realised it was Asher in powder. She remembered, she had kept it on the table, instead of the shelf.

'Oh, no Asher!' she yelled at him, and washed her hands. She held him by his arms and hung on her waist. While cleaning him, her sight fell on the reflection in the mirror and she was surprised about why wasn't Asher scared to see her, as she was almost immersed in the grocery. She turned left to see him licking the chocolate on arm that probably had hurled while blending. This act of his reminded her of Ryan, suppressing the emerging memories, she continued to wash. Also, kitchen was a sight worth viewing, the packets of butter were lying on the floor, The egg shells on the counter, flour spread all over the apron, pieces of fondant could be spotted everywhere, whisk, knife, spatula, whipping cream, food colour and of course the chocolate. Every item witnessed their presence and usage in the cake.

She carried Asher along her, up in the room and gave him a hot water shower, changed his dress and opened the toys box for him to play. Meanwhile picking up the white t shirt and pegged trousers, she took a shower too and headed towards the dressing area to dry her hair, thankfully Asher had been playing with a car all the time, she heard a dim a sound of her phone ringing it was still in the kitchen downstairs. She switched off the lights of the room and carried Asher along down, it was the service person from the event managers. She had booked an online ad, as it served her discount. She dialled him back as the call was missed. She messaged her then, he texted back 'I am fifteen minutes away'. She heated the water in an electric kettle and put three heaped scoops of cereal into the bowl. In a sipper she filled water, and sat on the dining chair. He walked towards the antilop high chair, and she bent down to put him in.

It was ten at night, when she had finally winded up with the next days tasks, the study room makeover had been done, new wallpaper, balloons and décor. She thought of preparing some pasta for herself and headed towards the kitchen, while cooking she opened the refrigerator and sneaked into the cake, it looked wonderful. A light blue coloured two storey cake, on which the white clouds look amazing, a big aeroplane rested on the top, above which she was going to place the candle shaped one. She clicked a picture of it, and sent to Camilla along with the previous snap of decorated room.

****

Olivia set the alarm, and placed the milk bottle near the pillow, so he would drink while sleeping. Invitation messages were sent to the kids of the neighbours. She kept turning over from side to side, though it was a tiring day spent, she found it hard to fall asleep even after switching off the light. The traumatic events of the past year wandered into her mind, the unexpected tragedy and what not. The past year had taught her many lessons including this, 'let go off the shedding petals, instead cherish and hold the leftover rose. The autumn season had come to drop off the weak ones and to show who is the real support.' she dozed off admiring Asher who was sleeping on his stomach, wearing a blanket over and his face turned towards right.

****

'Asher, show me your eyes!' she stood behind the cameraman, and he blinked his large twinkling eyes. Standing on the stool in the decorated room, he gazed around in amusement. 'Asher! Show me you eyes!' she called again for the photo, his endearing looks were complimentary to his attire, the dark blue colour was simply contrasting against his white skin. This time he wasn't blinking eyes as he got distracted by the huge golden balloon.

But where did this come from, Olivia looked around as well, 'happy birthday, ashy' A well modulated disembodied voice was heard. The man swept along the balloons and gifts and jumped up high, taking Asher in his arms, it was out of delight. He hugged him tight and the room had filled with smoke, creating a blurry vision, and his face remained hidden.

'Who are you ?' she shouted and the sound disappeared in the chaos of laughter. The man signalled some hand gestures and Asher was repeating after him. Till now the smoke had almost vanished and the face before it appeared familiar. He plucked his eyelash and placed it in the right fist, gradually Asher did the same. They closed their eyes and whispered some thing. Asher did the lip syncing along him. Her heart started pounding, within a minute, while she was struggling to figure out with the knitted brows, the man held him and made him stand on the floor, and whispered something in the ear again. Asher had a wide grin on his face and opened arms, ran towards her, and pleaded 'Mommy, let's forgive daddy!'

It was beyond imagination, and her mind was ready with a pile of questions about when did he learn to speak so clear and fluent? But before she could guess the answer for that question, she got the person. It was Ryan!

Again. In the tensed atmosphere, and the running white smoke, he approached towards Olivia and slid sitting on his knees. Her feet and knees grew restless, the ambience was turning edgier. There was some uneasiness as well, she turned both sides as the pressure was building consistently, to break it all she sat right, leaning at the bedrest. She took a breath of gratitude, it was a dream!

She placed her pillow beside sleeping Asher and rushed to the natures call. She brushed her teeth and her heart was still pounding, she had to give herself a therapy of calmness, it appeared as though her heart didn't hold the strength anymore to hold a new affliction. Her mind was still revolving over the dream, and she observed that how Ryan's face had blurred in her memory. She didn't want to refresh it by watching him in the pictures. It was a good sign she thought.

Returning from the loo, she switched on the light, wiped her face from the hanging towel and plunged on tippy toes on the bed to the adrenaline rush, it was the big day! She checked the time in the phone, it was still quarter to nine. There's plenty of time to sleep she decided, but once let me check the dress, she thought and opened the wardrobe, her blue dress hung decently on the rod. She adored the image in her head of how would she slay wearing it. A smile popped up on her face as she tied her open hair into a bun, she off the light and spread over the blanket, by stretching it, after adjusting the pillow and cushions. Asher's bottle was full, he didn't drink any, that was quite strange she thought and enveloped the blanket as her baby hair were annoying and she was shivering of cold. Only her face was visible and she was ready to dose off. She fought against the force of closing eyes to check Asher once, Lifting a part of it, she sneaked through, to see him sleeping on his stomach. How cute she thought. But wait, That's the position he had been sleeping since night, THERE'S SOMETHING FISHY! she climbed down from the bed and looked over from the other side, he was sleeping in the same position since midnight and hadn't drink any milk too, she was mixed up. Instead terrified. Tightening her loose hair strands into the bun, She lifted him in her arms and subconsciously waited for him to get disturbed or cry or just simply wake up or at least express sleepiness. But there was no response.

She rubbed her palm on his forehead checking the temperature for fever. He had turned cold, she could also sense a sort of stiffness. Her head was getting numb and limbs got cold and started to shiver, she called his name, 'ASHER '. there was no response still, his eyes were closed, she brought him closer to her chest and squeezed him hardest and again screamed in his ear, 'ASHEERRRR'. She was waiting for her heart to burst into pieces as there was no response again. She wanted to bang her head into the wall, the silence was slaughtering her. She held him tight before it gets very late, she grabbed a hanging shawl, his milk bottle, phone and took the keys from the table, she entered into the decorated room and picked up the balloon as she thought he might wake up easily to play with it. Waking out barefoot she didn't mind to leave the door unlocked, and started the car. She made him lie in her lap and started towards the city hospital. It was a five minute drive, yet the never ending one. If it would have been possible, she would have flew the car, to reach as fast as possible. It was morning yet there was a traffic on the main road, she wanted to bang into the boots or lower the glass and curse them all, for being so slow.

Simultaneously she kept an eye on Asher, he had still not awakened, she was howling of fear and screamed 'ASHER! mommy's got you a balloon, baby please wake up' her tones changed from to patient to highly aggressive, but nothing worked. The freaking silence continued. 'hope for the best Olly' she calmed herself. 'everything is gonna be fine' she kept whispering, talking to herself but nothing worked, her palms grew numb, feeling the rigidity. It was getting harder to focus, she reminisced the last time she banged in London, now she couldn't afford to do that, she had to be alive to look after him, as soon as he gets fine. She crossed her fingers, and kept driving.

They finally reached the hospital and the she parked her car and rushed in to the emergency centre carrying him in her arms, nurses laid him straight on a stretcher and wheeled inside, as she tried running along in the theatre, she was stopped by the staff apathetically. She tried getting rid of their hold to go inside. There was an over driving stress building as she had guessed this ambush of fate. She headed towards the reception still in numbness, furnished the details and made necessary payments. Losing consciousness, she felt it was impossible for her to write, and hence asked for assistance, when asked about father, unhesitatingly she replied dead. She scrolled down her phone and found no one to call, there was literally no one for her worst time. Camilla was in London..., viewing the log history with the racing heart and frozen palms, she had to trust Shawn this time. She called him, and the other side her tears knew no bound.

'Hello, '

'Hello', ' You are not audible Ma'am, hello'

What would she say? Sitting on the bench, she pressed her linked hands, after dropping the phone in her lap and holding the balloon. She laid her chin on her fists and wished for the least, that her son remains alive. She couldn't muster any courage to speak even a word. She cut the call and fetched for any support, her mind was blocked, with the falling tears she just hoped that everything goes well.

'May he remain safe, may he remain safe, may he remain safe ' she began to mumble with tightly closed eyes. Getting restless, she looked around in help and there she saw another boy, his head surrounded in pool of blood, being rushed into the emergency ward, he had probably met a car accident and behind came his parents fearful and tensed. Olivia cursed her fortune, that the lady was luckier as she had her husband's shoulder to cry upon, instead of crying in his arms, what she did had left Olivia surprised.

She raised her hands and prayed to someone, she literally begged with her words, her tears were on the flow, anybody could say the pain and grief she was going through but she lost no hope and kept praying. Olivia couldn't understand whom she was praying to, though there was an assumed god but how would he help her? How unfortunate was she thought to herself, none on land and none on the skies, she had no one for help.

There were a couple of people too, who were praying for their loved ones, this concept of praying seemed senseless and irritating to her. She texted Shawn and was looking desperately at the doors for the doctor to call her and say 'He's safe'. The door opened with a smooth creak and her heart started beating wildly, a nurse stepped out and called her in the counselling room. She ran behind her like a child and asked impotently holding her by her shoulders 'My Asher is safe, right?' she silently shrugged her shoulders and asked her to sit on the chair, 'Dr Emma Smith is coming, she'll talk to you' she continued. There was a fatal silence, after a couple of moments, she pleaded to the nurse, keeping the wrapped fingers under her chin and with a bowed head 'Please tell me my son's fine, please I beg you', she opened her purse and pulled all the money and put in the nurses hand, and with joint hands she begged again for her son.

'Have some patience' she said coldly and walked away, leaving the money on the table.

Dr Emma pushed in the door and entered, she was shocked to see that Olivia was his mother. 'Please have a seat Olivia! ' she offered a glass of water.

'Where is my son?' she shook her head wild, and cried loudest, banging on the table. Few strands fell from her bun, she raised the shawl wrapped around her white t-shirt, and handed the balloon to the Doctor ' I promise, he will wake up once you show him this balloon, it's his favourite' her eyes had already turned puffy. She sat on the chair, holding her arms.

'I m sorry. He's declared brought dead.'

Her subtle accent was an unsuccessful attempt of clemency. Her heart leaped out of her chest and clogged in her throat. The world seemed to spin around at the moment, putting a full stop on the time, her eyes dropped. Stunned at the statement, she tightened her jaw, paused breathing. It appeared as though her fate had determined to stab her throughout, before blowing to hell. She cursed every breath she took, and was rather astonished at the continuity of her existence. She could feel her heart beating vigorously, chills ran through her spine, freezing her consciousness.

Her lip moments and the words uttering from it, the sound echoed in her ears, creating numbness through ears into her head, her fear had come true. She had lost Asher! The vision began to gloom, she could hear his cries and guffaws, simultaneously, with sweat flowing all through her body.‘ that's impossible, how could he?’ she kept denying, her heart resisted, brain refused and her body disagreed. Her expression turned fierce despite the streaming tears, which represented her will to spear anybody through her helpless powers. If there was no mercy for, she didn't care to have mercy for others. Somewhere she was still reluctant to swallow the hard pill. She settled at the chair, tucked the hair strands behind her ears and adjusted her shawl, curving an uncanny smile, she crawled under the desk, to pick up the fallen balloon and handed it forcefully into her hand. ‘You are confused I guess. My son is not the one who was bleeding, he's that one year old baby, today is his birthday...’ she blabbered insanely, with a reduced tone, which raised suddenly with Emma's constant quietude. She rose from the chair and hurled the things from the table in anguish.

‘HE WAS ALIVE, I KNOW THAT, I DROVE HIM HERE, HE WAS ALIVE, I've SEEN HIM BREATHING IN THE HOSPITAL, YOU ARE FRAUDSTERS,YOU KILLED MY SON!!! YOU KILLED HIM.’ she wiped her tears and ran her palms, trying to rip her face off. ‘I am not lying, trust me, I bought him to get the vaccination...yesterday, he had cereal for dinner, I am going to sue you all for this...’ She retorted.

She was lying, out of helplessness, finding a way to satisfy her throbbing heart, everything had shattered before her eyes, the room she used to enter with hopes and happiness to learn about their unborn child seemed to be immersed in blood and gore, now had announced about his death in no time. The environment seemed to darken, the vision blurred, she took heavy breaths, to ingest as she fell short of breath, she sat on the chair, embracing the balloon to her chest, and squeezed it tight. Within a fraction of second, she howled loud, the balloon popped loud bursting out of pressure, consequently she collapsed on the floor.

****

Shawn stood by the corner of room, turning pages of the reports, waiting for the action duration of sedatives to end and Olivia to wake. A couple of hours later, she gained consciousness and sat upright, with a heavy head, figuring out the surroundings. He placed the reports on the table and sat on the hospital bed, opposite to her. He glanced at her eyes stealthily, as he didn't have words to console her agony.

Shaking her head for a while, she tied her hair and jumped off from the bed and questioned, 'Asher!, Where is Asher?', we have his birthday party, Right?'

Shawn held her by shoulders and made her sit on the sofa. He sat at knees before her, 'You know ma'am, he's no more ' His reply indicated the polite intention, yet inexperienced consolation.

'How did he?' she asked whispering, sweeping her fingers into her hair, through the forehead. The pain coursed down the eyes, faster than his heartbeat. Her red eyes expressed the excruciating pricks on her soul.

'Asher had died of SIDS, A very rare and unexplained death of children under one year of age, also called as crib death.' He cleared the cloud.

'SIDS stands for Sudden Infant Death Syndrome, for babies sleeping on their stomach, the exact reason of this is unknown, it has no detectable symptoms and factors.'

'Strange! I've never even heard of something like this' she looked into the air and commented. 'Are they sure about it?' she sat on the ground with folded knees.

'SIDS is undetectable, in the absence of any symptoms, and even after autopsy, when no reasons prevail, SIDS is considered to be the cause of death. Dr had performed autopsy and said they suspect SIDS, however the reports will take some time to finalize.'

'Autopsy?' her eyes widened! She jumped back in disbelief. 'they ripped off my ashy!! Now I'll show them how it feels'. It appeared as though she single handily trooped towards the door to conquer, however Shawn caught hold in time and made her sit forcefully on the bed.

'What's wrong with you?' she yelled out wildly, as her body resisted to agree, to follow and the capability to understand.

'Ma'am, please try to understand, we are helpless' he held her arms tight, until she struggled to get rid of his hold.

He got up from the floor and collected her discharge sheet and bag along with the medicines. 'let's go home!' he ordered as she was going insane.

Acting like an obedient kid she followed Shawn perplexed about how within a moment, a tick of clock had scattered her joys, burnt her pride and ruined her fantasies, leaving behind the ashes of dilemma, that whether the past twelve months, were a dream or this cruel day was a fatal nightmare.

There was an infinite mourning in every breath she took, it was still impossible for her brain to interpret such a calamity. Gazing into no where, trying to analyse the catastrophe she took baby steps, falling short of energy.

CHAPTER FIFTEEN

As her sight ran through the corridor, the clean atmosphere was pricking her heart, the luminous lights beamed into her eyes, Shawn turned around suppressing the doubtful surprise at her obedience, she stopped at the reception, bowed her head before her wrapped palms, and pleaded, with the clogged throat her voice turned out to be an unintended whisper.

'Where's my son?'. With the wrung hands in dismay, she waited for her response, and due to her apparently visible agony, the receptionist addressed her of the morgue. Shawn waited for the conversation to end as she poured her helplessness through her eyes and thanked her. It was in the adjacent building, the snapping of elevator doors, the sliding of entrance doors, the chaos of crowd, spiked through her ears, making it harder for her, to co-ordinate with her body and the protocols.

The cruellest moment had finally dragged their pace towards the morgue. They entered into the mortuary, it was a huge hall with ample of loved ones, and the spooky large walls seemed to drive her hysterical. She thought 'departed souls' because, her son was one amongst the bodies, otherwise any tongue wont hesitate, to say them ' Corpses'. Shawn presented the file, to the in charge over there and they followed him along as he walked in the rows of storage chambers, taking a few steps further he indicated the chamber with his right hand. Olivia marched like a zombie before him, or a refugee in search of camp, she could sense the pins in her head as a result of grief beyond measure. There was something sharp consistently pricking her chest, such that she needed to press her thumb against. It was the last but one from the bottom. With the scantily leftover ability to think and process, she imagined the sight would be terrifying, that he would lie like a silent angel descended from heavens! Wrapped in a piece of white cloth, looking as peaceful as dove. His curved lips, baring resemblance, as the way he used to sleep. Because, to be honest she had some large percentage of hope that she would give him a forehead peck and he would wake smiling at her. But the reality check had to creep into her false fallacies. She raised her shivering forearm, to withdraw the handle over, by her glued shrunk fingers, her eyes swept down at him from the handle, involuntarily crossing her fingers in reflex.

All of a sudden she jerked off, squeezing her eyes and masked her jaw drop with the glued fists, as she shrieked uncontrollably. This was a heart wrenching sight.

She took a large gasp of air, Her nails scratched deeper into her cheeks and lips stretched out revealing the tightened teeth. With a grimaced face and tonnes of pluck, she stepped forward to witness the cruellest reality of the her life. It was Asher, lying in the rack with dozens of cut marks and hundreds of stitches, his body had turned cold, and he lied with a piece of cloth lying over him. She immediately pulled out the wrapped shawl from her shoulders, and with trembling hands and overflowing tears, she put it over Asher, ' what are you doing?' Shawn interrupted.

'Can't you see, he's freezing ' she answered instantly and rolled her eyes at him for being silly.

'Since he was born, he never slept without a blanket on.' She took deeper breath and neared to the body, undoubtedly, it was a dreadful scene to witness. Without blinking an eye, she stood there and forced herself to look at him, ' if he has gone through all this, then it's the least on me, to look at these scars and wounds, and feel how much pain, he had gone through I am not a coward, to abandon him all the way'

She stood still for a couple of minutes, staring at her dead son, of course with the bleeding eyes of agony. She raised her fingers to adjust the shawl over him and forwarded the chilled hands to run her fingers through his fresh injuries, but before she could do that in an instant she blacked out.

****

'This was her second epileptic attack' Dr Emma read out the reports, to Shawn.

'This is a result of brain injury due to the trauma, these long duration of seizures is a matter to worry about. She gets unconscious for long minutes and in her case, the intake of oxygen is reaching the minimal '

'Is there a risk to her life?' he enquired.

'If she harms herself by any object, during the seizures, you must keep an eye always. I know it's not that easy, but it's the need to save her life.'

Shawn remained quiet, piling up the doctors instructions in his mind. A gigantic task stood before him. The day was no less than a nightmare to him, and there was no scale to measure the intensity of Olivia's tragedy he thought.

****

She was sitting beside Shawn in the car, when she woke to her conscious. He was driving the car, noticing her like species under observation, every now and then. Leaning head on the glass, sitting at the passengers seat, she gazed at the infinite passing street lights with puffy eyes, which ran short of tears now. She could feel her body radiating and signalling senselessness. Taking a turn at her to enter the lane, at Olivia's house, Shawn stopped the car. Without uttering a word or enquiring, she pushed opened the door, whilst he sat in a dilemma.

She stepped down barefooted, Shawn held her wrist, 'Wait a minute, Ma'am'

She sniffled and turned her head, as if asked about a proof of being alive, with her half dead eyes, 'I think there's no one at your home' he continued ' Its not a good idea to let you alone' his mouth twitched.

She pulled back the door hard enough to close, after sitting back on the seat, not even bothered to ask where was he planning to head, the unresponsiveness showcased her loss of fear, along the loss of her child. She had already concluded, now there was nothing more painful to lose, In fact there was literally nothing left to lose. It seemed as though he was determined to drive till the end of world. Somewhere on earth, in a dark place he parked his car. He raised his arm after opening the door, offering her help for getting down. She flattered before him into an apartment. It was under the influence of heavy dosage of medications prescribed, that she wasn't in her senses.

****

Shawn found it hard to sleep. The horrific scenes of the day flashed before his eyes as he kept tossing and turning. Olivia fell asleep, sitting on the floor of guestroom, still in a subconscious state. He gulped down a sleeping pill, his hands still trembled while he drank water. Her excitement speeches of his birthday echoed in his ears, burying his head into the pillows, he finally fell asleep.

A couple of hours later, he became alive to the monstrous screams in the apartment. It was a horrific scene to witness as he opened the door of his room, it was dark all over, except that dim yellow bulb. The broken crockery lied shattered before the threshold. The hanging frames and just everything from the dining table, the sauces and the bread, every single thing covered the floor almost. He switched on the lights only after putting on his slippers, his sight swept wildly from one place to another to spot her, as he tiptoed beware of glass. he neared the store room and the shrieks seemed to increase, there she stood in front, banging the door and screaming.

'Have some sense!' he yelled at the apparently insane Olivia. 'What's wrong with you?' he raised his brows and his anguish drilling into her eyes.

'What's wrong with me?' she pushed his arms away, tucking the strands before the ears she held him by his neck pushing him to the wall, almost choking. ' where have you brought me? Where's my son? How dare you abandon him in that graveyard and bring me along you?' she chided.

'You know what Shawn? This was the cheapest!' still pressing her palms against his neck.

Hit by the hard time, he finally got himself rid of her hold, as he took a breath to live, she hastened to fetch the exit and marched here and there. Again he cautiously rushed to get her files from the room and explained her about her health status, which was unintentionally responsible for her memory loss. She sat on the sofa in the guest room, stunned by the report of hours she unconsciously spent. There were things she wasn't aware about. There were instances she remembered as Shawn narrated, but none was as she hoped. Tired of the trauma she repeatedly wished that someone wakes her up and say ' That was a nightmare, honey'. Upon listening to him, she couldn't nurture the courtesy to apologise.

Resting her head against the wall, with closed eyes, she held her folded knees close to her chest, tuck sitting. He sat beside her and there was a long silence or a speechless consolation complimenting the silent screams of grief.

****

Though the next twenty-four hours weren't a threat to her life, but it couldn't be recalled on her memory book either. Shawn took the keys along to her house to get the essentials like phone charger, her clothes, switch off the MCB, also his pilot costume. Checking the plugs in the kitchen he opened the door of refrigerator, a two storey cake stood covered in a glass lid, immersed in elegance and perfection. The clear sky-blue finishing, the minute details and the startling aeroplane of fondant, described her enthusiasm and excitement. The candle shaped one, the room decorated with affection. Alas fortune didn't hesitate to conclude them waste.

Her phone was flooded with missed calls and messages. It was after two horrible days that she charged it. It was obvious that most of those were Camilla's.

'Wow, lovely décor and cake appears yum, must say you were not a bad student of mine'

'Happy birthday to Asher! Wishing him the happiness of the worlds and heavens, may he always succeed in life, and grow up to be a good human like you '

'I've been calling you all day for wishing my son, you are a cheat, don't tell me you were busy dating;), ok now quickly send me some pictures of his, love from Camilla xoxo

Love him to the moon and back'

'What's actually wrong with you, nevertheless I just wanted to share with you that slowly the things are falling into place, I mean john is now free from the work over here and soon we'd be there to bother you in Cardiff, this was the cherry on top, the actual news is there's a bun in the oven JJ (dancing emoji), john is over the moon and TBH I am beyond ecstatic'

'I am thankful to life for blessing me with the gifts but pregnancy isn't an easy task to deal with ...'

There were many other messages from the photographer about the delayed shoot. These added a race to her heart and rubbed salt to her wounds. As the clock ticked by, she awaited her head to burst into million pieces. It was astounding about how her heart was alive bearing the burning hell. She starved for hours until she collapsed or Shawn forcefully fed her.

This evening Shawn returned home. He walked in the guestroom to check her, and she was sleeping by the door like a homeless tramp. At the ringing phone, he thought to wake her up, but didn't. It was better that she escaped the reality, the more she ran far from herself. Though it was possible up to a minor extent only, but a little is more at such times.

He swiped at the screen and narrated the disaster to her, the conversation took turns with his introduction, heartbreak, tears, shock and compassion for Olly, her health updates, new residence and Camilla's decision to visit her friend in need or her son's burial. His right hand hung on his shoulder, as he held the phone, while he stirred the coffee with another. Almost an hour later, they had gradually exchanged well wishes for Olivia. Camilla announced to him of her pregnancy and also expressed the guilt of texting her before knowing anything.

****

The sun, rays and fallacies had sunk beyond sight, as the fathomless earth engulfed Asher within. His pure soul wasn't meant for this cruel world. Every one could hear the whispers of clouds and feasts of angels as the most beautiful flower of the heaven had returned there. He belonged to the heaven ever since he existed. He lay straight in the coffin wearing his favourite pilot costume. His skin had turned pearl white, his thin closed lips appeared to curve indicating calm and peace. His large eyelids neatly covered his eyes like a cling film upon his dark blue veins. Olivia sat on her knees and ran her fingers through his face, despite taking deepest breaths she fell short, with taut jaws and knitted brows, forcefully shut eyes, she kissed him on his forehead, a whole drop of tear slid from her lashes on his face, and she helplessly expected the reflex which she was habituated to (Asher used to wipe her tears, every time she cried and would widen his lips revealing teeth, indicating smile). This was just an instance, she had to understand that she must wipe all those memories along this tear. There was almost a small gathering of her colleagues. The cold breeze was pining her patience, as she witnessed his coffin being buried.

Regaining her consciousness, she found herself alone in the graveyard, the sky had turned darker but not more than her fate. Everybody left one by one, presenting condolences on tongue, and furrowed brows on forehead. She cried, she wiped, she thought, she sat, she drowsed, she howled, she fought; in short proving the state of being alive or probably questioning the reason of being one.

'Olly!' she heard a familiar voice approach her from her back, which radiated a pain in her chest, and hence she chose not to turn. With the nearing footsteps, the voice repeated and she felt a known touch on her shoulder as she leaned by the tree. At this she raise her eyelid to spot Camilla.

She too had joined the list of consolers, it seemed Shawn had guided them along, Camilla was accompanied with John and his dad, Alfred Whitaker, or to be more precise, Olivia's father. Camilla hugged the sitting Olivia and expressed her sorrow, yet she remained silent at the instance. Every act of their appeared no more than an ostentatious drama to her. She turned back and walked towards her father, 'Now quickly spew up the lines you've by hearted to make up the formality!' she chided. His lips were zipped and gaze lowered.

'Such a strong bond we share, Mr. Alfred! Every time I succumb to the wounds of fate, I always find you by my side. Infact not the wounds of fate, but the injuries caused by you, ever since I grew up, you were always the reason of my agony. Satisfied? Are you now happy finally or is there something remained to ruin that you've arrived here?'

'I am sorry, my baby, I am sorry ' his voice had turned weaker over the time, or maybe himself too, as the tears ran all along his cheeks and double chin. He was full of guilt and apology that day. A restless vibe took over him as he discovered her daughter in trauma. He stepped nearer and raised her palm to rub by his forehead as a sign of apology. 'Stop it!' she yelled pulling back her hand and rubbed it forcefully against the uneven trunk of the large banyan tree, causing her skin to tear and bleed. 'Don't touch me, you dare not to touch me, you dare not to touch any stalwart. You are dirty, you are filthy.' She stepped back screaming turning furious. He walked out of the graveyard without uttering a single word and john accompanied him too, while Camilla signalled them to leave as she decided to stay with her friend.

Shawn waited for them in the car. Camilla struggled to Strike up the conversation a million times, and gave up on being silent, but she remained adamant and sat beside her, determined to take her home. Till the mid of night both the girls sat before his grave with folded knees in her arms, When finally she let her tongue move,' shedding these tears or sitting as in a strike, you can neither save my pain nor can you share it'

'I can understand Olly, you are devastated.'

'Why would you understand?, By the way congratulations, you are pregnant!' her tone sounded Taunting.

'Oh no, was just kidding around ' she was puzzled.

'You think I am envious?' Olivia questioned bluntly.

'I'm telling you it was a prank' she tried to convince, widening her eyes to emphasize.

'Once you look into my eyes, you'll realise, that I won't be ever jealous of anybody throughout my life, I am not jealous of you, of anyone in the world, if at all I have hatred towards, then it's all those people who are peacefully sleeping in their graves, without going through pain as I ' she pointed around at all the graves in despair, while Camilla sat speechless and simultaneously she wanted Olivia to pour her heart out.

'Get away from me Camilla, Don't you see, I am a bane, for anyone around me. Please go and get yourself a life!' she yelped and it seemed now she was sharing her pain, as her eyes bleed with agony. But the moment after her shriek, she collapsed by fits.

This was another episode of her disease. Camilla hustled to wake her up, Shawn came running towards her and attempted the same. It took a couple of minutes for her to gain consciousness, yet both her true friends wished deep in their hearts, that she leaves this cruellest fate and doesn't regain consciousness, only last escape to the reality that had depressed her beyond hopes.

CHAPTER SIXTEEN

This evening marked a month from Asher's demise. It was a roller coaster ride for Shawn as he had a hard time literally bearing with Olivia. Some days were a silent mourning, while other were tangled with her health issue and therapy sessions; with a hope that things just get better, he made every effort. Olivia had turned pale, with large dark circles and lean body. Shawn left every morning to the office only after pulling the curtains apart, arranging her breakfast and directing her the pills after meal and returned late in the evening. The house was silent during the night and dead in the day time. After a series of consolation and moral solace he had now started to escape her. Today when he returned from the office, she stood in the kitchen, surprisingly without any trace of the daily hurricane. He took a breath of peace, as it seemed things were getting back to place. It was good for her as soon as she accepts the facts, maybe it be the bitterest. He walked in his room to change. Pulling the door of his room to open, from the margin he sneaked and his eyes fell out at the cathartic act. Her eyes wide opened in search, She placed the plate on dining and lunged into the kitchen with the punching flip flops, making some more and called out loud.' Ryan, your pancakes are ready, get Asher along, he loves the dripping chocolate. And remind me to get the bottle of honey, while doing the grocery, I am missing it from last three trips, and yeah this weekend I've planned dinner at the beachside. I'll get him the sand play set and I am sure he'll love it.' she flipped the pancake after pouring butter, and turned around, 'You're listening to me, right, Ryan?' she searched for him and marched into the rooms. 'Where are you, you are with me right? I can't see you!' she roamed around the house yelling his name. Shawn came out to plight and to him she enquired ' Wonder where this boy vanished, did you see him, he was just playing with the building blocks'. The childish tone she spoke with, skipped his heart and got chills on his spine. Not even awaiting the reply she headed towards the porch. Proceeding with the heavy steps he stopped her against the wall, 'I know where is he,' he continued after the expected desperate 'Where?' 'He's dead. Olly, why don't you understand? Why on earth are you complicating things?'

'Have you lost it?' she exclaimed.

'Just wait, I'll show you, he'll come from that room, wearing those lighting shoes' She pointed towards the guestroom and sat down leaning against the wall. It was a cathartic scene indeed. All those months Shawn had seen such a sensible senior, and now she was behaving like a psychotic patient, screeching her heels by the floor. Everything was turning beyond worse. Shawn wasn't used to all this. Extending a helping hand towards her had cost him his peace. He called Camilla at the moment and informed her of the slipping conditions in front of Olivia. Through his answers and expressions it seemed as though she had clearly denied to come. Well she wasn't very good at connecting the dots but she assumed what was apparent. Shawn found himself in a swamp, but he was empathetic enough to see her stuck in the bog below him. He had to think something out of the box, to get her back to life. After having pancakes made for the mysterious Ryan, he hit the sack.

****

'They were just heavenly!' Shawn complimented her pancakes. He woke up in mid of the night, she sat on the bed and swiped pictures in the phone gallery, leaning against the wall.

'Thank you' her lips barely pulled up suppressing the large dark circles. She sat on the couch in the guest room.

'How are you feeling now?'

'I m good' she nodded, and bowed her head after blinking back the tears.

'I had the whole two plates, and am still not over the taste, I swear! ' he continued.

'Ryan loved them too, and also Asher ' her nose turned red and eyes moistened mentioning them.

'So I am in a state of utter satiety, what about you?' he clearly put a diversion. It was not that he was fed up of her stories, in fact she wasn't ready to reveal anything about it ever. How many times had he asked her about her life, so she could feel light hearted after sharing, but she remained tight lipped.

'And more than the pancakes, he loved me ...' she continued not paying heed to the growling stomach. She was getting habituated to skipping meals and taking the acidity pills. This time it was quite apparent that she could no more resist the inner voice. The pain needed a way out. And now she had realised Shawn was the outlet. He glared in surprise as she was never comfortable narrating her past. Though silent, but inside he was all ears to get the mystery solved.

She opened the window and put curtains apart to let the air in. Swallowing the clogged throat she unfolded her sacred love story. She sat cross, wearing a t shirt.

'It was not so many years ago, that I too had a happy family. Life had blessed me with many happy moments, but never a perfect life. One or the other thing had always lacked in my way, and gradually I'm left alone.' She shrugged with a smile and blinking back the tears again.

As a kid, I remember loving my father the most. I still remember those moments thinking how perfect was my life, like fairy-tale. He was the hero of my life. Just like all girls love their father, I too adored our relation. He loved me too, but growing up, I realised, that taking to the parks, games, ice cream and chocolates never meant a perfect person. He was a well known professor of Rutherford University. Fame and proud took over him, and gradually took him away from us. He was a money chaser.

My father abandoned us, when I was only eight years old, just to marry Laura. She was his rich fellow worker. Mommy along her four children, have struggled many years to make the ends meet.

Being the eldest of all siblings, I identified my responsibilities in the worst times. I never wanted any of my siblings to become school dropouts. Mommy took the smallest of jobs just to fulfil our needs. I worked at the cafes, flower shops and not where, to get home some amount. A decade of our lives passed in dire straits. As the things started sorting out after a longest time, Ryan knocked on the door of my heart. I had taken lessons from Mr Whitaker, but in any of the qualities he didn't fall in that category. I took a long time to handle things maturely, and he awaited impatiently.

On the path full of pins and needles, also injured, bleeding feet, he promised me of the practical cake walk.'

'Was it a romantic proposal?' he asked. To be honest she was not expecting such question from him, but however it was successful enough to make her chuckle.

'No, he wasn't of that type ' she giggled.

'Infact, it might be listed under the most unromantic proposals. Or a Guinness World record of an awkward proposal. One fine day he called me up and said that if he gets married than he would get three paid holidays in a week, that won't count to his vacations, and then he asked about my opinion to accompany him Paris in February. It took me half a minute to analyse his intentions. He was daft at the anniversary gifts too. But we had one special place, that's the Klive beach, where we would spent hours together, and that was the real peace. The stars amidst the darkness and calmness submerged in the sea, how tiny we appeared as the creatures, appreciating the universe at the shore' she emotionally caressed the unfolding memories, pouring it out sacredly through her lips.

'Later on I discovered that Ryan was a nephew of Laura, with whom my father had fled away. His parents had passed away while he was a child, his brought up was done by Laura. When mommy came to know about this, she stood against Ryan. Actually against the idea of our wedding. But for me it was not the time to back off for such silly reasons.'

'It wasn't a silly reason, in my opinion' Shawn put forward.

'Actually back then Ryan had lied to me, that my father, Mr Whitaker had died several years ago. So I had no objection as the root of problem was dead.

But my family was against it.'

'Your family means? Your mother and is there some body else too?' he enquired curiously.

'My mother, my brothers Billy and James they were all against me, and when we married secretly they didn't lose the heart to cut off the ties with me, who had sacrificed her childhood for them. Anyhow my sister, Isabella was very young back then, either to support or oppose.'

'Wait a second, your sister Isabella?' He confirmed, joining the dots.

'Yeah' she agreed undoubtedly.

'Isabella Whitaker?' his raised eyebrows in amusement, pertaining his suspect got right.

'Yes' she nodded her head, confirming to his surprise and the right guess at the same time.

'I said you, on the day one we met ma'am!' he got intrigued.

'Neither did I deny!' she replied ironically. ' I think now we are more than colleagues, you can now call me, Olivia' she continued.

'This is she, smart, intellectual, Decent and modest, the real, Olivia. This was just one percent of what she was. I hope she hops quick on to the life and of course to the office as well.' Shawn thought to himself, until a few minutes, and Olivia broke the silence.

'I wish her all the success of the world's, today she is a star of Ireland. But as she grew up in the environment that was toxic against me, she too believes I am the reason of mommy's sickness and her death. I had also talked Clara, Billy's wife, a couple of times. She too believes the same. And hence no ties with my family since then. '

'Why did you two split up?' he regretted asking within a moment later as he couldn't resist the urge to know.

At this, her tears didn't resist either. With the flowing rivers on two sides she breathed in the blocked nose and continued with some pauses and resumes on the go.

'I believed we were the perfect couple with brilliant chemistry! And even then I thought, let aside all relations, we would be the perfect family' now it was getting harder, her heart pulled out in the throat, as she tried to speak. And again she took a longer pause, her eyes radiating pain, and face grimaced in agony. She was overwhelmed by emotions. Shawn was waiting for the story for the first few seconds but now he was awaiting her calmness. As the memories overpowered her, Shawn wasn't lion hearted at the moment and excused ' I'll get some coffee.'

Back in the kitchen as he stirred in to the mugs, her voice replayed in his mind, picturising as she said, it is miserable. The never ending thoughts build up sympathy in his heart, strengthened enough to roll down a tear at the other side of eyelid. A few minutes later he stepped back into her room along the coffee mugs and bunch of questions. He closed the windows as it had started to drizzle. Before he could even take his place, she resumed like a call retrieved. ' When I lost my family, I used to think, I may not get the family, but I've got the best partner in life. He was the best indeed.' this time she narrated with a fierce spirit, as though she had prepared herself to be mightier.

'Everything was fine until six years of our marriage, I pursued the diploma courses and got a job. He bagged his promotions perfectly. One by one we had set everything right. And I believed that one day we could also convince my family.

But I was wrong again. Neither did my family forgive for going against their wishes, nor Ryan started the relation, laying the foundation of truthfulness and honesty. Had he told me about the alive Whitaker, I wouldn't flee alike him.' her heart raced reminding herself of the sharpest thorns on her path.

'He used to be so excited about our unborn child! His day started with plans and his nights used to end with gratitude towards me. And over the time, I don't believe how a person could betray me like this. At times it seemed that he was more enthusiastic for the baby, yet he abandoned us in the need of hour, when we needed him the most, in an unknown city, with the unfamiliar people. And that very moment my soul saluted my mother, she deserved a standing ovation Infact, for the years ago prediction she made, was precise, accurate and flawless.'

She looked into his eyes and continued, ' You know what I used to say Asher?' before waiting for any reply she answered her question ' we both were unlucky in terms of having a good father... But to be honest there was a little hope struck up in my heart that, Asher wasn't amongst them. And now?' she widened her eyes with a painful smile, ' I swear on you, I don't encourage any false hopes. ' At this she broke her laughter and wiped her tears by swiping the thumbs.

'Where is he now ' he sparkled the extinguishing fire. This time, not guilty.

'I don't know, Camilla says he's alive! Yet I don't believe her. Is the living of such person not at question, who neither witnesses his sons birth nor his demise., Or maybe his humanity is questionable.'

'Stumbling on so many rocks, finally I was..'

The conversation lasted for a couple of hours and Olivia fell asleep after taking medicines. He put the blanket on her as she was getting edgy of cold, and switched on the heater. He turned on the lamp and felt relaxed for she had shared a percent of burden on her heart, though slow but it was a considerable progression, ultimately a sign of success.

****

'We don't want to be considerate John! If not us then at least I, can cross all the limits to seek revenge of my insult and disrespect!' Ryan jumped down his throat.

'You are getting misunderstood brother, there has to be a study done with calm nerves, and later you can avenge the culprit.' John explicated the furious Ryan, forcing his wide foot into the socks.

'Calm nerves! Spending over an year in that gaol! And returning to find out the horrific truths! I just can't be calm! My soul seeks revenge! Don't you get that?' his eyes turned red fuming in anguish.

He tied the shoe lace listening of him, 'got to go now, we'll discuss this in the evening' he closed the door from outside.

'Discuss this in the evening!' Ryan punched on the wall aggressively.

****

Shawn pushed out his fist from the pillow to press the snooze button of the ringing phone. Within a moment the phone rang again. Before he pressed the button again, Benjamin hammered the bell in his head. He sat tangled in the blanket with the drowsy eyes and adeptly messy bedhead for complete one minute.

He got dressed up and gobbled up the bread after spreading butter. Just before he was about to leave, he put an eye on Olivia. It was an unusual sight. She was still sleeping. He thought not to disturb her and order her breakfast whenever she wakes up. He also texted her the same to inform.

He took a start to the office, looking at the watch, as he was satisfied about reaching in time, he played the music and enjoyed the hassle free ride. Waiting for the traffic signal to indicate green, a thought bombarded the tranquil of his head and breaking the signal he raced the car speedily down the road leaving whirlwinds around.

He reminisced the missing medicine box from the shelf and the ever sleepless Olivia dozed off more than usual. He just hoped that they were coincidentally just two different instances. But a gut feeling prompted, that it wasn't a mere coincidence. He sprinted hastily into the room and called her out, to make her conscious. She responded dizzily, calming his pounding heart. Her parched lips twitched, 'Let me sleep' she murmured, turning her face the other side.

'Please call me as soon as you wake up, I'll order you a breakfast ' he instructed and stood up from the bed. A shiny foil or something caught his attention illuminating under the bed. Fixing up his belted trouser as he bent down to have a look, his heart skipped a beat and clogged into his throat.

It was the empty pharmaceutical blister pack!

CHAPTER SEVENTEEN

'I cannot talk to her!' Camilla declined.

'I just want you get any hint.' john spelled out, while driving.

'She's already so down in the dumps!, If I cannot stand her in her worst times at least I shouldn't trouble her.'

'That's your choice of not standing beside her in her worst time ' he taunted.

'John! You see how busy I am now, the work load, morning sickness, uneasiness and what not. I visit her once in a week and talk to her on phone, take reports from Shawn. Things were different an year from now, back then I was a single person, and now we're married, and as a matter of fact I am pregnant. We need time, how much ever we know each other, we need to give time to each other to let our relationship develop and evolve. I was a sensitive person earlier yet I've learnt so much and now I get it that the smallest of things matters. This is real life john, here people don't revolve around the victim all the time. The side character has a life too. May be a bigger one. There's no ONE motive to achieve in this world, every life is struggling over a million milestones. Every one life has its own journey. In real world, there's a difference between consolation and rehabilitation and I am not ashamed of being her best friend and still fall in the former category of people. Its how hard I try to reach her out even in challenging situations.'

'And in a huge interaction you cant interrogate her trickily.' His tone filled with sarcasm irrespective of the heart winning and mind unlocking speech.

'No, but I can be of one help to you that is on her behalf, I can make you aware of the truth. Does that make any difference?' she exclaimed.

'Does that make any sense!' he threw a fierce expression at her for being stubborn.

'I m ready to bet about it, she is definitely clueless.'

'You are defending your friend, and there's nothing wrong in it. Flip the coin and see my side, my cousin has been jailed for absolutely no crime for over an year. He has his right to conduct the investigation.'

'It is about the night before Asher's birth. When the two separated, later at that night, the cops raided at our house and illegal firearms were recovered. Ryan was charged of smuggling illegal weapons and sentenced to 1 year jail without any clemency. Have you ever thought of him, how had he spent every single night and day longing for freedom, paying for doing absolutely nothing. There's a need of mercy for him. He has loved and lived with her, he knows to how much extent a person can fall or rise.' He stopped at the red light of signal and in the dark night in the beaming lights, he turned at her, his deep hazel green eyes gazed intensely into hers as he continued giving a pause.' And he's pretty sure that Olivia is behind all this.'

'Why would she do this?' she interrupted.

'How would I know that?'

'John! You are driving me crazy. Let me assume for a moment, that you are right, so why would she go mad before that cheater, consulting psychiatrists, even neglecting her son in the starting days, I still remember.'

'How come Ryan is a cheater now?' he objected.

'His cheat is unjustifiable. He had no right to lie about her father.'

'I am not here to defend his mistakes but in my opinion, it's no big deal. Everything is fair in love.' He parked the car and stepped out to get prescribed medicines from the pharmacy, and as he sat into car after getting them, Camilla's phone buzzed followed by answering Shawn's call and the debate toll an involuntary end.

****

Shawn riffled the pages of her diary which was found under her pillow, and read the last night's entry,

The way is not mine, neither I have destinations to unfold,

I am a straying passenger whose journey is on the threshold.

What do they mean to me the quakes, the storms or the tornado

I am a lost passenger, yet leads to its shadow.

I've brought along some belongings without a penny to pay,

But I've been repeatedly taught, they won't help me on the way,

Witnessing the guilty smiles, and wicked sighs,

I carry bubble of joys, made up of stealthy cries.

The load of these has compelled me to drop the wishes and dreams from eyes,

Which is why, the moon wept last night and people assumed it rained from the skies.

Let me return to there,, at the heaven's call

And world remain in false fallacies, that it is mere rainfall '

The bees of confusion and shock, buzzed around his head. A woman who was sagacious a night ago had taken this extreme step of taking her life. He was taken aback by her beyond predictable decision. All thanks to good luck and DR Emma, for getting to them in real time and treat her before adverse effects of the over dose. She was admitted to the hospital that very morning and was under observation. The day was disgusting and exhausting for Shawn. Lying on the bed, gazing at the ceiling, he tried to analyse the life. Not his, Olivia's.

He was hurt. And realisation of this had started to annoy him now. There was a difference between being concerned and hurt. She was a friend of his. A bit closer one after yester night. But it was not a strong bond, not even mutual. It was a one sided favour of being merciful, towards a helpless woman.

The thoughts stimulated the other and he began pondering over the fact, that if had he not shown mercy on her, where would have she gone. She has literally no one in her life. Camilla being in the city itself, hardly visits twice in a week, what would she do when she needed her the most. The more he thought about her, the more he felt for her, and also equally was he getting heartbroken at her. These were two different things. Scrolling down the phone and replying everyone's messages, his mind quenched for the answer of his uneasiness. He moved to the mirror and looked at his flushed out face. He raised his foot on the table and his elbow on the rested leg. While his chin pressed against the loose fist. ' Am I in love!' he asked his reflection with a demented smile and pulled apart brows.

****

With the hurried steps Camilla proceeded to the room no. 16. She gently pushed in the door and marched towards her. Olivia was sitting on the bed, gazing at the tray of food, muddling up the carrots and broccoli. At the step of Camilla, she raised her eyelids and dropped them down, swallowing the pit in throat, likely to preparing herself for this, ' You know what Olly! I want to punch on your face and knock you down ' Camilla chided as she fed her pushing in the spoon of salad. Camilla had tied hair red hair, a cute bump sneaked from the loose pink t-shirt. Olivia couldn't help praying for the long life of it in her heart. she had gained weight in the past months. Moving plate to the side, Olivia bent forward.

Her eyes watered at one statement of her bestie. In the instant, it was evident, she was craving for love. She parted her glued lips, and closed again as she couldn't pick any word to begin with and ended up with biting her lips. Her brown moth like brows glided over and pain beamed from tears flowing by the pale cheeks, and dark circles. Her pursed lips narrated the agony that she couldn't express with all the words in the universe. Camilla jumped on the bed and wrapped her arms around Olivia. Both the girls, sobbed embracing each other.

'Ah.. its all my fault, I should not have left you with that fellow,' Camilla was immersed in guilt.

'Not at all, your doing more than you must. You have a life to live, don't spoil it all for me.' She emphasised.

Her tears flowed steadily. 'I m sorry for being self centred, I forgot to take good care of you, I am sure loneliness has compelled you to take such a step. I thought that Shawn is a fine guy, but it was my irresponsibility. I am sorry.' she apologized.

'How's john and your health now?' she enquired.

'I am thankful to life, for everything is amazing, we are planning the gender reveal party and you are coming, there must be no excuse.' She insisted.

'I can't take a few steps to corridor even, ' She resisted.

'I am not inviting you tonight either!' joked Camilla. The girls cackled at each other after an awkward silence.

****

Collecting the discharge summary from Dr Emma, the duo left for a day out. Camilla lent a wheelchair from the neighbours and wheeled it for her, as Olivia sat on it. They started the day with café coffee day, where Camilla had the coffee and of course Olivia was restricted from drinking, so she stared at her and realised the intensity of her fault. Elementally, sitting on the chair in café, and not having one was quite a punishment. Their time revolved around the gossips of colleagues, as Camilla had resumed her job. How Hannah was caught ditching Richard, how Neil's hairdresser had turned him into a complete cartoon character, Alex's fake account "miss_ marina", and his messages to the staff, especially BENJAMIN! They binge watched web series at Camilla's. Ordered Olivia's favourite pizza and cheesecakes. And last was seemingly every women's first love, shopping. Olivia suggested a mauve column gown for her. And she readily accepted seeing her friend coming back to life. She selected a floral printed dress for Olivia, behind it hung a blue ankle length gown.

'Look, this is amazing!' she raised the hanger at her shoulders to check the size. Olivia pushed her hand and hung it back on the rod.

'What's wrong?' Camilla objected.

'I already have one like this' her voice lowered and eyes watered.

'You didn't show me ever' Camilla looked around for more dresses.

'It was for Asher's birthday' the statement stunned Camilla, she wanted to kick herself for reminding her of him. She clenched her palm and wanted to divert her, 'look at this, am sure you've never seen this' she pulled out a mustard dress from the corner.

'Hic!' Olivia took a hiccup and burst into tears aloud uncontrollably. Camilla rushed to her hold her tight. The sale boys and everyone at the store stared at them perplexed.

****

'I am sorry Camilla!' Olivia interrupted the hundredth time, while they watched an Irish drama.

'I said you it's fine, you are disturbing me ' she threw a cushion at her. 'look at your sister, she's such amazing actress.'

'Today was the last day of annual sale,'

'So!' she threw a frustrated look at her.

'So what? You missed that wonderful dress, because of me. Because I started sobbing you had to miss it.'

'That's no big deal Olly!'

'I'll buy it next time'

'But that plump bird fled away with it, while you were condoling me.' She dropped her forehead into hand in embarrassment.

'Never mind focus on this *Eimear,* '

'Who's he now?' she asked.

'She! Your sister, Isabella Whitaker in this drama, the name of her character! Any more queries!' Camilla reprimanded.

'Yeah, one last, why is she crying?'

At this Camilla covered her head in a cushion and later her ears, for such a silly question. They had great time together, Camilla was loving the interruptions and distractions she was creating. She was thankful to see her laugh and speak her heart out. It was like the old times, when Camilla used to watch, Olivia would disturb her asking million questions. It was once in the theatre that the staff had thrown them out because of the continuous disturbance and complaints from audience. Since then they watched at home. But Olivia never changed, in this matter only, else every habit had witnessed a terrible change.

****

Camilla was half asleep when the door bell rang. She walked to the door, yawning and tying her hair. As she was unlocking, her phone rang, it was john.

'Open the door '

'Yeah I am ' she whispered.

'Why are you whispering' he asked aloud mysteriously, stepping into the house.

'Its Olivia ' she whispered again, and pulled him out in the lawn.

'Oh' now he had lowered his voice.

'Dinner? ' she asked.

'Yeah, had it with Ryan.'

'Shhh!! we have to be alert, Olivia is at home and you are not going to ask her anything about that night. She's not in any condition to get more depressed, I am trying hard to keep her happy. Please don't ruin her happiness.' They murmured sitting on the swing in the lawn.

'Of course not, I am blessed with a little common sense if not as much intelligence you are blessed with.' He taunted. 'You are such mischievous' she pulled his cheeks teasingly.

Olivia overheard the entire conversation from the window of kitchen, as she had come to take the bottle of water from refrigerator.

CHAPTER EIGHTEEN

The next morning, before Camilla broke her sleep, Olivia had started to Shawn's house. She wanted to take the keys from him and return back to her house. She was tired of taking favours may it be from Camilla or Shawn. Camilla had her heart, but the thing she hid about Ryan, wasn't justifiable at all. Whatever may it be, it was driving her crazy. Everything at Shawn's was wonderful. His house, his company, food on time, but it was also impossible to forget her pain. She stopped at his house and pushed in the door, after ringing the bell twice and calling at his phone. The door was unlocked. And there was no answer to the door bell as well as the phone call. She entered in the his room and searched in the cupboard, shelves, wardrobe, locker, everywhere, she couldn't spot the keys. Shawn wasn't taking the calls. She went in the room where she was staying, to pack her belongings. What all had she gathered in a month and more. She packed the bag and checked the phone later.

There were 5 missed calls from Camilla and 3 from Shawn. She forgot to remove the silent mode, after waking up. Awakening was possible only if she could sleep. The discussion about Ryan could not let her sleep all night. Forget about sleeping, she couldn't even distract her mind to anything else. The thing that had pricked her the most was Camilla stopping john from informing her about Ryan.

How could she do this? This wasn't a true friendship, despite of beyond measure kindness and every effort she made, this deed had cocked up all. ' Where is that bloody Ryan on earth, doesn't he understand how I need him. Didn't he come to know that his son has died!. No active social media, no response at the phone number. No sign of being alive at least. This day, I feel so alone in the world. There's no single being whom I can go to.' With folded hands she sat cross on the floor, leaning by the wall and held her shoulders tight, as the thought process took a flow, her conscience popped up Shawn's name. But her experience and heart turned their faces from seeing any false hopes. She closed her eyes and her eyes poured the intense pain gently, tear by tear. She wiped her tears with Asher's napkin, and held it close to her chest. She could still smell Asher's fragrance in it, which was possibly a hallucination to anyone else. This is life. Every one creature had a different horizon of perception, millions of different views, opinions, beliefs and hopes. She rubbed the napkin against her cheeks roughly to wipe away the tears and dialled to Shawn.

'Hi Olivia, I am on the way to Camilla's house, see you in five minutes.'

'No' she almost hid the pain in her voice.

'I mean I am at your home, I actually want my keys, and' she hesitantly continued. 'I want to return to my house'

'The keys are with me, ok, I am coming there.' He agreed and disconnected the call.

Half an hour later, He reached home. Olivia had almost fallen sleep, tired of weeping. He knocked at the door which broke her sleep. As she opened he entered with a flower bouquet and a shiny wrapped gift. She was ready to leave, in a black t shirt and denim jacket over on black jeans. Her neatly braided brown hair, indicating first step of strength, organisation and determination.

It is human nature, presents and praises please them. A very small percentage of her got happy, because she was expecting Shawn to be furious at her for eating the pills. She was happy equally, for the gift as well as that their bond was intact.

He handed the present to her, 'this is for you'

'But why?' her lips lifted a bit.

'Because you are going back, maybe a souvenir from my side ' he grinned ear to ear

'Well then, I must immediately leave, this might be the polite signal to get lost' she smiled back.

'Do you think you got strong enough to reach your home?'

Olivia gave a puzzled look.

'Are you ready to get everything started from the beginning, I am happy that you are taking this decision, but it's too early Olivia. You think you can overlook Asher's absence? You think it's an easy task to do? I know you've already done this before, but the situation was different earlier, now it is not gonna be an easy task to do. There's no one along you, how would you gather yourself after breaking infinite times, there's a life ahead of you, think wisely. Offering you an unwanted suggestion, you can stay here for some more months, after you resume your job, a little later, you can go back'

Olivia listened silently to him, gazing in annoyance. 'I agree that I allowed you to address me by my name, but that doesn't cover-up the difference between us of a senior and a junior. Don't try to teach me what's wrong and what's right. I am well aware of it more than you. Mind it that I am announcing the decision and not asked your permission.

You have many favours upon me and I am keeping the courtesy.' She paced out of the house, taking along the handbag and stretched her palm before him. 'My keys?'

He put his hand in the pocket and lifted the keys up by the heart shaped key chain, which had a photo of Asher and zoomed it into her eyes. The sky turned dark in a moment, and it started to rain heavily with thunders. Looking at the her beloved, her heart skipped a breath, numbness grew over her head and neck stimulating pins and needles in the arms, that very second blocked her thinking capability, straight away her body started to sweat, the pain turned effervescent in the pounding heart, she could listen her heart beat wildly. The picture of his, freshened her affliction. Tears filled in her eyes, but she tried to look brave. Her legs wobbled like jelly and giddiness developed, eventually resulting her to fall insensate on the door steps, wringing wet in water.

He sat in the threshold, panic-stricken at her stagger, 'Olly! Olivia!, what's wrong?' he lifted his head from the ground and laid it in his lap, he repeatedly moved her chin left and right, and got horrified at the no response. He lifted her up in his arms, while her head hung on the other end. He hustled to get her into consciousness by spraying water on face. Her jaws became rigid and eyes closed firm with tightly clenched fists. She dropped her body freely, as Shawn laid her on the bed. He removed her shoes, and dried her hair, with a hair dryer, whilst calling her aloud simultaneously.

Twenty minutes later, she opened her eyes, upon vigorously shaking her and slapping on her face. Shawn was nearly swamped in sweat. He hastened to get a glass of water. She regained conscious and the tears held in her, started to pour. Shawn had brought her a sandwich and fresh orange juice. She had the stomach filled and went to sleep. Shawn got ready, and started to office.

****

'Where are you now?' john enquired on the phone, driving his car.

'Long back where I should have been!' Ryan retorted, sitting in the backseat of cab.

'Are you going to meet her?' he questioned stopping at the signal.

'Of course my boy, I'll meet and settle a score' he flung back.

'Good luck ' he hurled the phone on the passenger seat.

****

'We honestly had a good day, last night she talked me so seriously, about resuming her job' Camilla wondered.

'I am not sure what's exactly the problem, but she wanted to leave my house either, It took a hard time making her understand that she cannot, she's not even in a condition to live alone, even for a while. But I am helpless at this point'

The two sincere well wishers of Olivia, conversed on her behaviour and instability, in the lunch hour, while sipping coffees. The news of her attempting to commit suicide had also spread like fire. People threw weird gazes on Shawn, as which act of his had made her to do so. Or whatever. There is no one to put a period to assumptions and gossips. He was one of those people who believed never to bother about what people thought or said. But that was his belief, now when he underwent such odd talks, he felt uneasy about it. Yet, there was no way back. He had his career before him. Quitting up now meant quitting forever. Thoughts of resignation also wandered around his head, but there was a stomach to fill, and dreams to be fulfilled.

Working at Johnson's was a dream for every intern. And he had to pay for living his dream, may be. So is the unjust life.

****

'Ok, so one last question for today' Olivia giggled, for annoying the sleeping Ryan once more.

'Please proceed ma'am' he blabbered with shut eyes.

'Do you love me, you've got to answer honestly' she demanded with her widened eyes and involuntarily curved lips.

'Nopes, you aren't good' he answered.

She was sure about the incomplete answer just then he continued.

'You are the best ' he smiled back, and wrapped her arms around her, curling into the warm blanket.

'I nearly died in the pause you took ' she pinched his arm and placed her head on his arm, squeezed it tight of affection, believing deep at heart, never to set apart and cherishing the moment simultaneously.

'Oh you, who has
Proved all myths,
And broken my beliefs,
You still owe my breath,
And now I am choking of grief'

Olivia shut the diary immediately as the door pushed in. Her fake make over on face had failed to restrain from rolling a thick drop of tear on the cover of her diary. Shawn pretended unnoticed,' hello ma'am ' he announced to the room, that he wasn't informal any more, by not taking her name.

'How are you doing now'

she grinned unwantedly back at him, avoiding his eyes.

He presented the unopened gift to her once again. She secured her thoughts (diary) in the bag, and zipped it under the brown shawl. She accepted the gift hinting letting go of the morning's argument. Her face expressions weren't normal. He could easily figure out her disturbed mind. May be a lava was fuming under her smile. She unwrapped the present not so gently. Oh, yeah the minimal thank you was also missing, while taking the gift. It was the trending zecho dot (6th gen). Placing the device beside on the table, she read the details on the box aloud that described the incredible sound system, sleek, compact design, balanced bass etc.

'Wait a second' he jumped from the couch, switched it on and placed it on the centre piece of the room. He raced back to the couch and commanded with underlying joy.

'Alexa, what's the weather forecast for tomorrow ' he stretched his brows towards the table, staring at her, like a child's enthusiasm for a new toy.

'There's a chance of isolated thunderstorm on Monday, with seventy percent humidity.'

'Alexa, play me a song of Aviva Mongillo.'

'Boys they're handsome and strong But always the first to tell me I'm wrong Boys try to tame me, I know tell me I'm weird and won't let it......

The song played and Shawn enjoyed the music, he had started to dance to cheer her up, he stepped on the floor and making random grooves and steps, wearing a sky-blue shirt, contrasting his white complexion and blue eyes. For a while Olivia had an obnoxious expression later as she lifted her gaze, to look at him, a small smile slid onto his face and the dance got energetic. He had a crooked teeth, which made his smile a different yet attractive one. She had never seen him, smile so much earlier. He was not a good dancer at all, but his attempt seemed to be an interesting one.

'Cause a princess doesn't cry (no) A princess doesn't cry (no-o) Over monsters in the night Don't waste our precious time On boys with pretty eyes'

He repeated the lines along the speaker, threw his fingers into air, rotating his arm while the other rested on his oscillating waist. He grabbed her phone and scrolled down into the album's, to click on Ryan's picture, he expanded to focus on his eyes, while singing the lines towards him *boys with pretty eyes'*

Olivia waited for the whole drama to finish, she was so annoyed by the behaviours of every one. It was a different stuff before her, but just before the interest seemed to strike, she felt odd, maybe like betraying someone, but who was that? Ryan? Her head was growing numb in confusion. As the song stopped and Shawn slowed his steps and flumped back on couch, placing palm on his racing heart.

'May I know the reason of this?' she rolled her eyes, pointing at the device, quite ungrateful to the presenter.

His cheeks blushed at the question and lips took a curve simultaneously. Biting his lips like a shy, he answered raising his bent eyelids, which almost scared Olivia, ' At first I thought, I was in love with you ' he confessed. The statement echoed in her ears like a buzzing bee, until he added further.

CHAPTER NINETEEN

'I thought so, because, I was hurt, when you attempted to kill yourself. It pricked me in for a very long time. So I made a stupid guess, that was I falling for you. But I was wrong. This only appears in movies and tales that you fall for a person, for whom you feel. Glad, I solved the mystery on my own. It's the human nature. I helped you in your bad times, I passed through all the ups and downs to pull you out of the depression for straight one month. And this decision of yours has put a fail stamp on my hard work. This feeling of failure hurt me the most. Now that I've known you for a few months and you are also friend of mine, my heart goes for you. Your action has put my prestige on stake. People throw disgusting looks at me. I am not counting the favours I did. But I think you must be back into your life. You have an amazing job awaiting you, your friends are waiting for your return in life, there's so much in life to do. Clinging on the tragedies is not the treatment. Do you remember, once I said you about the priorities to be maintained in life? The topmost priority is you. And next is you as well. Please come back to life.' He counselled the depressed Olivia for a long time, giving her all possible reasons and inviting her back to the earlier lively version of her.

She found it strenuous to remain calm enough to listen his speech. He was a young lad, with many different perspective towards life. All his lectures had started to suppress his favours. At this point in life, she stood at a place where she had no shoulder to cry on except him. But she was done with it, she was traumatized and afraid of letting someone caress her broken heart. And hence didn't want to share her tiniest feelings with. Now she only knew that she wanted to go back to her house. That's all. Anyone who would become an obstacle between her and her house was her bitterest enemy now. But this boy was stubborn, he was reluctant to let her go, despite she insulted her. There was one last option and it was to escape this prison. But she would never want to be like her father. A coward, who would quit to escape the challenge. She had already done this at Cam's house. But there were million other challenges she had in her life, she couldn't gather the positivity to take every opportunity as a challenge and triumph over it by accepting it and facing it. All these thoughts clouded her head and robbed of the ability to answer or understand the chattering Shawn.

A couple of minutes later she realised, that he was done mingling the entire English vocabulary.

'Yeah, I understand, but Benjamin was the lout since the start, he's never going to change' she answered in air.

He sprang back at the irrelevant reply, and suggested her in embarrassment

'I think you need some sleep' with a forcefully nailed grin.

****

'I got late because of the ultrasound scan, but thankfully, everything is going great' Camilla sighed as she narrated the doctors visit to John, she pulled hard the door of car, placing the files and purse on the dashboard. John had reached there to pick her from the hospital. Though he was an alert driver, and a responsible citizen specially at following traffic rules, he couldn't help smiling eye to eye, so grateful for everything.

'That's really great ' he was pleased. As the couple turned quiet after the exchange of news and feelings, their ears connected to the anchoring host of the playing radio.

'T*he steps to success or the backdoor cheat entry, the hard-work and patience or the auctioned industry, rumours of relationship or the fake PDAs, we are here to let the cat out.*

A new radio show that has created buzz in the country and controversies in fans of every celebrity, starting very soon, make sure you don't miss it,

Be it on the way back from office, or while baking your cake, you are only a few finger clicks away from us.

The grey man show, every weekend only at five pm.'

The two listened to the promotion of interview program, and enjoyed the music along side.

****

She returned from the counselling session and decided to go for a walk in the local park. Even this step was tough for her to take, as it would remind her of Asher, but that was the end of her fear. She decided to take this courageous step, though she herself knew she wasn't in the best of her mental health conditions. She wore a grey t shirt and white joggers, embedded those ear pods in to her ears and pressed to play music. After taking some lethargic steps she settled at the a bench in isolated part of the park. There she sat for almost an hour, but thinking absolutely nothing. She thought maybe, but she forgot. She felt like a rabbit sneaking into cruel world from behind the toxic burrow. To live in her egg wasn't soothing now, it had began to consume her. Living with John was getting annoying day by day, she needed some time to let all the pain out, let the tears dry in her, to let her eyelids stop paining of shedding tears, to let her cheek muscles loosen as she smiles once in a million years. How much time? She didn't have an answer for that. If at all she goes to her house, what would she do, she didn't save even a penny, what would she do. She wasn't allowed by her psychiatrist to resume the job either. Brett was another big creep she thought. As he counselled and consoled everything seems perfect, the moment she steps out of the clinic it would get impossible for her to calculate even two plus two. What was her mistake to suffer all these. Loving her family, being loyal to husband, being an over protecting parent or what?. Children of all age groups ran around in front of her eyes with the heartiest smiles on their face. She unlocked her phone by tapping the finger on the sensor and slid into Asher's photo, his golden curls covering almost his forehead and two little teeth that sneaked from the pink lipped window. His deep eyes, in short a flawless angel he was.

Where did he go but?

She paused the thinking over it, as she remembered, about Brett's instructions, he had asked her to note down what she thinks. She took a notepad and a pen and started jotting down.

'Where did he go, I mean I know that his body is in the coffin, but where did exactly he go? And when no one entered into my house that night then who did take away my son.'

She look around, scratching in her braid, making many folds on her forehead between the two brows. And she raised her brows later at remembrance of something.

'I remember locking the doors, the shut windows, then who came into my house. There must have been someone in that day. No, even Ryan doesn't have the keys to the door. I didn't even check the jewellery and valuables since then. Must check

now.

There's no point of checking it now Olly! Two months later to the death of your son.

But who said, he can't come back? He might come back. No but my mother didn't return either, after she passed away. Huh. Must be a trap for the people.' She raised her head from the pad and turned left and right to see if someone was spying her. She bent totally into the paper and continued.

'My son. Can't believe now that once I was a mother. Who had given birth to a son. My womb carried the baby for whole nine months.'

She ran her fingers on her stomach, reliving the past beautiful moments. She raised her bent head and gazed around at every one. It was comparatively a sunny day in the wet season, the chirps of birds making rounds in the sky were acting to soothe her. After inserting the pen in her bag, she closed her eyes and rested her head on the back of the bench as her braid lingered on the shoulder. She tried taking longer breaths, but those deepest breaths couldn't erase her agony. Until she heard a disturbingly familiar rattling voice behind the large oak tree.

'I had filed an application for the loan, please make sure that it gets approved.' The conversation seemed to take place most probably between a bank fellow for recommending his name for approval of loan. The guy on other side must have enquired about his name. But till now she didn't have to listen the man's name to identify him, as he emerged from the bushes, wearing a mint green oversized t-shirt. Round framed glass rested on his widespread nose. And there was the man she still hated in the universe.

'Alfred Whitaker, I had filed it a month ago.' This was the confirmation stamp to her answer, it was again her father.

'It's not for any business purposes, I'm telling you, I need it, I am going through a lows from quiet a time now.'

'Lol, who would ever trust this fraudster.' She thought, as she listened him convincing someone for money.

'I am a retired professor from the reputed university, you must know that, before interrogating me!'

'His habit of boasting hasn't changed over the decades ' she concluded.

'They still leave infinite messages and calls, to pay a guest visit, but now I don't really feel like to, you know...' His swanking continued.

'Give me a time of three months, I promise to pay it all at once'

'Bragging like a royal and begging better than a tramp. Poor guy' she thought.

'Earlier I used to stay in London, but after the death of my wife, I've come here in search of a new start.'

'Oh, I am residing in the Age Cymru, that's the organisation for accommodating pensioners.'

'Oh, yeah I get monthly pension of hundred pounds sterling.'

'Hello! You there,' he threw the phone in the grass in frustration indicating the abrupt end of call. And sat down holding his forehead, and his huge cough series added to his pain, as he clenched his chest tight and sat in despair.

****

Camilla paced into the living room carrying along the bowl of popcorn. Lights were turned off and the huge screen was projected on the wall, the sound system was also arranged. It was another Irish web series. She had grown her red hair long and tied them into a messy bun. She wore a pink woollen night gown. Her cute little baby bump, manifested her gravidity. John was already there slumped over the couch, half asleep. She placed the popcorn on the table, sat gently and raised his hanging head, to make him lie down and sleep peacefully? No! She was Camilla, she raised her head and tossed the moisturizer lotion bottle in his lap and pointed at her arms implying her dry skin needed to be moistened at the first. He flipped the bottle and poured a little too much on his palm and started applying on her arm. He smiled heartily at her, pleased to work for his royal Merida lady. His beady eyes clashed with her big blue eyes, the time decided to stop at the moment, as the time chose to pause, and the moon blushed as love was in the air.

****

'They say girls find their father in the man of their life, but my case was completely opposite. I loved every habit of Ryan's, which differed from my dad. I always loved to see him following a path other than him. And I never left any stone unturned to change all his habits that resembled him. We were the best couple in the town, Infact in the world. I was so addicted to him and it wasn't easy for me to overcome the pain, gradually I realised it wasn't mandatory for a woman to be happy if she has a happy family. She could also live happily, if she was a blessed mother. What more could I need? Asher! He was the one stop of happiness for me in this cruellest journey of life.

Alas! He too bid me without even leaving behind a reason to leave, and live.' This gentle old man in a pony, wiped her tears with a napkin and gave a forehead peck. She tucked the loose hair strand behind her ear and the old man's soothing voice, pulled out her pain, following which her eyes filled with sweat, sweat released from being to tired of sad and broken. The two sat on her favourite bench in the park, near the large oak tree. Far from the chaos of city and in the minimal chirps and plants squeals that made realise her of being alive.

After a tedious fortnight, the fortune again seemed to fool Shawn, or is that it was that every thing was falling back to its place. Olivia attended the Brett counselling sessions and would go for a walk in the local park. She had begun to get all the grocery done. Exercises prescribed were being followed. Morning meditations and noting down of whatever she felt. Of course not in her sacred diary, that was maintained separately, this was her new notepad. Her dinner also met the requirements suggested by the nutritionist. Nuts, seeds, beans and lentils along with the fruits and green vegetables contributed to her healthy diet. She had also tried avoiding sugar intake, up to the possible extent. Oh, yeah, Alexa, it was a not so good present for her to cope up with depression. Period.

She had also started to take sleeping pills to fall asleep, sometimes coffee overdoses and every other day she caught hold of a stranger in the park and narrated her life story as she did today.

It was evident that she was following Shawn's advice of '*put yourself first*'. It wasn't possible for a personality like Olivia to become self centred. But she had to try a method to get out of the ditch. Depression was a marsh, if didn't find a way out, it would trap you deeper and deeper, until you reach to an end that's gonna harm you and eventually to the society as well.

CHAPTER TWENTY

'Since the last two weekends, the Grey man show has been the internet sensation, Breaking the records than ever. The interesting stuff is that, the guy hosting this is a disguised person, unrevealing his identity. Pictures and videos on Instagram show him covered in a sort of grey costume, and an ash mask. The most interesting part is, that any one could guess, it's not an scripted interview show.'

'Ok' Olivia replied tying boxer braid in her head, looking into the mirror.

'It's aired on the radio channel no. 5, and your zecho dot would also play it for you.'

'Fine.' she rolled her eyes while applying a gloss on her lips and tied the wrist watch.

'You okay?' his eyes shrunk, as the forehead waved into frowns of confusion.

'Yeah I am good, your lectures sound boring' she retorted bluntly, looking in the air, ready to go out, after tying her sneakers.

'That's way rude' he threw out honestly.

'As you said, put yourself first!' she finger quoted by lowering her index finger and middle finger twice, curving a fake smile, she marched out of the house carrying along her bag, which she hung on the shoulders. While Shawn was awestruck, by her reasoning to a horrible behaviour once again. He put one heaped spoonful sugar in the coffee mug and began to stir, cautiously about his finger getting burnt if dipped deep. Unable to feel the steam, he touched the mug, resisting to understand that it had already turned cold. Pondering over the new issue, he sipped through his pouted lips.

****

Camilla laid on the tilted seat of the car, followed by an unusual Monday blue. John drove the car yawning and rubbing his eyes every now and then, the past night hadn't been a good one in terms of sleep as well as peace. There have been a long list of conversations, debates and arguments over several subjects between Olivia and her.

A couple of days ago when she witnessed her father poorly in need of money, she indirectly enquired about his whereabouts, to which Camilla replied in utter ignorance showing lack of interest in revealing her the reality. This has perplexed Olivia a bit more. There was no clear track that she could chose, that would lead her to *eternal peace and happiness.* To strike up the already geared argument, Olivia slipped off the nights secret before her, about eavesdropping Ryan's discussion. The words were manipulated and tones worsened as she realised the cause of her mysterious run off from her house. And then there was an eternal silence of fuming lavas.

'I agree I never asked you about that rascal until Asher's death. And you didn't inform me either. This makes complete sense.' She gulped down the dripping saliva from her lips as she spoke non stop and pulled back her hair to roll them into a bun. Letting out an *enough of drama* expression. A pearl rolled down washing her eyes and reddening her nose and as she chose the speak an intense grief and complaint had overtake her voice. 'But since the last three moths, was there anyway left that I begged you of his absence?, of missing him? of dying to meet him!' raising the voice till the last word nearly blasted on Camilla with two droplets of unintentional spit on her cheek and head. Yes, Olivia had noticed that, no, she wasn't sorry or embarrassed for that. She wiped her face with John's sleeve, grimacing at the act, meanwhile he glared bewildered at the timeless cuddle.

'I swear on you., I don't know about him.' Her tongue stammered and eyes radiated confidence. Besides the fact that she was aware of the truth, Olivia had turned into face reading expert in case of Camilla, and she could detect some honest and guilty vibes from her at the same time.

'I heard you! I am not a mentally retarded patient, its no hallucination, if you don't want to reveal anything just say you don't want, there's no need for cheating on me or lying on my face!' she wasn't ready to trust even her shadow, this time not even a bit.

'Please be calm, and keep some patience, let's sit and have a talk.' She suggested holding her pretty grown tummy as she took her place on the ottoman that was nearest seat to her. John rushed into the kitchen to get her wifey a glass of water, and her medicine box.

Olivia interpreted her health issue and kicked herself for being ignorant, until her ego added on all the thorns and pricks received from her. She sat at the chair, as if making one more unreturnable favour on them. Her temporarily sympathetic face turned into the rigid nailed lips and fierce eyes. Tossing the three tablets into her mouth one by one she sipped the extra water to calm herself.

'Okay!' she looked into John's eyes as if asking his permission before bursting the bubble. While his face was stunned with dropped jaw, in utter blockage of nerves. Camilla inhaled all the air in the world through her mouth and cleared the pit for the millionth time before announcing the truth. Olivia forced her spirit to not leave the body, and contracted her veins to stop circulating, awaiting her answer all ears.

'The truth is that, we never knew about Ryan, since the birth of Asher.' She took a pause. A long pause. Thinking that there was still the time to mix it all and conceal the truth. The bitter truth. Then there was a sudden instinct, that she felt a push on her back, so she just threw it up.

'The night that you were admitted to the hospital to deliver Asher, Mrs Laura had fallen unconscious. An ambulance was called next to yours to take her to the hospital. Mr. Whitaker had accompanied us on the way to the maternity, and John left along her. Ryan remained alone at home.' She took a perfect speed to narrate the incident which although didn't match with Olivia's impatience.

'He says that as he took start towards the hospital, the cab had to stop as the other vehicle screeched speedily, almost banging it's bumper into his head. It was the lonely dark street, two blocks away from his house. By the time he picked up his phone from under the shoe, he was surrounded by dozens of cops and three cops cars. He lowered the glass to enquire and officer Chris informed him, that he was accused of storing illegal weapons. Hearing this, he allowed them to check his vehicle. Upon no sign of it, they demanded a raid on his house and despite his denial and refusal, they forced him. As they searched in the house, several weapons without an issued licence were found and he was arrested on the spot.'

As she narrated the story, Olivia glared at her in disbelief, still lingering on the decision to make, whether she should believe it or not. But she didn't have any other proof to decline it. There was no choice to make, but to believe on this tale. While john wiped his runny nose, and sipped hot coffee, displaying agreed expressions on all her statements.

'Mrs Laura passed away on that night, I was busy with you, Mr Whitaker also stood by your side, until john informed him of her demise. Yet on the third day, he came to pay a visit to you and Asher despite being in the pain of losing her wife.'

'I never asked him to show up ' Olivia rolled her eyes in disgust.

'For a couple of days we thought, Ryan must be at any one of his friends and didn't know about auntie's death. But he never showed up, until he was released after an year ' she lowered her gaze and voice before revealing, ' After Asher's death actually. '

'As soon as he was released, he came to meet us and narrated the entire tragedy. That was a trap for him and he believed you were behind it all.'

At this she widened her eyes and dropped her jaw, Yet she spoke nothing and waited eagerly to listen.

'I tried a lot to convince him that you weren't involved in this mess, yet the fire of revenge that he held within was unbeatable. It had blocked his ability to think or understand. After a few days he came to know, that your sister Isabella Whitaker had been behind this.'

'What the! How could that be possible? I mean why would she, on earth fall into this guy's matter, especially when she knew that I am married to him.'

She stood up from the place and started to explain on her behalf. Camilla kept quiet for a couple of minutes just the way she was prepared for this reaction. John got busy over the continuous phone calls.

'This is your problem Olly! Why do you think she won't do it. It is her. It was her. That's the truth!' Olivia wasn't in the best of her mental state, and such harsh realities hitting all at a time, made it hard to process all these news.

'And now, I can swear on my unborn baby, we don't know about Ryan. He was always on the urge to seek revenge from his sinner. And maybe he left on this path.'

'Does he know about dead Asher?' her trembling lips finally dared to announce these words in air.

Camilla nodded in agreement, ' he thinks that your sister is responsible for that as well.'

'Has he gone crazy? Why would she be responsible for it. It was all...' she paused while arguing, defending her sister. Standing upright, she pushed her feet into her shoes and rushed out of her House. This time Camilla didn't call her from behind, not even once. She ran straight till the car parking, while the people looked in confusion and she sat in the car, the continuous stream of tears fell from both the eyes. This was again hitting her hard, pricking her sharp, to her already shattered soul. The facts that she learnt all at once had started to make her numb, she felt dizzy as she pushed in and twisted the keys to start the car. Instantaneously she pulled it back, as she had realised it wasn't safe for her to drive, and surviving out of surgery twice wasn't possible either. She wanted to sit and analyse what was exactly throttling her. 'Is it Ryan's ignorance? But that wasn't ignorance! Or the guilt that I misunderstood Ryan all this years? He was still not a clean chit on his part, he could have informed me. At least once? How would I know that he was stuck in some hell? I tried every possible way to reach him. He was found no where. After being released from the bars, his duty was to approach me. Consult me once, before he assumed all the story. I know he thought of meeting me, but the news of Asher's death must have stopped him from doing so. It means he cares for me still. Is this what it means? But who is the sufferer in this tale? me! Is Isabella really the culprit? But why would she need to do this? And who's responsible for that rascal Whitaker running down and out? That must be his karma for sure! There was a hurricane of thoughts in her mind, and she fetch an answer to any of them, even if she does, it didn't get her any satisfaction.

She rested her head, with an aching heart, tilting the seat down and closed her eyes. Just then a thought clicked into her mind, she pulled her phone from the passenger seat and texted Shawn.

'I am at Camilla's, pick me up from the parking on the way you return home.'

And she threw back the phone on the seat beside. Moment after moment pressure built in her head. She could literally feel the heat radiating from her scalp. She blew out trying to exhale the tension, but nothing worked.

'Ok! One last time' she yelled at herself, feeling impossible to resist her from that one thought, though she kept neglecting, but which has managed to raise through her ego and common sense most probably. She picked her phone and with sweating palms and chilling fingers she dialled to Ryan.

'Damn it! Bloody switch off!' the call didn't connect, his phone was out of network area or switched off.

****

All the way to home, she sat silently weeping in the car, while Shawn drove the car in quietude too. Entering the house, he took way to his room, not taking notice of her sadness, or maybe pretending unnoticed.

She never felt the need to do some drama to catch his attention, nor was he Ryan, the earlier Ryan, for whom she would do such things. She paced into her room and laid down-turned, burying her face in to the pillow, hanging her legs in the air, as she flipped out the shoe of each foot with the other toe. There was no possible way out of this mess. Shawn was probably tired of listening to her sorrows. But why wasn't she. Why every wound of her, appeared fresher than past to her. She unzipped her bag, and picked her pen and pad. Turning the pages to the new, she realised she isn't in a state to write either and slammed the hardcover, leading it to bounce and drop behind the bedpost. She dropped her head once again in the pillow and struggled through her not so thin palm to pick her notepad, ending up in getting her fingers scratched against the wall. Resting her head on the straightened arm, she glared in silence. Yet again Camilla's words echoed on her head for the hundredth time, with her leftover ability and talent to imagine how the things might have taken place. There was eerie silence in the world. She could presume this from her window side. Not a single being proved her to be alive. The lightened streetlights and the moonlight was just an attempt to fool the citizens. Because they could only lighten the pathways and roads, they could never strike up a dark life, they couldn't give directions to a soul. A broken soul. Her thought process was constantly being interrupted by the ticks of clock. She crawled and neared the shelf beside bed, to grab the paperweight and turned, making a position to attack her target and BOOM! The glass on the clock had broken into smallest pieces and the falling paperweight made the loudest thud, followed by crunches of the glass pieces and as anyone could logically predict, the clock fell from the nail and banged on the floor. She closed her eyes and a small smile crept onto her lips as the bothering sound at last come to an end. After a split of second, her peace of mind was being disturbed by her pounding heart, she jumped down from the bed to get it done right, ignoring the piercing glass in her soles and then there was the third sound disturbance. It was Shawn thumping continuously on the locked door.

She darted to open the door and before he could utter a word,

'Who locked the door?' she roared with high pitch and her fierce eyes locked into his, until he analysed the situation looking at the broken glass behind her, the wetly substance his foot sank into as he neared the threshold, and the red floor flooded with blood.

CHAPTER TWENTY-ONE

'Duh, get your senses?' he was sure the underlying catastrophe wasn't an accident. 'You have the keys inserted in the door from your side and why would I bother to lock you!' he exclaimed helplessly looking down at her disdainfully, as if on a mentally challenged person. Cause she was becoming one. She was losing the mental health and balance. She lost control over her limitless anger and what ever she was doing under its influence.

Her constant untamed gaze, produced haunted vibes, as if possessed by some spirit, although he never believed in such, but the situation compelled him to reach a conclusion. He got goose bumps at the glimpse. 'Olivia, I am just done with this daily damages you make' he pulled her hand, and made her to sit on the chair. He got the first aid, and sat by her feet, cleaning the excessively bleeding toe and heel.

'By dressing up just one wound, please, don't pretend to be my well wisher. There are million other bruises on my heart, every new day I end up with one more tear.' Her nose reddened and eyes filled as she let the smallest part of her heart out.

'I don't care for you?' he dropped her ankle and his jaw wondering at her statement.

'How can you be so ungrateful? If not me, than whose looking after you since the last three months. Without a single benefit to me, irrespective of any condition, I kept caring for you, the obstacles you made in my career, in my job place, ignored all your mistakes and even presented you, called you towards life every time, just don't test my patience levels Olivia! You are just beyond tolerance.!' He shouted at her in anguish.

'Your job place!' she smirked sarcastically.

'The job for which you almost begged before me, which you got only because of my mercy! Never forget that!' she pointed her finger at him and warned with a lower tone and raised brows.

'And if I am staying at your home, once I resume my work, I can throw its ten times on your face!' she boasted.

'It's not about money!' he attempted to correct.

'Oh, and this silly gift of yours, is of no use to me' she abruptly interrupted and picked up the zecho from the table, switched it on by applying infinite times pressure than required, through her finger nail.'

'WHY AM I CREATED?'

'WHO CREATED ME?'

'*No results found in 0.544355 seconds*'

'Have a look at your gift! Lol!' she smirked at him.

'Whats wrong with you? What are you asking?' he glared in confusion.

'It's all your fault ' she neared him, holding him by his collar and banged to the wall, as he stood beside her.

'Why am I held responsible for your Ill fate, for your misfortune?' he yelled back at her. Pushing her hands behind.

'I tried to kill myself, to end my life, but you messed up the plan at the eleventh hour! And my misfortune? Who writes my story? Why am I destined to be depressed?' she pressed her palms against her head, turning around the in wilderness.

'Instead I must kill you, you are my biggest enemy!' she continued. Her tremendous limb movements made it difficult for him to manage, and her untamed approach towards him, made it way scarier.

He rushed to the main door, turned the keys and wide opened the door, ' that's it Olivia! I am sorry. the doors of my house are closed for you, for now and forever.' He put his right hand in the pocket of his joggers, pulled out a key and clapped it into her hand.

'Where would I go at this hour?' she resisted into the house until he forcefully pushed her out, glowering and squeezing his jaw together.

'Thats none of my business, just go to hell from my side, Or I have a better option, you belong to a mental asylum!' taking heavier breaths he jutted.

She bugged, pushing him inside making her way and dashed into her room to get her shoes, and darted even back faster out. Not waiting for a second he slammed back the door hard, not even caring what the neighbours would think.

He moved to the kitchen and poured water into his mouth, tilting the raised bottle. Taking deeper breaths he leaned over the couch in the sitting room, glaring at the mess she left behind. He was now guilty of his behaviour, he was tired. Exhausted. Of all the mess she had spread In his life, it wasn't an easy task to deal with that sick lady. She radiated negative vibes. It has been three months now and there was no tolerance left in him. Specially for a career oriented guy like him. He closed his eyes trying to *forget* her. He did everything for her. Everything meant everything. Just a moment of peace had become a big deal for him. It wasn't available at home, at office, no where.

This had to be done, someday. He consoled his rising conscience. Rising as an objection may be. Consoling or muffling may be.

He walked in his bedroom, after locking the door and threw himself on the wrinkled blanket. Pressed the lock button of the phone for any random notifications, and turned it back. There was no call from her. ' Oh yeah, she didn't take her phone along'. He thought to himself. Her shrieks echoed in his ears, as he tossed on the bed, for thirty eight long minutes. He grabbed the phone and dialled to Camilla as he raised from the bed, strolling around the house, as he chewed a finger nail along the pinch of t-shirt between his teeth.

'Pick up the call, Camilla!' He tapped the phone on his palm, turning the speaker on.

****

'Three calls and fifteen messages in the last two minutes, you need a to revise the calling etiquettes specially to a pregnant lady.' She let out the daunting statement that took a friendly end. He rolled back the steering, taking a return from the block 26 lane, in an attempt to fetch her.

'Umm, yeah.., had your dinner?'

'Absolutely done... 'he replied. The amount of anxiousness she had to listen didn't translate into her voice.

'Err John? What about him? Is he okay?'

'Cool, wait a second, I'll make a video call for your confirmation, that he's sleeping peacefully.'

'Noooo! We..., I mean, me and Olivia had a fight and she left the house angrily ...'

'How could you let her go!' she yelled at him.

'Actually I forced her to leave ' he confessed.

'Damn it, Shawn! Where is she now?'

'I don't know, just wanted to know, if she came to you, but'

'No, she isn't anywhere here, and the way she left us in day-time, I am sure she won't return here.'

'Ooh. Whats the problem actually? What had upset her now?'

'You. Forcing her out of the house.' She slammed him.

'I got an idea, wait I'll check if she's there.'

'But where..' he disconnected the phone before listening to her question and speeded the car into the right lane, breaking the traffic signals and almost dashing into the old lady crossing road with an open umbrella when it wasn't raining at all.

****

' Take a right turn and keep driving until reach your destination in 3 minutes.'

Shawn tapped off the GPS locator and drove straight as directed. Pulling back the hand break hard, he parked the car on the rising slope and jumped down. He turned his head from side to side, trying to find her. The night was quiet and however the moon had decided to reveal its full face into the sky. And there she stood, as Shawn's sight fell on the shore of Klive beach. Burying head by the elbow, casting pebbles into sea, scrutinizing the landscape, she noted down something in the booklet. He approached her from the back, with slightly pressed feet, an unsuccessful attempt to not disturb the universal silence.

Standing still behind her, ' knew, you would be here' he announced, expecting her to freak out or at least surprise at his presence. Contrary to his assumption she remained unaffected. In a moment he realised she must have seen his car already.

'There's no part left unbroken within me, for you' taking a long pause of courage to speak she continued ' to hammer it and shatter into some more million pieces'

'Let's go our home' he ordered ignoring her usual complaints.

'You can go to yours and I'll reach my house, worrying about that isn't a part of your job'

'What's wrong with you Olivia?' he fumed at her for resisting persistently, and reached by her side taking heavy steps in annoyance.

'I repeat that's not a part of your job, you may kindly get lost!' she was trying hard to be gentle, also Shawn wasn't intentionally testing her patience.

'Okay I am sorry.' He tried to make it, placing his palm on her right shoulder, he embraced her from the side sitting on the rock.

It was the darkest of nights, illuminated by the tiny street lights. The sluggish waves crawled gently towards the shore bathing their feet as the duo sat clueless about their next breath.

He breathed through his blocked nose, that made a sniff, to which Olivia uttered, completely unrelated to her psychotic behaviour at home.

'You must return to your house.' She looked at the farthest wave emerging, pointing at the sand beside the large rocks. 'You know, every time I came here with Ryan, I would press my feet in to make footprints in the sand, and we would wait until the dawn to see if any wave of sea damages it. But never in those seven years, any wave damaged my footprint on the shore. He used to say this land was his heart and that my footprints were carved on it.'

'You must return to your life' he answered, trying to figure out the mess in her eyes.

'It's impossible for a person to live a life, who is stuck infinite miles from life and only a step away from Death.' She replied, gazing at her feet hopelessly as she tucked in the hair strand behind the ear.

'It's possible, only if you give it a try. May be just one push.' He clasped her palms. There was a warmth in his palms, it was genuinely a helping hand. But she was beyond exhausted of trusting again. The surrounding breeze radiated giving up vibes.

'I am clueless, unaware, baffled, speechless, lonely, weak, powerless, incapable to see, think, process and at least die. I m sorry for the behaviour, but you are the culprit.' She turned towards him, making contact with her agonised eyes, running down chills through his spine.

'You are the culprit, for not letting me die in peace' she continued looking at the sky. 'I would have met my son, my Asher baby.'

'Nonsense. How could you ever meet a corpse?' he asked.

'Didn't your soul even quiver, to say him... Him a... *corpse?*' pulling out her hands from his grip.

'Indeed it didn't, for it's a fact. You are perished after you die, and chapter finished, story over, book closed.'

'That's exactly the point, what's the purpose of the creation of this book, what was the need of creating this story and what does the writer get killing the protagonist over and over again.' She questioned with the curiosity of philosopher, and innocence of a child at a time.

'Listen, I don't have answer for such questions, I only know, that you only live once. So just enjoy the life in your own way. Sky is the limit, at least learn to crawl. Just don't stop on the way. That's all. I have a set of goals, some inspirations which fancy me, and a stomach to fill. There are no rules, but it's a race.' He appeared more puzzled than Olivia while explaining what is life to her. Actually it was a point of realisation to him, that he never thought on this topic. He was never taught about it. Because it never became an obstacle to his success. In a case where there's a question to the proper definition of success.

'You are a sensible person, but this time your explanation didn't strike my satisfaction. You are not able to convince my conscience. It's a simple question.

WHY AM I SUFFERING SINCE A SMALL AGE TO TILL DATE? WHO WRITES MY FATE?' She air quoted, widening her eyes at him with crawled eyebrows.

'Oh Olly, do you see anybody writing it? Have you seen someone creating a human, all these discussions suit in the tales of folks. Get some senses! The world runs on its own system, and that's the way according to which a body is born and a life is welcomed. And eventually a person's body weakens due to any medical reason and a person dies. He loses his life. It's just that simple.'

'No rules? So why did you stop me from killing myself, and even from killing you? My life, my rules!' there was a fire in her meaningless speech.

'Morals. Ethics. You can't just go against them, those are which classify you into a good and bad person. This marks the difference between animals and humans.'

'You are fool of an ass!' she yelled at him for not understanding her simply not so simple question from a few hours. ' just leave me alone!' Shawn stood firm at the rock, preparing defence methods in his head because she could stand up to push him down the rock and introduce him to the underwater world.

Contrary to his prediction, She continued speaking, pointing at the sky,

'Look at the moon held so high, with its changing phases, look at these twinkling stars, which is the icing on the huge cake of sky, the sky so vast and huge, out of range of an human estimation. Let alone attempting, I'm sure no human force could have even imagined of such a beautiful world. Why are these created? Such a largest spread of land, which comprises of hundreds of countries. Can't you take signals from such signs of nature? You can't fool me by saying there's no creator. There is. There is.' she emphasised of the latter words, exploring everything she could.

She pulled him by his palm and the she walked deeper into the sea and he followed timidly. Frightened of drowning, he remained at her side and out of her grip diameter.

'I never took the swimming coaching idea, very seriously and that may cost me my life' he thought staring at her.

CHAPTER TWENTY-TWO

At the edge of dawn, the sun light burst into the sky amidst the clouds. Olivia pointed at her reflection into the sea, as the waves took rest and surface was still. ‘ look at these beautiful eyes, better than all the cameras in the world, my nose, I can smell and differentiate a million different things. My symmetrical pigmented lips, and a tongue beneath it. A brain in my head, with an ability to think.’ She continued running her fingers over her stomach, ’this piece of flesh, gives birth to a new life! You understand! I am blessed with these senses, I just can’t resist myself, to use them. You say morals differentiate a human from animals? No. Observation makes the difference. You all are busy as animals as those creatures, running behind their selfish goals. Yet ending up with none.’

‘Olly‘ just come out of the shell and see there are million people out there suffering from huge problems, disasters and what not? Look at them and get some inspirations...’

‘You think I have reached this point, being self centred? No. I’ve considered of all those cases, just before you suggested and it kills me in. Why do the superpowers suppress smaller, why does the innocent natives lose their lives, homes, children just for the ego of politics. Whose in charge for the newspapers flooded with crime news? Whose responsible for a nation striving of poverty and countries doing so well? Whose responsible for rotation and revolution of heavenly bodies? For rising of sun from east and it's setting in the west? How are all the things connected together? The rain, climate, drought, famine, food, health, poverty, trees, fresh air, animals and eventually happiness and if one gets privileged to have all of this things, then a guy can break your heart after six long years of marriage. So you got to be ready for it. That's what I am trying to understand, there has to be a system. System for everything.'

'You think you can run the world on your new rules' he smirked.

'Of course, I can't. Listen.' she gulped in to explain. 'You bought me a gift, that zecho dot. Right? The salesman didn't just handover the machine? He gave a box along with It. With instructions to use. With dos and don'ts. With warnings. And if I use it in the same way, it won't damage, but I threw it yester night. And that was not supposed to be happened. This is my point, as the human beings, animals, land, water and the whole universe has been created there might be creator to it. There might be a user booklet. There has to be something. I just wish if I could fetch it anywhere.'

'Your ability to think has stopped and that's making you believe in myths. Basically, you are Over, over, over the top, overthinking.' He interrupted..

'These are not myths!' she concluded without a second thought to give.

'I can prove this to you, just look at my dad, a man who ran endlessly behind money, who even abandoned his wife and kids, now, is a skint, begging every one on earth for a few bucks.

Ryan! The huge narcissist whom I had failed to recognise all the time, who had made a timeless effort just to make sure that the things linked with his name don't sink. He chased vanity, setting up goals in the society, show off and ruined everything midway. His tarnished image was a result of him being jailed. Even after getting freed, neither did he bother to throw a visit to his namely beloved, nor at the grave of his son. When he learnt the fact that Isabella is the culprit he could have approached me. Ask me once, how do I live? His ego didn't let him forward the hand of peace.

Let's not forget Isabella as well, she hungered power and I am sure before she could get the crown she abused the prominence. Few days ago, she was invited on the grey man radio show, and it was as if the interview was determined to raise her to the noose. His twisted cross questions, and her answers that mismatched, became a sensation and she has been restricted from some stuff until the court announces the decision on the complaint filed. Her lawyer says it's a conspiracy. But her psychiatrist says she's guilty.'

'How are you informed about every minute detail?'

'Day before yesterday, I attended the counselling session of Dr Brett Adler and came to know that even Isabella is consulting him. She had burnt all her boats to reach that position and probably, she can never afford to lose her highest standardised life.'

'Isabella is her patient and you are nothing more than a patient to him either, how could he disclose secrets to you.?' he protested.

She smirked at the silly question. 'Professionalism, privacy, purity, honesty, humanity, ethics, morals and etiquettes, these are only those little things what the whole world lacks.'

'Hmmm' he nodded in despair, looking at the rising sun.

'The list goes on still, Shawn.

Why not consider me, the biggest threat to my life. All I longed for since the youngest of my age as far as I could recall, I remember I craved for love. Not a penny more than that, and see today I stand empty handed, with pulled out and torn pockets. Every face of pure and unconditional love has abandoned me to crawl on this shore, like these crabs.' She referred at the underlying creatures which emerged from the rocks.

'Let's include you too, listen, you claim yourself to be a philosopher. Right?'

She asked her the already known answer, and he knew something hard was coming through her unpredictable mind.

'You know what, you look the most confused person on earth, when I ask you about the meaning of life, and the reason of being created. Let alone the philosophies.'

'You can't assume everything on your own, Olivia. You can question me whatever you wish, I am sure I won't disappoint you.'

She unfastened the flap of the bag with Velcro and pulled out her writing pad, riffled through the crumbled torn pages and handed it to him. It was a page full of writing cum scribblings. Upon forcing his eyes and refreshing his brain, it was discovered that those were a list of complaints.

'*1) I am lonely.*

2) I am a failure.

3) it's too difficult.

4) No one can help me.

5) I don't have much.

6) I am always sick.

7) I am overburdened.

8) I feel lost.

9) I feel ugly.

10) Who created me?

11) Why created me?

12) Who and why created the moon and the sun, the stars and the skies held so high, the under water creatures, the air creatures, the animals that reside on land, Infact the land and the water and everything which includes the million species of plants as well.

13) Who created the day and night, how do they take their timings, the mountains, flowers, oceans etc.

14) What's the proper way to live a life, amongst the creatures whose supposed to be dominant, men over women? Or women over men?

Rich over poor? Or poor over rich? The government over citizens or the citizens over government? A single path which can bring about peace in the entire world throughout the issues!

15) what happens after I die? After any creature dies? Book closed or what?

16) why do the natural calamities occur?'

He turned the page to make her feel it was worth reading, which was actually not for him. And to his misfortune the list continued yet he closed the book unable to gear up courage to explain her. He was drowsing by the time. If it were anybody other than her, it was possible that he might slap the papers on their face.

'Olivia let's go home, I am feeling sleepy.' He voice changed as he yawned.

'Only if you could give answers to these...' he raised his hands before her 'I surrender,' Yawning once again he neared the car, at which she followed her hanging the bag around and holding that notepad pad close to her chest. As she approached the car, her sick face wasn't the same anymore. Her dead spirit had finally rose back and there was a determined spirit that took over her.

She sneaked from the lowered glass window of the passenger seat, pushing her hand into the holder. 'We are two different people, with two different perspectives, so let's take our own paths, and test the fate of the two different destinies.' She picked up the keys of her house, her phone from the passenger seat and making an eye contact, she waved a concealed good bye. Deep in their hearts, both were aware of the fact that despite a formal hand wave, there bond has come to an end. Their friendship was taking its last breath as he waved back silently. Waiting for her departure and not wanting her to go, he stared blank in the air. Her hair strands were flying by the passing wind, as she waited for a power packed goodbye. Finally she turned back, and walked away. They were habituated to each other, but they also knew that their separation was destined and mandatory to let each other grow.

Wiping of a tear, he turned his face to the other side. Don't know the reason why, but he didn't raise his voice to call her, as she turned without awaiting his response. How would she go? Where would she reach? Whats her next step? He was as clueless as her. But he let her go.

****

'Long time no see,' Mrs. Agatha greeted with a toothless grin, as she walked in the gate after a really long time. She was an old lady with a croaky voice, sharing the same block number in her residence. Olivia had built in a strong resistance to let go of all the things that's going to remind her of anything. She smiled back at her and headed towards the door. Inserting the key into the keyhole, she turned to the right twice, and before she could enter there was a blur image of what her home looked like while she left. As she pushed in the door, stepped into it and raised her head, her heart pounded and she quickly bounced back reverse to check If it wasn't her home.

But it was her. Yet it wasn't the same. Before her mind could clear the clutter of confusion, an old man showed from the kitchen taking feeble steps. Her heart skipped a beat as that man was none other than Alfred Whitaker.

****

'Have you tried explaining her?' Camilla enquired about her friend.

'We talked the whole night, I am unable to understand what's in her mind....'

'Where is she now?' She wondered aloud.

'Don't know! She's becoming a warrior day by day, and now it's getting impossible to hold her back, let's leave her to explore, avenge and whatever she wishes for.' He presented.

'What do you mean by don't know? If she's not with you, it means she will go back to her house and that's not we want right?' she expressed her fear.

'This had to happen someday, and let's see what happens. You are her friend and you never intended to double cross her. It was under some impotent situation that you chose that place for his residence. Still, I am not sure of how she will react to it.'

'Ok talk you later, it seems john is at the door.' She ended the call, as the bell rang in the background.

'Good morning babe' he neared the dining with a bag.

'Glad that you finally extended your jogging time.'

'You are aloud to rejoice, but not for my jogging, instead for these freshly made rissoles I had' he emptied the paper bag into a snacks tray.

'Only if I could...' she silently picked one, as he offered the plate.

'What's Wrong Camo?'

She narrated the entire incident to him.

'I think you must talk to her about it. After all I warned you earlier also, that this is not happening good.'

'But I took this step thinking well of your dad! He found a place to live, all those old age homes are so pathetic.'

'Because you never agreed to let him live with us. That would not have been a problem bigger than the one this is.'

'The entire possessions aren't divided fairly, Ryan got the greater percentage even though he is a nephew and you? Being a son, he treated you partially. And that selfish son is enjoying somewhere behind the bushes.'

'You never know Camilla! Maybe he is in a situation worse than before.'

'I don't believe it. How could he just disappear. So coward of him.'

'Nevertheless, Its high time, I think you must call Olivia and inform her about the same.'

****

'Oh for God's sake, what has brought you here?' she stood by the flower pot placed beside the entrance door. Her soft tone wasn't totally expected.

Her house was not an inch like what she had left, the previous one. The sitting had changed, the colour of walls, furniture, electronics, wallpapers, interior and what not.

'Please take a seat, it's a long story, I need to explain.' His wobbly chin and loose cheeks defined his edentate jaw. To be honest he had grown too old in a short time. May be the death of beloved Laura had turned him so.

'Oh no, I am not so keen to learn your fake sympathizers.' she looked around the room to locate the wall clock, and there hung a black round one, ' its quarter past seven, you have one hour to pack up. Sharp at quarter past eight I must not see you in my house. Out!' she yelled at the old man ruthlessly, and he dared not to utter a single word except expressed an attempt to speak some by shaking lower lip. His previously grey hair could hardly be spotted on the dusky scalp. She wandered inside, exploring her new house. Just then she recalled her favourite bubble swing. Oh, yeah her couch? The previous dining table set. Where was all that. She marched from the gallery downstairs to check at him, and ask what was actually going on. At the moment she stepped down the last step, her phone rang. It was Camilla.

'Good morning Olly.'

'Hello,'

'How's it going?

'Absolutely perfect, just like it should have been quite a time ago.'

'Breakfast?'

'mmm'

'We need to talk something, important.'

'Please proceed, I m listening.'

'Till now you must have encountered uncle Alfred at your residence...' she listened the whole incident calmly.

'I know you won't tolerate his existence, and that's why I called you to inform about his new place to reside. I'll text you the address, just explain him and get him a taxi to reach there. They'll adjust them in the housekeeping staff and also arrange for his accommodation.'

'Fine, I'll do that.'

'Bye'.

It was eight in the large wall clock, as she glanced at the old man he was already done with his packing and, widening his pupils from the rim of his spectacles, he was probably noting down his medicines.

'Since how many days are you at this place?.' she questioned glancing at his eyes for less than a second than gazing in air.

'Twenty five days including today' he answered promptly.

'You may live here, if you wish to. No need of shifting to another place.' She commanded and the old man stood in awe. She turned back and left the room after completing her statement. Leaving Alfred in utmost astonishment and a sense of belief to the rumours he had heard about her mental health.

CHAPTER TWENTY-THREE

As he feebly unpacked his little belongings, he remembered to dial John.

'Hello' his trembling hand rose towards the ear. Upon listening to the not answering answer, he long pressed the cut button. Lowered his glasses and confirm if he was dialling the correct person, as he made sure, then dialled him once again.

'Hi dad.' John picked it up at the last ring of second call.

'Hello'

'Camilla sent her the address, she will direct to you towards it.'

'Oh yeah, first listen to me,' his quivering voice continued. 'She says that I can stay here, and that she doesn't have any problem with it...'

'Well that's unbelievable and great at the same time, wish you luck.' He cheered him.

****

'Thank god, everything is up to the mark and in no time we'll meet the tiny camo in our arms, god I can't wait to see her.' John rubbed his palms together in excitement after wiping with a napkin.

'Touchwood' Camilla knocked her head smiling about it.

'Well to be honest I've always wanted my first baby to be a girl.' John expressed, leaning by the chair and allowing the waiter to place their plates on the table. He picked out a fork and was about to poke it into the plate before getting stopped by Camilla.

'What do you mean first child?' she frowned at him.

'First as in first of all' he replied thinking.

'Kindly explain the term 'of all',' she stressed at the words, giggling inside.

'Maybe sixteen!'

'Sixteen!' He hushed up her for being so loud. It was a dinner at restaurant or a treat to themselves after her routine check-up and upon revelation of their baby's gender. While she burst into laughter, letting go the superficial objection, and the blush took over her cheeks as she grinned ear to ear. He crossed the two fingers of both the hands symbolising hashtag, winked and whispered, 'hashtag squad square'

'I see ' she nodded still red.

'What about a gender reveal party?' he proposed taking a spoonful of soup into the mouth.

'Sure! Not a bad idea.' She faked enthusiasm at the answer and it wasn't a big task for him to figure out the reason. It was Olivia for sure. 'You were right Camilla. The world can't stop for one person's grief, nor can everyone dance as happily at our joy' he thought aloud.

'What do you think, would she attend it?' she asked.

'Who?' he questioned pretending unknown about her thoughts.

'Olly.' She uttered with a pause.

Then there was a silence, except the clinking of plates and spoons, and Camilla's chewing.

'Wonder how did she accept uncle Alfred at her place.' She reflected on.

'I guess she's used to heart pricking days and she's seen grief and pain beyond limits, it must have melted her heart for him. After all he is her father too.'

'Four children with Mrs. Victoria and one with Mrs. Laura, and out of nowhere Ryan becomes the heir to him. He is such a bogus.' She rolled her eyes.

'At times I feel, the one step treatment to all her problems is Ryan. I wonder if he just visits her back and all the things get normal.' He suggested ignoring the statement.

'It means you know where is he?' she interrogated suspiciously.

'Actually he called me from an unknown number, two days ago. Again, didn't give a hint about his whereabouts.'

'It's so miserable to see these two persons lives worsening in front of my eyes. They were an ideal couple for me. He wasn't perfect nor was she. But together they made it worth. I just pray for her.'

'Salt sprinkle?' he offered.

'Just a pinch.'

****

Monday 7:30 AM.

'Memories in mind, Burn me alive
The sharp broken dreams,
Pierce through my eyes,
Stars don't feel heavy in dreams,
Until The sky seems far
And well wishers farthest,
There's some in between, And I still hope for the best.
Resting my trust on the one,
Paying every breath, I buy one moment,
To stumble on the bond
And struggling all along, I make an attempt
To reach my lord.'
Sitting by the wall,

My soul travels all,
I follow the conscience,
At every small call,
To keep it alive,
Amidst the chaos.
Any dimension justifies, All the falls and rise,
Yet I strive to Find the cause of life,
The day I know,
Is indeed a celebration,
Beyond the sky is Not too high,
The Grave of mine, Might be within a mile.'

She leaned by the newly lilac painted wall, and scribbled through the pages to end on this diary entry. Within a couple of minutes she fell asleep, which was obvious under the effect of her medication, which would act more heavily when she hadn't dozed off for even a minute. These night outs were different from previous ones. This was a different approach she made herself to get out of the mourning, but not into the life once again, not into the same delusion, the world was living in, instead she wanted to quench the thirst, feed her curiosity. And thus, she had to pull herself out, and in the journey she learnt that none could help us out, until we trued it full heartedly. However this extraordinary outlook towards life wasn't sure to lead her to a happy and peaceful life. After all it was all she ever craved for.

****

Pulling out the keys after twisting them to lock the door, Shawn glared at house in peace and contentment. It seemed after an eternity that the walls took a breath of peace. He was a philosopher, not a warrior. He tugged off his shoes one by one and flumped over the couch adoring the peaceful environment. It doesn't mean he had no more soft corner for her in his heart, it was just that he had almost pledged himself to assist her from a minimal space distance. Infact for anyone, he was a man of helping nature but not at cost of almost everything. He decided to make a call to Dr Brett and take her health updates. This is world. Neither bad nor good. Neither Black nor white. Neither villain nor hero. Neither culprit nor victim. These are mere words which have place in the kids opposite words. That's all. The head is filled with grey matter. Similarly every one creature on its own makes a contribution to the society, thus everyone person is a protagonist character in its book and the fate acts antagonist. On this battle of a soul and it's fate, Olivia had set her boat to discover what a battlefield would look like if there was a third character present named faith.

****

'Good afternoon'

'Hello, good afternoon, Shawn here'

'Hi, How you doing?'

'Great'

'Hope I've not disturbed you at the wrong time'

'Not at all, if I am not wrong, this is Olivia Whitaker's Friend. Right?'

'Exactly you got me right. The topic of my concern is, that actually it's almost one week since she shifted back to her house. So just a little update thing you know...'

'Ok she is actually showing improvement, it's a long process, since she was traumatized multiple times. And also epilepsy can be treated but not cured, so she is showing improvement and also takes medications and exercises as prescribed. I hope this improvement remains progressive.'

'That's nice, actually just a week ago, I came to encounter her extremely unpredictable and unexpected behaviour followed by some unrelated and illogical conversation.'

'That's my point. This is a disease. At one moment, this epileptic person may sound the most intellectual person on earth and the other moment you may find it hard to stick at the tolerance levels. But I can assure you, that she is surely improving.'

'That's a great news, Infact a treat to my ears. Thanks a lot.'

'Anytime'

****

Within a span of two years, this was yet again a new chapter in her life. She realised that all the rays of hope, were connected to a common sun, which had eventually settled beneath the horizon.

The first five days had Olivia sleeping in her room all the day and night outs surfing on internet, ordering meals online, weeping reminiscing good moments, dreaming about a happy future with opened eyes as well, Meanwhile senior Whitaker had his own way of spending time. He would go for a walk, read books, prepare breakfast, have it, going out for hunting jobs and like wise spending the day in an organised manner. Being a long time employee of the Johnson's, she was eligible for the paid sick leave. She checked for the balance amount on her account. Now it was the next step, while she would be busy with her project, she needed an assistant for the housekeeping. It was half past two, the door opened and Alfred walked in. He bent his head pacing into his room, while Olivia sat tucked at the bean bag chair with her pen and pad. He crossed the way in front of her, as quick as crossing a busy road.

'Hello, you!' she could never say him *dad* ever again. He didn't deserve it either.

'Me?' he turned verifying.

She nodded indicating positive response. He neared the dining table with bowed head.

'No jobs?'

He remained silent raising his eyes indicating agreement. 'Camilla informed you about one, what about that?'

'They have a condition to stay there, in their provided accommodation.'

'So why not go for that'

'The working hours could exceed even up to eighteen, lesser salaries and small rooms obliging over six workers in each.'

'And what was the lesser salary?' she put forward, with her crossed legs, fidgeting her hands.

'500 pounds for a week.'

'What do you think they'll pay you thousands for a week, that too for housekeeping?' she smirked mocking at his expectations.

he continued to remain silent.

'I've got a job for you' he raised his bent head.

'Monthly payment, would be three-thousand pounds, will that work for you? Or you expect the fifty thousand cheques from Rutherford University?' she clapped in the air and chortled.

'The work includes, cleaning, dusting, laundry, cooking, lawn and chauffeur. In short housekeeping for this place' her pointed finger, rotated around.

'You have one hour time to think' she commandingly said.

'Aren't you amazed how I am trusting you with my life, you may poison the food, rob me, bang the car, or just simply shoot me! I know you are capable to do beyond this.

But trust me, the only thing is that now I am no more scared with what ever my fate unfolds. I've seen them all, I've lived through the black, so why afraid of brown and grey. My life is already a hell, which is why I won't hesitate to torment a person who had ruined my mother's life,' she continued.

'Tomorrow morning I'll reach the address, Camilla had texted about.' He informed without even wasting a moment. As Olivia was about to respond, the phone in her lap rang. She picked it up and talked for a couple of minutes, while Alfred stood still all ears to the phone call with an apparently bowed head.

CHAPTER TWENTY-FOUR

The moments he stood awaiting her approval, his weakened memory reminded him of the other night he overheard, Olivia crying in her room, when he couldn't sleep because of the asthma attack. After ending the conversation on call, she dropped the phone on the cushion.

'You said something?' she questioned.

'Yeah, I am ready for this job.'

'Good, you still have a time of an hour, because people like you are bound to stick to your commitments' she replied sarcastically.

He headed towards his room without uttering a single word in defence.

****

Later in the evening, as she sipped her coffee, standing in the gallery, she spotted Alfred going out somewhere. '*preap*' she whistled with a higher pitch to catch his attention, and it was a successful attempt as well. He rose his head with a crawling brows and involuntarily opened mouth in curiosity. She ran her fingers into air '*come up*'.

He entered the house, unlocking the door with the extra keys he had whereas she tramped down the stairs. Holding the railing, in her night suit she looked at the clock, 'if I am not wrong, an hour has actually passed since our last conversation, and if I am not wrong again, you were supposed to answer me'

He sighed listening at her every now and then.

'I already told you Olly, I am ready to work here.' He rebuked.

'Ma'am, it's ma'am for you' she rolled her eyes in the air, disgusted to listen her name.

'Where were you going?' she continued.

'To get myself some groceries.' He explained.

'Okay, so if now that you've joined this new job, let me introduce you to the rule book.' She cleared everything loudly as she stepped down the stairs.

'You are supposed to ask me before you leave the house, I have two sandwiches for breakfast with a glass of fresh juice. I am going to resume my office work from tomorrow and you'll drop me before time. While I return I'll have some fresh fruits and a cup of coffee. Make sure that you get all the things in one go, I love to see my house crystal clear and cleaned. See to it that dinner is served on time, you may eat after I have. You are allowed to prepare for yourself whatever you wish to. And special attention to my wardrobe, laundry and dry cleaning of dresses. Wardrobe includes shoes, bags and watches.

Remains the study room now, in which you are living, so please, you should empty it and shift yourself to the cell in basement. No cycling road trips can be entertained here, and do you think there's a need of you to remain fit still. Dirty fitness consciousness ...!' she murmured. 'I think, it's clear to you now.'

'Yes ... ma'am' he raised his thumb, pretending to act normal, because he was actually shocked by the stony hearted behaviour. His lips hesitated to call her daughter in a way.

'I've understood everything ma'am, but let me make one thing clear to you as well, that all the tragedies in your life weren't caused by me, every stone on your path and every cloud on your horizon isn't mandatory to be associated with me, so stop avenging and punishing me for the your Ill fate.' He announced confidently, turned around and continued ' I am going out to get the grocery.'

****

Olivia broke her sleep at the ringing alarm in her phone. She turned it off and sat by the bedpost, her little sleep consisted of the dreams mixed up, blur picturing of her previous house and Alfred forcibly entering her room to kill her. She wiped the sweat off her forehead, her eyes were sticking back to close and she was full of sleep. Yet she chose to throw the blanket away and set an alarm for fifteen minutes from now, and lay sleep. A moment later she checked the time, it was half an hour already, had another person informed her the time, she would never believe it, but the mobile phone, she had to trust it. But it was only a moment ago that she set a snooze alarm. Grabbing a bathrobe she moved into the bathroom, took a hot shower and dried hair. The dress today she would wear was already pressed. A lemon yellow and ivory checkered shirt over an off white long skirt. An oversized ring in her ring finger and wavy hair. A gloss on lips and her beige handbag, which had her pad, pen, and charger as well. Stepping down the stairs, she was reminded of *him* again. He stood with the tray of breakfast and the dining table. She marched with her high heels all the way down to the dining. Chewing the toast, she gulped the juice in two sips standing in a rush.

'Start the car' she ordered and he walked out, wearing a mint green pressed shirt and jeans, 'seems like he's not out of the professor avatar until now.' she thought as he headed unboxing his sunglasses.

He opened the door and sat on the driving seat, without waiting for her to sit. It seemed through his actions that it was just a tough situation that made he do this job and he wasn't happy with it, maybe a list of debts and loans to clear. She slammed the front passenger seat door and opened the back door for herself and closed it gently after sitting. As he drove passing by the way after a long time, she couldn't help remembering about the last time she drove back from office to the home. She had butterflies in stomach, as they neared the office.

'Johnson's bookstore. Right?' he confirmed taking a left turn from the main road.

'Oh yeah in the third block, I work as a manager over here.' She intentionally flaunted.

'There was an assistant lecturer of mine working here,' he shared.

'It must be somewhere else, only professionals work here.' She boasted.

'I am not sure, but he informed me many years ago, Benjamin said he worked as a supervisor there.'

She remained silent, sure about he was reverse boasting. He stopped the car in front of the main gate and she opened the door herself waiting for a second, if he could get down to open for her.

'I'll finish it by 3' she informed as he lowered the glass of front seat.

She stepped on the stairs for first time in a while, with confident steps and ready for pretending unnoticed of all eyes glued to her face. It was there. Moving into the elevator, she encountered the same or a little more than expected. The first face she saw heading on the third floor was non other than Benjamin.

'Mrs. Olivia you are not allowed to work until you get the healthy certificate from your psychiatrist.' She was ready for the answer, but the looks everyone threw, she could feel without looking at them. There was Shawn, Neil, Katie and above all, Camilla seated in Olivia's cabin. Keeping everything aside, she answered raising her pointed chin and making a self assuring eye contact.

'Of course, I'll look up to it when or not I am going to resume my job and I'll make sure to follow a certain procedure, in the mean time I realised I am privileged enough to use the library and I want to make some good use of it.'

'That's so thoughtful, please proceed.' He was blocked by the unexpected reply. While the scene replay ran in her mind as she verbally defeated him in front of everyone.'

There was pin drop silence in the hall, and she chose to remove her sandal outside to avoid further embarrassment. She walked through all the sections of the library, and stopped at the last one. It was a huge rack full of books under the name plate ***'spiritual'***. Maybe this is what she needed. Taking a few books she walked back to the table and raised her head, after switching the phone to silent mode. This time she could notice more eyes stealthily glued to her face and actions. She opened the hard cover of first book, taken aback by the continuous glares she checked her clothes, it was not odd. Her hair weren't messy.

'Oh, they must be looking at a mentally ill patient. That's how do they look.' she raised her head from the book at the murmuring voices, her eyes rushing back into the book could spot faces smirking at each other. Tucking the strand of her hair, she could sense Ciara sneaking into the book from behind the chair, walking tip toed.

'So there's the problem. Reading about spirituality was a evidence of me being mentally ill. Or was it a joke to read and discover about it.' She thought. This time she decided to oppose the flow, and follow her conscience. However this was not an easy task though. She placed her pad aside and started to read the books. In no time it was lunch break and she decided to studying. Sitting in the canteen, would simply add more fuss, she was rather comfortable being silent and busy in her own work.

****

'Alzheimer's' She overheard the gossips, behind the book rack. A fellow colleagues soft voice whispered.

'Not Alzheimer's, it was something else.' An adenoidal voice corrected.

'Leprosy, I think.' This time a croaky whisper.

'Oh no crap' there was a buzz in the air as they gossiped and giggled.

'Its epilepsy idiots' then there was another buzz of giggles.

There were five minutes for the recess to end, Camilla walked in the library and pulled back chair beside her. Until she voiced out, Olivia didn't realise her presence, awestruck about the conversation.

'Hello' she greeted with a plastered smile.

'Hi'

'What's up'

'Ceiling' she looked up and replied flustered.

'I mean all okay?' she questioned.

'Absolutely perfect' she answered coldly.

There was an awkward silence for a minute. After which Camilla chose to break it. 'I've been temporarily designated your post, I wanted to inform that long ago, but couldn't...' she stammered while providing explanation.

'Poor sense of analysis' she expressed disagreement. 'I feel sorry for myself, that you couldn't understand me over the time, out of all the losses in my life, you've come to consolidate me for the temporary loss of my job, give me a break.' She turned her head back into the book, rereading the lines waiting for her to leave.

'It's not about consoling, it's just informing you from my side...' she understood her explanation was meaningless.

'Anyways good luck' she gestured thumbs up with a smile. She forcefully grinned back at her.

****

Shuffling the books according to their sizes, she moved to the librarian counter to lend them. Mrs. Sophie sat on the chair, with her glasses pulled down, about to fall from the nose. Her grey hair tied into a bun and her eyes seemed to shrink over the years.

'Good Evening Miss Olivia.' She greeted and an awkward smile crept onto face. She looked at the books and scowled at her, of course for choosing that subject of books and pulled out the drawer below the desk, taking a napkin she dusted the books, representing their uselessness.

'Are you sure you want to lend these books?' she pulled her face.

'Yeah' she nodded with a smile. She took her card and issued those books.

'Strange ma'am, it's been five years since you are working here, and it's the first time you are using your library card.

'They provided me this library card, as a staff of the bookstore, I can borrow any of those books without a buck to pay' Olivia announced. Ryan was dusting his bookshelf and turned back at her to have a glance at her card.

'What if you lose it?' he questioned, dropping the broom down and clapping his hands to dust it all.

'I can issue a new card, but not for free.' She answered tossing it in her palms.

What are you doing?' she yelled as he jumped from the stool and grabbed the card from her hold.

*'Saving your thirty pounds.' He climbed over the stool and placed it in the book, closed it and rested in the right corner of uppermost shelf. 'page number twenty six of the book***I've met your soul'**

'How does that save my money?'

'Because as much as I believe that the sun will set, and the moon will rise, I also believe that you'll lose this card.' He smiled stepping down from the stool and settled at the table, while she was seated on the study chair.

She rolled her eyes as he teased her, turning her face the other side while he enjoyed the scene. 'you know what there's one more thing that I believe in 'he continued. 'Oh please, keep aside your beliefs and facts' she turned again tucking a strand of her hair into the ear.

'More than every fact, I love to believe and I believe that this bond of our will never fade.' He completed his statement placing his hand in hers as she stretched her arms to hold him by his collar. He caressed her chin as usual she couldn't help but turned crimson.

'It's not strange miss Sophie that I am using it for the first time, the thing to ponder on is that I preserved it for five years.' She concluded reminiscing a sweet but bitter memory.

****

It was half past five and she has been waiting for ten minutes, sitting in her car. She didn't have his number saved in the phone, how could she call her. There was a man strolling his dog, in the garden opposite. She decided to get down and ask him if he had seen her father anywhere.

'Have you seen an old man who drove this car? She asked pointing at her car

'Yes, he walked in the bookstore along with a man' he answered.

She headed to the office and searched for him thinking why did he enter her office to embarrass her anymore. But to her surprise things were too more different than her expectations.

She spotted her father sitting in the cabin with sir Benjamin sipping coffee, and chitchatting with him. She wasted no time and entered the cabin, without considering it necessary to seek permission. As she pulled in the door,

'I never knew this is your daughter, sir' Benjamin remarked.

He chortled silently drinking coffee.

'I've seen you working well, but there are a million things to learn from your father, girl. The way he was passionate about his subject, work ethics and professionalism, he always stood out in every field he entered.' He continued to brag while she could only silently listen about it. It might be the bitter truth that he wasn't boasting and why would he either. But the past experiences made her impossible to digest his praises. Ok but there was a thing that, he wasn't lying this morning about his friendship with Benjamin. The praising and enjoying session continued for more fifteen minutes after which she chose to leave just the way she entered. (Without seeking permission).

CHAPTER TWENTY-FIVE

Tuesday 9:30 PM

I am a mislaid river, Who hasn't explored itself,

Every time I try, I find a whale or an elf.

I am a mislaid river, who knows the hometown but unaware of its identity.

I won't trust either they step me down or identify as deity.

I am a mislaid river, who remains optimistic in spite of all flaws,

I owe the courage to flow but a little more courage to pause.

I am a mislaid river, who believes art is free of demands,

But to succeed set your way and rush, they command!

I am a mislaid river, through cherishes it's journey through harsh waves,

And can never forget the still in puddles and caves.

I am a mislaid river, who exists high but lives underground

Addicted to lights and happier in towns,

I am mislaid river, who awaits the helping hand to call me,

Although I witnessed the rescue boats, departed floating upon me!'

She closed the diary and dropped the pen into the stand. It was no more a sacred treasure to her. It was just a record of any humans feelings and memories which wasn't an emotionally important stuff to preserve for her. It was a hard day after a very long time. She decided not to waste any time browsing through the social media, and set an alarm for the other days early morning.

****

'If you say she behaves discourteous then I think you should not live there, I'll make some other arrangements for you,' he decided.

'That's just her apparent face, I know deep down what she thinks, and feels, after all whatever may have been the consequences, I am her father. Besides, I am also sure about the fact that she will melt over the time, and also let me live to see the day she forgives me. Except that I don't have a reason in this life.' Alfred retorted.

'I would have surely asked you to live with us, but then our long working hours and you know this small apartment...' john justified while Alfred chose to remain silent at the dissatisfactory explanation.

'But remember dad, whenever you need anything please inform me or Camilla, we will always love to do anything for you.'

'Sure son, take care.'

'Bye'

****

The next day was the same, waking up late despite of sleeping early, quick shower, breakfast in a rush, and off to the library with the books she had lent except for a change that she wore her flat shoes over a black bell bottom and pink t-shirt. Her hair were neatly tied into a pony tail and a broad bracelet on her thin wrist completed the look. Alfred drove her to the office. Mrs. Sophie greeted her as she entered the library and she could feel the stares and glares as she walked in, deep down she felt content for not wearing the noisy footwear. She had to get used to it, just as once she was used of getting compliments on her good looks, carrying on responsibilities efficiently and leading a happy family life. Indeed she used to be a treat for eyes those days. Beauty has been always amongst those things which faded over the time, yet so much chased and cherished.

****

'Mr. Alfred, had your dinner?' she asked chewing the last bite of her pizza.

'No ma'am' he answered from the kitchen counter.

'Come and join me, also get my purse from the room upstairs.' His happiness knew no bound when his daughter called him for the dinner. He sprang on the stairs to get the purse like a child. Placing the purse on the dining table, he pulled a chair beside the place opposite to her still nervous to near her. She pushed forward the dishes and water bottle. Unzipping the purse she pull-out her cheque book, filled in the details, put her signature, tore a cheque from it and placed it beside his plate. She was done with her dinner still waited for him to finish. Alfred was over the moon, to be alive and privileged to see her daughter grow closer to him.

'You may go and sleep, you are tired... ma'am.' He didn't forget the limits, or may be the cheque in front of him reminded him about the same.

She chuckled upon hearing the statement after uttering an exasperated snort. It was after a moment of dilemma of deciding whether to connect with him or not, that she signified, 'Etiquettes! these are the minimal, taught by my mother. However how would you know, who never learnt to value values.' She smirked.

His signature reply, silence. He remained quiet again, provoking her to disclose some more. 'My mother had struggled a lot to raise us to successful beings, whatever we are today it's only because of her. But why would you care?'

she rolled her eyes.

His heart throbbed at such blames, 'it's not the way you think, why won't I care for you.'

'Oh really,' she guffawed clapping her hands in air.

'Let the cat remain in the bag.' It was evident she wasn't in a mood to clear anything.

'That's your opinion. But I think its my responsibility to make it clear to you, about the false fallacies. I agree about being disloyal to your mother, but never had I cheated on you all as a father.' His voice remained in a lower tone, indicating no compulsion on her to believe him.

'Of course, Infact I am surprised, why didn't they reward you with an Oscar for being the best dad to John' she completed the statement to mock and taunt him.

'Your mother never allowed me to' his eyes watered narrating the past he was guilty and helpless about 'I always begged her to let me meet you all and help you financially too.'

'Agreed,' she swung her face, openly representing that she knew he was faking around. And he continued his dinner, trying to teach himself it would never make sense to her'

She walked in her room as he finished his dinner and changed her clothes. Putting on a cotton night suit she hoped on the bed connecting the earphones to the phone. Waiting for her eyes to stick, she would meaninglessly scroll down. '*Rumours has it court may issue an arrest warrant for the Irish onscreen fame, Isabella Whitaker*' she must get arrested her mind said. Her heart said the same. The fumes rose from her hardly extinguished heart. It was a fact and none could deny it that she was responsible for their separation. Flinging the phone on the bed, she dropped her face in the pillow, but immediately rose to see where did it hit. A breath of peace she took as it landed on the blanket. She slept burring her head into the cushions, wishing to escape her life likewise.

****

'Are you in a rush or on a plan to wipe me out!' Olivia wailed at the driving Alfred. He chortled, 'What would I get you for murdering you?' while slowing down the speed.

'May be a few more pounds!' she shrugged off.

'And who'll give that?' he enquired hilariously.

'Isabella Whitaker' she answered after thinking for a few moments.

'Why would she do that?'

'Power abuse, you know. Just as she had jailed Ryan accusing for some thing he never did.'

'And are you unaware of her being jailed?'

'Oh, yeah thanks to the grey man show. But today jailed, tomorrow bailed, that's a powerful celebrity.'

'Hopefully.' He crossed his fingers, resting on the steering wheel.

'Praying for your daughter, yeah?'

'She doesn't even know me. But yeah I would wish the best to all my children.' There was a long pause, while her mind was pondering over a thought. She broke the hesitation and let it out. ' where is your nephew now?'

He stared at her face for a moment. 'It seems that Ryan is punishing me on your behalf.' She remained quiet. 'He disappeared into nowhere after getting all the stuff by his name. The case made on him isn't over yet and hence all his properties are under the police custody. And here am I driving homeless.' She sighed listening to him.

'Isn't it an irony that, you chased money over everything and today struggle for every penny.!' she treated with contempt.

'Do I have the right to defend myself in the conditions of this job?'

She nodded positively.

'I never chased money over everything ' he looked into her eyes, Pausing the car on the right side.' I always tried to remain connected with you, nevertheless that was a bad time, that had us separated.'

'Bad time for me , for mommy, not for you Mr.!' she retorted.

'Because of your mother's wrong decision, it is that you are suffering until now.' He concluded.

'Her wrong decision or someone's wrong actions?' she taunted as the car took a start.

'I am not denying my faults, but it isn't always the one wrong person, do listen to the two sides of the story.' He raised his voice as the conversation got deeper.

'Well in this case, I would love to consider the three sides! Mommy's, your and Mrs Laura Wilson's.'

His face reddened with embarrassment, it had been an era ago but he felt insulted in front of her daughter.

'The struggle we went through you could never imagine about it, and even if you were a bit of considerate about your children, then this third side of the story would have never emerged. I dropped my school, worked a s a waitress to feed your kids, and you were there enjoying with that witch.'

'She has passed away now! Have some mercy!' he corrected.

'Oh really? This thought didn't visit your wise brain while counting the mistakes of my mother and as a matter of fact she died too.'

'I feel sorry and guilty, about what all you had to suffer, and I also understand that it can't be changed...'

'Oh that's a biggest favour on me thank you for understanding when it wasn't least required.' She interrupted with a higher pitch.

'Let me complete, madam! I just want you to know that it could have been better, if your mother would have allowed me to.'

'As if you were dying to...' she smirked.

'Indeed I was.' he stared at her,

'Then you should have!' he raced the car turning to the road no. 12, and pulled the handbrake, parked in front of her office, waiting for her to step out.

****

Days passed by and like wise the books she had completed reading from the spirituality book shelves. There was the last rack remaining and she would probably finish it in a month. This wasn't a six month leap exactly, because this period comprised of all the highs and lows she overcame yet chose to be a warrior. She had learnt and studied about all the different scriptures and mythologies pertaining to the life on earth and reason of creation of mankind. Colleagues had started to believe her mentally ill, whereas it was the last session scheduled today, she was supposed to have counselling with Dr Brett Adler.

There was an evident increase in the number of arguments she had with Alfred and alongside an increasing habit they were getting of each other's company. Days weren't tougher for Alfred anymore although she didn't stop accusing him of every pin that pricked her to till date. Ryan was still nowhere to be found. Dreams of Asher and old pictures of them as a couple still hurt and broke her many times, the difference that arose was Alfred learnt to console her daughter. In short she would allow him to solace her. At times both would cry together, one because of the bad fate and the other reminiscing bad deeds.

It was a common afternoon, when Olivia sat in the library after the lunch time. She already gave up coffee long time ago, but utilised the break time in a different way, by taking a walk in the park opposite to the building. It would refresh her mind, after all reading for the longest hours wasn't an easy task to do. She picked up the pen beside phone to note down some point, just then her phone beeped, it was a random notification she thought.

On the second beep she decided to put her phone on the silent mode, and as she pressed the button reading the text on the screen she sprang up on the chair, shouting, 'Hurray, I can't believe this'. As a matter of luck, there were only two people in the library, one was Mrs Sophie and the another was some random colleague. Mrs Sophie didn't deserve an apology or explanation and one person, ok let it go, she thought and hurried twirling around the building, taking the stairs and dialled to Alfred.

'Hello, where are you.. on the way.. ok first pick me from the office... It's an urgency... I'll inform you later... To the city hospital make it faster.'

The car raced up to reach the location in not more than five minutes. He lowered the glass to enquire but she sat on the seat beside him in a hurry.

'What's the matter Olivia, are you fine? A sense of discomfort took over him, as he took her name, but it was purely out of concern. Declining second call from John he kept enquiring the same.

CHAPTER TWENTY-SIX

'Tonnes of congratulations on being a grand pa!' she turned ninety degrees towards the driving seat, and announced to Alfred.

'Grandfather?' the baffled old man asked.

'Camilla got a baby girl!' her mouth opened widest in excitement, bursting the eyes out.

'God Gracious!' he exclaimed rejoicing the news, his rheumy eyes brightened all of a sudden along with the widening of lips into a smile

Thinking for a few minutes, she popped up with another order for him. 'Don't call me ma'am in front of them..'

'And what would I say to address you' he made the later situation easier.

'Olivia, obviously, mommy used to say that she loved my name. That's the first gift she gave me, and no matter what I will preserve it..' she got emotional at the joyous moment.

'And what will you call me in front of *them*.. Alfred?' he asked glancing at her expression while driving.

'I'll try my best to avoid calling you' she retorted. Her brain jumped into he previous dimension, ignoring him.

'We will stop at the nearby store and get some gifts and flower bouquets and chocolates' she had no control over anticipation.

'I just don't believe it, that how did I forget of her due date!' she palmed her head. Olivia expressed utmost joy while Mr Whitaker silently drove in merriment. They walked in the hospital room as informed by John, holding loads of presents and flowers.

'Congratulations, she threw her arms on the lying Camilla, placing the presents on the table. Her voice wasn't as feeble as expected, it still radiated that *Camilla* enthusiasm vibes. 'Same to you!' her dry lips curled up causing the eyes to wrinkle, as she smiled from her heart. Beside the bed was Her daughters cradle. A glance at her involuntarily, unintentionally and helplessly reminded her about her angel. She looked at her baby, while knowing that Camilla, John and Alfred were looking at her. Her smiling lips slowly reversed and the squinted eyes opened up, as her brain froze into the sharp pricking memories. However her hands made way below the little baby and picked up in her chilling arms. This feeling of holding a baby, automatically curved up her lips, letting go of the storm beneath. It wasn't just a piece of flesh, it was a tiny human, created by her creator. She wanted to thank the creator for blessing her bestie with best. She deserved nothing but the best. She held her close to her chest, while the heart and brain coordinated and communicated.

Placing the baby back on her cradle, after pecking her forehead, she sat dragging a chair near to camo's bed. She caressed her forehead asking, ' how's your health?'

'I am fine,' her voice fluctuated over the pitches as she whispered trying not to awaken her daughter. 'That was a real quick transformation though.' She pulled her leg. After that john offered her an open box to of sweets to have, which she hesitatingly accepted.

'I am sorry Camilla.' This was an epiphany to her. 'Wait. what?'

'I am sorry, it's a shame to be a friend and far away in times of need.' She broke down before her. 'I must have been by your side, at least for the sake of an attempt to balance the favours you made for me. I know it's impossible to return your kindness, but I should have stood by your side, to make your hard time easier.'

'The greatest favour you can make for me is to open the closed doors and windows of your life. Let the fresh air in. Allow the opportunities to reach you.'

She patted her shoulder, encouraging and wiping her dropping tear. ' friends again?' she asked with a clog in her throat with a clean heart. She closed her eyes as the tears rolled down her cheeks and she nodded. It was a clearing moment for her. She also wiped out all the grudges from her heart. Camilla adjusted her hair, swallowing the clogged throat. John was going in and out for the baby essentials and wife's medications.

'And what are you going to name the princess' Olivia paced to the cradle and adored her best friend's daughter.

'She is Heidi Whitaker' John declared as Camilla redirected the question through her eyes.

'That's a good name' she commented genuinely.

'Had my mother been alive she would have been the happiest to see' John reminisced with teary eyes. Upon listening to the name of his beloved, the lost charm of Alfred's face had returned. His lips took a namely uplift, yet his eyes could narrate the entire story.' This is a special moment indeed, she must have been there to complete the family celebration.' Olivia added. There was an astonishing expression arise on face, as they all knew the unlimited amount of hatred she had towards Laura. Camilla was getting restless as everyone spoke aloud and that might awaken Heidi. Olivia could easily sense the fear and spoke comparatively slower. She also felt the need to leave early and allow the mother baby duo to rest.

'I'll take your leave and visit tomorrow, I think you need to rest.' As she finished the sentence, Alfred stood straight and walked to the cradle. It seemed as if he awaited his children to show him or place Heidi in his arms, but no one did. He picked her up in the arms and looked at her face, his eye to eye grin, brightened an unattractive face, the illuminating smile, also warmed up her heart. 'Both of you stand beside Camilla and we'll take a selfie.' She decided. Alfred and John obeyed her and stood on the either sides of her. While Olivia took two steps back, adjusting the frame and angle of photograph. After clicking the pictures, she slid them over before Camilla 'this one has my sharp jawline'

'No but my eyes are blurred'

'See, this is perfect, except john, he is staring at the box of chocolates you got with his drooling tongue out.' She giggled.

'I was actually looking at my ringing phone beside it.' he corrected.

'Camilla, I think you got to hire a detective, something is suspicious about this phone call.' she pulled his leg.

'Oh, I can do that single handily ' she boasted to tease him along.

'Heidi wants a treat from the loaded aunty.' He joked.

'Who's loaded here?' she winked. 'Anytime for Heidi, as soon as she grows capable of having a burger!'

'Oh no, I won't mind, accepting treats on her behalf. Later when she grows up, I would return the treat twice, I swear.' Camilla continued to joke.

'You need to join the fitness club as early as possible, have a look at your double chin.'

'And you need fresh fruits diet. Look at those dark circles' she zoomed the captured selfie in phone. The two girls laughed insulting each other. It was the push opening of the doors they had closed for each other in the past span of time. John was beyond happier to see them reunited.

'Ok now I must leave.' She lifted her purse from the table, and walked out only after wrapping her arms around the mother and giving a peck of love again for her niece. More than the bond of an aunt and a niece, it was her gal pals daughter. She sat in the car, followed by Alfred.

****

She returned to the house, tired and exhausted after a long day. Her study was also incomplete for the days part. Rolling over the bed after completing her nap, with her head at rest, her palm moved under the pillow, fetching for her phone. Pressing the side button, she read the time. It was half past nine, and a missed alarm reminder. Pressing her finger against the fingerprint sensor, she unlocked the phone to read about the notification.

'Oh no!' it was the missed appointment of her psychiatrist. She rose from the bed to sit upright, retying her hair, she checked the time once again. It was too late, and there was no chance of adjusting it in any slot. She still couldn't believe it that how did she forget such an important event. Oh yeah, it was a very special day spent, after an era she thought. Interrupting her thoughts, the phone rang, she flipped the to check and it was Alfred's text message. 'Dinner is ready, you must take the medicines on time.'

Keeping the phone aside, she woke up and slid her feet into the flip flop, and picked up a night suit from the closet. Washing her face after getting freshened up, she looked into the mirror and Camilla's words echoed into her ears as she noticed her dark circles. Walking out of the washroom she got her phone from the bed, and scrolled through to select her no makeup and no filter photo, she then again headed towards the wash basin, and rubbed her thumb on the under eyes. It had turned dark indeed, And her eyes, the freshness she could spot in the picture, wasn't alive anymore. Her eyes had tilted to the sides, wrinkled. Curving her lips, didn't bring back the charm of her smile that could be seen in a lifeless picture. A lifeless picture, yet narrated thousand words of the bubbled fairy tales through her eyes and smile. She wasn't alone in the photo obviously, the betrayer, Mr. Ryan Wilson was standing capturing the mirror selfie when they visited Manchester and resided at a hotel. Looking at his photograph, still pricked her heart and she hated it now. To a person who was trying her best, to make her way out of the bog, memories weren't a present of life. Bad memories throbbed her heart and good ones made sure to stab her alive. Depression was a disease with no visible bruise. How many of the incidents and memories would she muster up the courage to let go of. She knew she had done it almost and it was natural to break down, but what about the innumerable times her heart, brain, soul and eventually her whole existence had to shatter and scatter. It hurt her every time she broke it, though every time she rose like never to turn back into the past. She let go the hatred towards her father, allowing the day of humanity to enter. But at the breaking point she abhorred his presence too. As these thoughts hurled in her mind, the piercing pain, already pushed the pain out of her yes, but in this strive only the tears flowed through the eyelids. She stood up putting weight on the sink by her palms folded into fist at the end of platform. She sobbed looking subconsciously in the mirror.

Probably a shoulder to cry on, that's all she needed. She gargled and washed her face once again, splashing the handful of water, rinsing it not until the soap was over but she rinsed until the need of a companion faded and the emerging faith in her heart overpowered all her lows. Wiping her face with the towel she moved out of the washroom, and brushed her messy hair. Taking the phone along her she unlocked the door and walked down the stairs. Alfred sat asleep at the couch, while the TV was on. The tray was placed on the dining table, it was evident that he slept awaiting her This thought made her to uplift her head to glance at the wall clock. 'Wait. what! It's ten thirty!' not sure about wasting or investing, but this crying thing consumed a lot of time she thought. Arousal of guilt took place for making him wait for so long.

Nearing him with a hesitation, she patted on his shoulder. She felt dubiety calling him by his name. After all he was her father. But how could one let go his misdeeds. He woke up and stood at the second pat, coughing nonstop and headed out to wash his face.

'Let's have dinner,' she broke the silence.

'It's very late, I waited for a long time'

'I'll get it for you.' He headed into the kitchen, along the tray of food. Heating up the pasta, he selected the duration of microwave and opened the refrigerator door to get the bowl of salad. Taking out pasta from the oven, he heated the soup for a while and arranged them all in the tray. She waited for the dinner scribbling the dining cloth with her blunt short nails, already into some or the other dimension. The clinking of crockery, brought her back in to the world. And she pulled up the plate on her side, then noticed the soup and picked the bowl and spoon. He served the soup for her, unable to hold back for it to cool down, she sipped spoonful. ' the best treat one can get on a freezing night of winters. It s mind-blowing.' Praising the dinner, she asked him, 'when will you eat?'

'It's very late actually, I think I must skip it.' he declared.

'Have a spoon of it, and I bet you will change your mind.' He was happier getting praised by his daughter.

'Just a spoon of it' he forwarded his plate sitting on the dining chair. She served white pasta to him and the duo continued the dinner silently. She had so many things to talk about to him, but she couldn't help remembering Victoria and her childhood. All these things were still a barrier between the two. Alfred made efforts to make the things normal as he thought he existed for that cause. At some point she also considered his efforts, but he was getting paid for that, and then also didn't make sense for her to *trust* on anyone. Later while eating her mind revolved around the study she was doing. It was the concept of spirituality. It sounded odd, uninteresting and illogical to all, yet when she read deeper into it, it was the most obvious things about life, that one should be Infact obsessed with. Endeavours were required to jump into this field out of nowhere, she could reach to the point where she was only because of the infinite determination. Various languages, and scriptures were present before her eyes and she followed the all of them until she could find the answers to her noted questions. She started this study with the belief to find answers to her questions. And until she wouldn't get satisfied with them, the research would go on and on.

CHAPTER TWENTY-SEVEN

'How's the champ doing?'

'She's a warrior, like her aunty' said Camilla.

'She has two aunties by the way' Olivia gathered all her notes and files to assemble and place them in the bag, while talking on the phone with right shrugged shoulder.

'In that case let her be a princess like her mother' she jokingly took pride.

'She can grow up to be any one from the family, except her grandfather' she whispered, and both the girls giggled.

'And how's everything going?' she continued.

'Great, we are returning, after getting her vaccinated.'

'Aww my cutie pie! She must have cried a lot.' She grimaced on listening.

'Yeah she did, but now she's smiling looking at her mama! You like mama, do you like your mama..' she continued talking to the one week old.

'Right now, I am starting to the office, catch you later and send me Heidi's pics'

'Bye! Take care.'

'Loads of love to the baby' she lowered her shoulder and dropped the phone in the open purse. Placing her tab in the bag, she zipped it and wiped the sweat on her phone and the ear, after pulling out a tissue paper. Turning towards the entrance she saw Alfred waiting by the door. Her hand face palmed imaginarily as both were occupied carrying a purse and office bag. The reason was that she hoped that he did not listen to their conversation on phone and jokes about him. She made an eye contact with him expecting him to throw an offended look, but his normal expression made her believe that he didn't.

****

'What about your missed appointment Olivia?' Alfred put forward while driving. Him Calling her by the name had been normalised in the past week yet she would take an eternity to call her *dad* even once.

'I dialled him the other day and he asked me to visit this Saturday'

'Ah that's good. Tomorrow I'll drop you there and get my hair cut in the salon nearby.' He planned.

She remained silent as the car slowed nearing the office, taking hold of the bags, she opened door to step down. Mrs. Sophie greeted her with the same smile as she made her way to her chair, although it wasn't an isolated place, but no one would sit at that particular place, reserving it for her. Keeping the bags on the desk, she neared the wooden bookshelf, bent to the lower level, opened the door of the last rack and gathered the remaining books in her arm, to pace towards her place. She unzipped the bag to take her belongings out. Unboxing the spectacles case, she opened her glasses and pushed it amidst the open hair strands. It was in the recent past that she was diagnosed with hyperopia after a consecutive compliant of watery eyes and blurred vision.

****

At the lunch break, closing and assembling all her paper work and files, she searched for her sandal, by dabbing her toes below the desk. Pulling them nearer she forced her feet into it and rose into a strongest girl as she walked. It was an unusual sight to find Shawn in the library, which was happening today. He paced towards her and neared slowing down his steps, as a casual greeting,

'Good afternoon'

She nodded as a sign of exchanging the same.

'Coffee' he offered.

'Thank you, that's sweet of you, but I would rather go for a walk'

'Not a problem,' he grinned, scratching his hair. Olivia proceeded to the main door and he took some quick steps to get by her side and continued,

'Actually, if you wont create mess of it, then I wanted to talk to you.'

She rolled her eyes at the condition he made, it was quite offensive, but then he wasn't wrong from his perspective. She continued to walk ignoring his permission, and he continued as they stepped into the descending lift.

'I wanted to apologise...'

'For what?' she let out her curiosity.

'A lot of stuff but basically for not letting you to return your home, on Camilla's word..'

'Oh that's no big deal, I've learnt to deal with things far more worse ' she retorted sarcastically.

'And for forcing you to leave my house, in the mid of night... situations were getting worst and at moment I thought that would be a great solution.. '

'Oh if that's the case, then I'll have to apologise for a lot more things than these'

'No it's completely fine.' He answered as she walked. Standing still at the same moment watching her as she headed to her way. Waiting for a moment to get a reply from her, he returned back to the office, as the conversation did not strike up. He was clueless about which direction was she proceeding in. He was sincerely sorry for all the bad times and was genuinely concerned about her as well.

'She appeared happy and content, wonder if she had reconciled with Ryan' he thought. The next moment his conscience doubted upon him, if he was turning green with jealousy of her happiness, that he could not digest her peaceful life. But then his heart justified it by declaring concern for her friend as a true well wisher.

Sitting on the chair in his cabin he dialled to Camilla,

'Hello Camilla, how are you?'

'Hi Shawn, I m great and sorry for not replying to your messages'

'It's perfectly alright, I thought to call you and congratulate since you didn't answer to the texts, congratulations on the birth of an angel..'

'Thank you, that means a lot,.. hush.. hush baby Heidi, mama's girl doesn't cry' She silenced her crying daughter.

'Oh.., how's everything else..' he indirectly enquired about Olivia's whereabouts.

'Hush.. Baby... everything's good, thanks to God.' She answered quick, sounded disturbed by the exchange of needless conversation and calming her baby.

'How's Oliva nowadays?' he disclosed the main subject.

'She is healthy and happy. John can you please switch on the heater..'

'Carry on please, call you later' he ended up the conversation annoyed by the disturbance.

'Sure, till then take care. Bye.' He placed the phone on the desk and extended his trunk, leaning against the head rest, he rotated his chair putting weight on the toe. These were the subconscious activities while that of the consciousness were involved in investigating about her.

If Ryan had come back to her life, then it was her duty to update her. If she cried about her worst times before me, then it was the least expected to share her happiness too. What if, I am assuming all this and there is no such twist in the story?' he twitched his lips and breathed out exasperating through the pout, fidgeting his fingers.

****

She stepped on the three stairs and pushed in the door of the clinic. This was an unusual sight as there was no one sitting at the front office. The lights of his cabin were switched-on, so it would not be wrong to assume that he was in. She sat on the bench in the waiting area, as she could listen Dr Brett's voice, speaking to someone. The words weren't clear and the tone was of speaking to a patient probably. She concluded that there might be a patient inside. The time slot appointed to her was four forty pm. Waiting for fifteen more minutes, she doubted if he was vocal on a call. Passing two more minutes in May I or may I not she walked in the cabin, and before her eyes could co ordinate with the brain, she sensed a familiar smell of fragrance. Later as she rose her eyes, it was a patient sitting opposite to Dr Brett. He gazed at her silently for a moment and informed, 'I'll call you in five more minutes.'

'Sure,' she was embarrassed to get in the midst of a counselling session. As she pulled the door back, the female patient turned back at her voice. It was again Isabella Whitaker! She was taking the counselling session. This was again a may I or may I not moment for her and she chose to leave. Within a millimetre span of the closing glass door, she heard her name as she turned back. 'Olivia' Damn this voice melted her heart instantly, she could take no step further getting emotional upon listening to her voice.

Entering through the glass cabin with hesitation and mixed feelings, she saw that Isabella was already walking towards her. She was indeed an epitome of beauty. A tall body, with the long tresses falling along her long neck and perfect collar bone. The dusky complexion which was a resemblance to her father. Her sharp and thin glossy lips trembled, as she stood clueless, her perfectly shaped brown eyes with large lashes rose and stealthily bent over again to drop a dense drop of tear, guilt, helplessness and what not. Her heart pounded at this and pressure built in the head, after all she was her baby girl, beneath the layer of beauty her deep eyes spoke about the hell she was going through. There was a gap of one feet, and several standardised materialism between the two. Well those were apparent, and internally they never lacked a similarity. Both were undergoing a hard time on their paths. Olivia tried to speak, but her tongue couldn't dare because of the prejudice. Just then Isabella's lips turned of trembling and one by one the tears rolled down, warm enough to melt Olivia's superficial expression of rigidity. She broke down as well ignoring Dr Brett on the chair observing them. Isabella wiped her tears takings step nearing to her, threw her arms around the sister and broke leaning by her shoulder. The two cried aloud unable to control the sound and emotions. The flowing tears from the four eyes cleansed both the hearts and Adler shed a tear looking at the reunion. It was a fact that both were his patients, but a human heart is naturally bound to rejoice in others happiness. Olivia's head rested at her shoulder while Isabella's arms wrapped around her head. After a few moments, they moved heads back, wiping each other's tears. Olivia didn't know when she neared the couch and sat beside her sister. While she sat with crossed legs and the tears continued to run by. Holding Olivia's hand in her chilled palms she rubbed by her forehead as her low pitched voice spoke ' Sorry. I am sorry Olivia. Sorry for ruining your life. Trust me I never intended to do so. And I am also paying it's price now.'

'It's ok Isabella.' She forgave her without giving a second thought and not waiting even for a moment, wiping her tears from the face.

'You are just making up the formality. Right? You forgive me from heart.' Isabella spoke with a varied accent, as a result of her working in different places.

'I forgave you just the way, when you apologised me for breaking my dolls and I used to say no problem' her lips curled along with trying to stop the tears. Listening to the answer Isabella broke crying and embraced her sister again. There was a knock at the door from the patient with time slot half past five, Olivia looked at the doctor and left without speaking a word. The sisters walked out of the clinic and Olivia thought she would go back to her way, but proving her assumption wrong she walked with her in the café opposite, pulling out a face mask from her pocket, she covered her face to avoid all sorts of attention by putting on the sunglasses too.

'I had actually planned this trap for dad. And Ryan got stuck in that unfortunately.' Her voice filled with guilt and lowered eyes narrated regret as she sipped through the shake from straw. Olivia listened to the entire story silently. There were not many things to speak, as Isabella was a well known celebrity, Olivia knew everything thing about her, and it was no big issue for Isabella to keep count of her sisters sneezes and coughs, let alone the biggest turns in her life. What would she answer to this narrative, she only knew what she had been through the times, how she managed to live by every means. There were many options, she could even go mad at her or let it go. And she chose latter. Everyone was equally involved in her tragedy, if because of Isabella's mistake Ryan got jailed, he had also hurt her by betraying about her father's death. And if he was so keen to apologise or reunite with her, it has been almost a year that he was bailed and yet never showed up till now. There was no single person that she would hold by the collar and hang to death. Every one made a contribution in making it worse. Everyone had done their part and they might not feel as wrong to themselves as much as they have wronged Olivia. She concluded that there was no use of digging up the buried.

'I came to know about your son.. I feel sorry for it.' She offered the condolence. Olivia nodded, tucking her hair behind the ear.

'Asher. His name is Asher. Ryan thinks that you are responsible for Asher's death too.'

'Oh god! I could never be so cruel. Damn. How could he even think like this.' She banged on the table. Olivia continued to be silent as she would get the answer herself pondering once more on the situation. Unfolding the fist she caressed her manicured hand, and rubbed her fingers over them. Pulled out the diamond ring from the finger and wiped it with a napkin, after which she slid the ring after cleaning it with a tissue.

Olivia stealthily glanced at her hands and crept them under the table. The skin was dried, wrinkled, unfiled nails and she could spot tiny growing hair on her fingers. Fidgeting fingers on her lap, she decided to be comfortable within a couple of moments. She knew the growing faith in her heart was more beautiful than those polished hands.

'It means you are in contact with Ryan' Isabella Investigated raising her eyebrow.

'No, I didn't even near his shadow since the night he got arrested. Camilla said me.'

'How come she knows about it?'

'Through john, probably.' she shrugged.

'Where is he now?'

'I don't know.' She squinted her eyes indicating suspicion, 'I can swear on you!' Olivia continued to clear her doubt.

'According to my information he is traceless, since last year.'

CHAPTER TWENTY-EIGHT

'Hmm' Olivia's face shrunk at the talk of Ryan. A few years ago she used to believe that he was the biggest earning of her life, but he turned out to be the biggest failure of her life.

'I came to know lately that dad has been sharing your house since a few months?'

'What's the colour of the dress that I am going to wear tomorrow!' she retorted coldly.

'What does that mean?' she squinted again. Such expressions of her reminded Olivia of all the scenes she saw in her dramas.

'You are reported about every single detail related to me!' she huffed.

'I could also have pretended unknown, and listen to your side. Well I am not so informed these days. Power is a beautiful dimension of life, which I am losing day by day. Thanks to the grey man show, that my career is perished. I wonder who is that grey man in disguise. Every alternate days I pay visit to courts, lawyers and psychiatrists.'

'Why don't Billy, James or Clara help you out.'

'After mommy's demise, our last meeting ended on a bad note and we really don't share that siblings bond you know.' She air quoted by her fingers. '. I hold a larger percentage of fault for this poor bonding, which I realised after the down rise of my fame. Power is an addiction, an intoxication, I never realised what I was doing until these harsh days of life slapped on my face. I didn't choose this path with joy and contentment, my childhood forced me to do this. Little did I know about the do's and don'ts of it once it is achieved. Any way, What about Alfred?' she continued after a breath of exasperation.

'He's good, and also claims to have been changed over the time. You might also be known that I hired him for the housekeeping'

'Oh no! I didn't know about that!' she chuckled and expressed shock simultaneously. ' that's a wonderful job!' A moment later she rotated her wrist to check the time, and continued 'I am getting late, we will meet later.'

'As accurate information you hold about me, hope you might also have an accurate phone number of mine....' she taunted.

'Of course I have.' She smiled. ' my driver can drop to your house if you wish.'

'Oh no Alfred is coming to pick me up.'

'Alfred..' she stared confused. 'Your dad!' she said sarcastically. 'He said he will be back after getting his hair cut in the nearby salon.'

'Well I doubt at this excuse' she touched her pointed finger at her chin, 'Don't know' Olivia shrugged her shoulders.

Olivia paid bill for the two and she stood straight, ruffled her top to dust of the brownies particles. Picked her purse and hung it on the right shoulder. The girls shook hands and bid off while walking out of the door. Isabella pat on her shoulder and rolled her eyes to the right corner, Oliva turned her head as signalled and witnessed a sight that disturbed her to the core once again.

Isabella waved her hand and made her way to the car. She too walked out to the entrance of the clinic and dialled to Alfred.

'Hello Alfred where are you, its already six thirty.'

'Just a minute, I am almost done at the salon, will reach you in a minute.' She cut the call after listening to the fake excuse.

While leaving the café Isabella showed her a couple sitting and sipping coffee from straws while placing their hands in hands, where love was in the air. It was Mr Alfred Whitaker and Mrs Agatha.

****

'There's so much in the gossip about your meeting in the conference room'

'You got it right, try as much as possible to attend it.' Olivia answered, while the connected ear pods were plugged in her ears and she worked on the laptop, preparing the presentation.

'Ok, that's quite exciting, and wishing you all the very best.'

'Kisses to Heidi! Bye' She removed the ear pods and placed them on the table. Alfred sat on the opposite chair while she discussed with him.

'E invites are sent to all, my notes are ready, and the presentation is being prepared. Conference room has been booked and what else remains..'

'I think you must call Mr Benjamin and invite him personally.'

Olivia plugged in the ear pod as the phone rang again, she pressed the button to accept the call, leaning by the bean bag, she answered the call.

'Hello Shawn'

'Good evening ma'am'

'I received this mail from you about tomorrow morning, what is it about?'

He posed a question.

'Actually its better if I disclose the subject, at the venue, but it would be of great help to me, if you try to attend it.' She answered staring into the laptop screen.

'And what else?' his curiosity translated into voice.

'Great..' she gave long pauses, making changes in the presentation while speaking to him.

'Seems like I've called on the wrong time'

'..No' this was also announced giving a pause, which eventually led him to cut the call furious about how he wasn't able to gather any information about her, which he had been trying from a long time. May be a reunion party with Ryan, it was. His mind created few lame guesses and many logics to prove those guesses right in his head.

She shut down the laptop, finally after completing the presentation. Scratching her scalp from a messy bun, she adjusted the cushion and fell asleep on the couch, hanging her legs from the arm of it. Alfred walked out from the kitchen to see her sleeping. He switched of the lights of the living room and spread a blanket over her. He checked the alarm, and walked down into his room to sleep.

****

8:17 AM

Wednesday

Passing through the rottened hearts and coward ears,
Spineless conscience and thankless tears,
Let my words percolate through your eyes,
To reach your soul surrounded with lies!
The feeble faith under the delusion,
Accountability burnt down, humanity deep frozen,
The storm of era was too charged?

Or our believes held very hard?
For the faith which was supposed to be preserved,
Is lying underneath within dust and dirt!
It has become very weak to survive,
Creedless! No reason to live otherwise!
We are all purposefully created you and I,
Solely of a duty to worship the most high,
Rest all is here and gone tomorrow,
Lest it be breeze of joy, of clouds of sorrow,
Let's cleanse it with patience, prayers and apologies,
In these blessed darkness, do forgive!
I pray almighty to strengthen my faith very hard.
Until and after, my soul and corpse are spread apart.

Closing the diary, she stretched her arms and yawned once again. Past night was spent with not so sound sleep, still she needed lots of courage to face the crowd, luckily she felt ready for it. Pushing her feet into the flip flops, she plodded along the stairs, to freshen up. Pushing the door in, she saw her ironed dress, hangered on the rod. It was a baby pink top and off white bell bottom. Alfred had already prepared for her big day and she was satisfied with the performance. Heading towards the washroom, she slid open her closet to throw a glance on some more dresses from her collection. Amongst the many her mind short listed only two dresses, the factors that contributed to rejection of all other dresses, was that she just wanted to dress up, but not beautify herself, for the one whose praises mattered had abandoned her long ago. Without an intention to impress, she just wanted to dress suitably according to the situation. Running her fingers on the sleeves of dresses, her mind decided in a while, that she would wear teal coloured ankle length bodycon dress with an overcoat. That would surely suit the occasion, she jumped into the bathroom, had a quick shower, blow dried her hair after putting on a bathrobe. After twenty minutes the mirror of her room was blessed to show a graceful reflection of a twenty eight year old woman, teal dress and her light brown hair tied into a pretty chignon. A neat stroke of black winged liner on her large hazel eyes. The dense pigmented curve shaped brows contrasted with the mauve lipstick she applied. Long silver hangings in her ears and white heels completed the look. There were changes in the reflections over the past years, she wasn't as thin as before, double chin and an inch baggy tummy sneaked through, making a small curve in the shaped wear. Yet the confidence in her eyes and faith in her heart were heavier on the weigh of beauty parameters. She twinkled looking at her reflection, pinning up the falling strands of hair, its simply human nature of being impressed by beauty, especially if it belongs to oneself. This latent admiration was interrupted by a knock on the door.

This was the third time Alfred knocked her door and called her for breakfast. She opened the door and tramped down the stairs, with utmost elegance. Alfred's eyes glared her continuously feeling proud for her daughter. Ignoring his sight on herself she sat on the chair gently, to have her breakfast.

'Isn't it funny that a human treats himself or herself the way he thinks, the clothes he puts on, the tasks he completes.' Alfred thought as he saw days, Olivia wore joggers and munched the salads bent over the bean bag, and her wildly messy hair. 'Where's my silver watch?' she asked wiping the fork between her teeth so as not to spoil her lipstick. He rushed to the study and bought it along her handbag. 'Wonder how it made its way to the study?' she shrugged her shoulders, raising the brows taunting.

'Two days ago, you left it while video chatting with Camilla.' She did not speak while being reminded, as the burden of anxiety had started to grow in her chest. She hastened after then and proceeded to the car, carrying her bag and putting on sunglasses. It was already nine and at dot half past nine her meeting was supposed to start. A freely jammed route to the office would consume straight fifteen minutes and the remaining time would suffice the period to settle her panicking. Alfred started the car, it swept through the smooth path. She caught a glimpse of his dressing, it was a red checkered shirt and blue denim.

'I didn't send you the invite, but if you attend it, it might add to the crowd and as you know, I want the maximum people to join me.' She explained being mean.

'Ok, as per your wish' he answered, primarily focussing on driving speedily.

'What about Mrs Agatha, can we take her along..' she proposed sarcastically.

His face reddened with embarrassment and he raced the car, almost banging into some Jeep.

'Oh I see' she answered politely, kicking herself inside for being so cunning.

****

It was a room temperature environment in the conference room, containing a huge table and lots of chairs. Butterflies launched into her lungs like that of rockets, as she saw all of her colleagues getting seated one by one. Starting from the right corner, Sir Benjamin, Mrs Sophie, Alfred, Neil, Alex, Camilla, Katie, Ciara and exactly facing opposite to her was Mr Shawn, whose face narrated how anxious he was to let the cat out of the bag. The other side was occupied by the office members as well. Taking a sip of water, she peeked at the clock, it was nine- thirty five am.

Laptop was connected to the projector, ruffling the pages around, she dropped her pen in the mid, and placed it on the table. Her heart skipped a beat, as she started.

'Good morning to all my seniors, colleagues and friends'

At the completion of this phrase, she could sense all the eyes glued to her face. This wasn't the first time she was facing the crowd, yet it was different. Camilla gestured thumbs up with both the hands and a smile, that encouraged her. But she smile back at her, and hence continued. Pressing the remote button, she turned off the lights, this helped her in focussing on the subject. No doubt she was a good orator, but this time it was entirely different. The topic and the crowd to which she addressed.

'First of all I would like to express gratitude for investing your precious time on my call. It makes me feel pleasured.' After this, as instructed the lights were switched of, to gather attention on the screen. The first projected slide, said *welcome.* Turning the lights off, she increased her focus,

'To begin with, I would like to give you an example of a zecho dot sixth generation.' The second slide swept, projecting the image of a circular device, that was being mentioned by her.

'This is a device, an electronic device invented by a company. This product has been launched at the given time etc. But is that information suffice for the sustainable usage?' without waiting for another moment of silence she answered the question by her own,

'No! We are provided with a user friendly manual, that describes the two big things as follows; why has it been produced and that how is it supposed to be used' On the discussion of zecho, that was his presented gift, Shawn grew even more restless to learn what was she up to.

CHAPTER TWENTY-NINE

'About its quality, along all the do's and don'ts, it's features, sound system, battery back up, the warranty period and what not, similarly I would love to share a bit of my study which I've done in the past months, we as a human being are also a product. A creation of the producer, a product of creator which we all cannot deny' she slid to the next slide of the presentation which displayed the heading '*CONCEPT OF GOD*'. Ciara's phone beeped in the mean while.

'My research is based on to fetch the one track that leads me to the ultimate facts and realities of the purpose of creation and the way to lead it. Just like the producer of this zecho dot has published a book alongside for the easy understanding and usage, I believe that the creator who has created these whole huge universes, who has created you and me into beautiful faces must have sent us the guide to walk through our life. This route is not so easy to be tracked, for it is underlying the million myths, deviations, objections and rejections damped over it in as the centuries passed stamping and almost ruining the meaning with which it had been revealed'

She swiped right to change the slide, that read ' *need of research*'

'We are sitting comfortable in our homes, working, earning, stuffing our stomachs, completing our desires. Are we really satisfied with our quality of lives? In this dark room I urge you to ask your hearts this question. We are just existing by sticking the Newton's third law to our hearts, i.e. every action has an equal and opposite reaction. Action, reaction this is how we are even breathing. Subconsciously chasing our ideals that we won't accept we do, but we do. And who are our ideals? For god's sake! Where are we heading towards. She has done a thing, I'll do something better than that, he lives a life like that, and I must get provision of the same. He's got a cool life, I must grab something cooler even. No! We need to put a biggest full stop to this approach. Look at the sun, the moon, the stars, this is the investment God has done exclusively on us, we need to understand it's rights and be dutiful and grateful to him. This point where I invite you is the midpoint of impracticality and materialism. There has to be an explained system of life, of every action we do. We will never feel the need of imposing a system on us until we make an effort to glance out of our comfort zones and look at how the world is suffering from injustice and iniquity, news flooded with crimes, poverty, domestic issues. Being a part of this world, how can we act ignorant to these innumerable problems taking place in the world?'

She played a video of the population of countries suffering injustice under superpowers, orphan and homeless children, that was sure to melt the toughest of hearts.

'If we try to feel their pain, their agony then we can surely understand the immediate need of revolution, to change the systems we have evolved with to grow in our circle, that routine of life which develops us and is only beneficiate to us. Instead we must acquire that system, which makes us responsible, compassionate and above all evolve us to succeed as a society.' She had prepared notes, but chose not to look into it, these were the words that came to her from heart.

She took a pause, to change the slide. This was the page filled with a few questions and their answers to it. Throwing her glance at the crowd, she noticed Ciara, typing in her phone, Alex sitting with hanging arms. She gulped the stage fear, confidently raised her chin, tucking in the hair strand, that was exactly in its place.

'I know my beliefs are not enough to prove my words, I have this solved questionnaire. This set of complaints and questions was recorded by me when I was feeling the lowest after a series of tragic events I passed through. And one by one I found answers to all of them, in a peaceful religion. Without any intention to share my personal life with you, my only aim is to spread this mislaid aspect of life. These phrases or questions might appear meaningless when we are tied in to the wealthiest cloths, but at some or the other point in life, when we are low, our conscience questions us, our weakened faith complaints about it, and our heart grows curious to find the answers. Camilla can you please read out the questions for me?' she asked. Lost into some where, Camilla lifted her head and walked near her hesitatingly.

Facing the screen, her voice shook as she started to read and turned into bold one 'number one, I am lonely'

' "And We have already created man and know what his soul whispers to him, and We are closer to him than (his) jugular" this is an statement from a scared book, which had beat all other scriptures in infinite terms. Here we stands for the creator himself, who calms his creation by claiming to be nearer than his jugular vein, closer than a person's heart itself. Isn't it soothing even to hear that your creator is closest to you also in your worst times.' She read out the quoted statement from the screen and explained further on her own.

As she stopped speaking Camilla continued, 'Number two, I am a failure'

' "Believers are successful", this is such an inviting statement to the religion of. that's it. The creator of the galaxy says you, promises you, that if you believe you are successful. What more do you want' She continued to read and explain.

'Number three, Life is too difficult'

' " With every difficulty is an ease" this statement belongs to the sacred book.

'Number four, No one can help me.'

"It's upon us to help the believers." The God himself takes the responsibility only on a simplest condition that we believe in him.'

'Number five, ' I don't have much'

' "For those who believe and righteous things is a generous provision"

'Number six, I am always sick'

"We have sent down the holy book as healing"

'Number seven, I am overburdened.'

"Lord will not burden a soul more than it can bear."

'Number eight, I feel lost'

"And he found you lost so guided you"

'Number nine, I am too ugly'

"We've created the man in the best make and appearance."

'Number ten, who created me?'

"We created man from sounding clay, from mud moulded into shape"

'Number eleven, why created me?'

"I have not created the jinn and humankind except that they worship me"

'Number twelve, Who created the sun, the moon, the skies and lands, the stars and seas, the mountains and the oceans, and all the creatures?' Camilla finished reading.

"It is He Who created the night and the day, and the sun and the moon; all (the celestial bodies) swim along, each in its rounded course.' She sat on the chair to drink a few sips of water, but accidentally spilled some on her face, which flowed through her nose and her eyes. Pulling a napkin from the purse, she wiped her face, till Camilla spoke.

'Number thirteen, how does the sun rise on its timing and the moon disappears beneath the clouds?' the bold and curious tone of Camilla remained constant, and she seemed to be surprised by the doubts which were always overlooked. As Camilla finished reading the question, Olivia looked at the screen, it was time to change the slide and she also decided to increase the brightness, as the spilled water was blurring the vision. To read it clearly, she swiped up the button on the remote. Due to the unclear vision, she accidentally switched on the lights of the room, while dabbing the napkin on her eyes. She opened the eyes to see, the lights turned on and as her sight travelled through the table Alex was looking at watch, Neil's head tilted back, Ciara sat with hanging arms, Mrs. Sophie was spotted yawning, Shawn used his phone under the table and was caught red handed giggling over something. Katie could be seen twirling a pen, Sir Benjamin was doodling, slouched on the chair and Alfred was sitting up with furrowed brow, making points of the lecture. Every body erected their postures as the lights turned on, Pretending to be impressed by the program. Olivia turned back at the screen, it was a message from Shawn that was mistakenly projected on the screen, as she had connected the phone screen to the laptop. *'I was wondering day and night that what is this lady up to, lol, spirituality lessons, these are the same questions that I had informed you earlier about. Just can't believe that her Dr said she's doing great.'*

Shawn was still into his phone, as she turned back after reading, the whole room had till now gone through the message, and she was waiting for him to lift his head up and observe the blunder he did. And he did. ' Oh NO I am sorry!!,' he jumped up from his place and eyes popped out after a moment to analyse the sin. 'I was about to send this in the group, and I mistakenly sent this to you. It isn't related to you in any terms' He opened his phone to unsent the message, and left the room bowing his head down, followed by giggling Ciara swinging in the Bob cut hair she had. Mr. Benjamin pushed the chair by his legs and walked gently out, looking at her, without speaking a word. Mrs. Sophie smiled and patted her shoulder, ' You looked absolutely heavenly gorgeous' And walked striding before them.

Camilla neared her as she sat dragging the chair, with her head hung on the fingers of elbowed upright hand. She closed her eyes to digest the moment of insult and embarrassment to cross her mind. Her lips pressed tight, and a period of block hit her mind, she wasn't in a state to analyse or accept one more failure, that too in this way.

****

Alfred glued his ear to the wooden door of her room, post they returned from the office soon after the meeting ended abruptly. No she didn't marched up the stairs stamping all the way, nor she flowed a single drop of tear all the way. There was an expected silence in the car, and the anticipated rejection to the lunch, he offered to get from the way back. She said that he could get for him, if he wanted but she was stuffed and would like to have it later in the evening. As soon as they reached home, leaving her belongings on the table unfastening the sandals, she walked up as calm as ice. Like nothing happened. This attitude of her had started to freak Mr Alfred. Waiting for half an hour he climbed up and knocked on the door. There was no response. He couldn't hear any sound from the room as well. There was higher chance that she could be sleeping. He walked down, deciding to wait for some more time, thinking about the dinner menu.

Dusting the Study room, he felt the buzz of a phone vibrating from her purse. Unzipping it he picked it up to see Camilla's call. Unhesitatingly he answered the call, ' Hello Olivia, Why aren't you replying to the text messages?'

'Hi, it's Alfred this side.'

'Oh hello uncle, how are you doing?'

'How's Heidi' both questioned simultaneously ignoring which she enquired about Olivia ' Where's Olly?'

'I think she sleeping, after all it was a bad day spent'

'Are you sure she's sleeping?' she had a doubt on the father in laws report.

'Not really, I knocked the door to check, but neither did she answer nor I heard any sound. She does like this in her lows, I'll handle it.'

'I think I've known her a bit more than you, and her unstable mental health can be a risk, you must check her immediately, is the room locked?'

'Yeah, but I'll look for the extra keys, bye' he flung the phone on the chair and rushed to the kitchen, pulled the upper cabinet door and picked up a bunch of keys. Flinging on the stairs he unlocked the door, switched on the lights and saw her lying on the bed with blanket spread over her feet and her face partially buried in the cushion. He exhaled a breath of relief, because she was sleeping. It was a deep sleep as she didn't move upon switching on the light. Standing on the threshold, his footsteps involuntarily pulled towards her. He neared her, with an affectionate and fatherly emotion in his eyes. Her dull skin and dark circles expanded the soft corner he had in his heart for her. He didn't dare to sit beside her, he could actually, but she would never like the idea. He stood adoring his doll, and noticed the vibration in the blanket. 'What was that?' He thought. Walking towards the other end he lifted the blanket, he could spot her shivering limbs. He immediately closed the fan, and called her ' Olivia, Olivia!' he sat by the end of pillow, moving her, shaking and knocking, pulling out his phone from the pocket of denim, he dialled to Camilla again.

'She's shivering, what do I do?' he grimaced.

'Oh no, it must be an epileptic attack, check for medicine blisters around her, I doubt she might, she has become so unpredictable, God.' She yowled.

'I know that! Shall I call the ambulance?'

'Start a stopwatch to note down the duration, lay her straight and remove any sharp and hard objects out of her reach.'

'Done' he picked up the scissors from the mattress and placed it on the shelf, scrolled through the phone and tapped on the stopwatch.

'Make sure that her airway is clear depending on her posture and clothing'

'Oh yeah she's lying straight.'

'Don't put anything in her mouth'

'Fine' he placed the phone on the table and tried calling him. This disease had been treated but not cured, unlike the people in her life, it was destined to be with her life long. He stretched his hand to the table, and grabbed the water bottle. Pouring the water in his hand, he spilled some on her face, to awaken her. Making way through her long hair, his wrinkled fingers touched her scalp, to lift her head, while stroking his thumb on her short forehead. All through this he remained calling her, every moment felt heavier on his heart. Her unresponsiveness was freaking him out. She lay idle with her limbs hanging loosely, as she had no control over them. A drop of sweat flowed from the forehead through the back of ear to reach his neck. He didn't care to switch on the fan. It was getting harder for him to sit cross legged, due to the bump on his stomach he had. He turned her face side to side, holding her jaw, there was no response. 'My baby' he broke down on the spot, pouring his head on her, lifting her chin. The panic took over him, he couldn't differentiate between the drop which poured from his eyes and the sweat that dropped from his forehead. His frozen hands, were trembling as he bent over attempting to touch, her wrist, to check the pulse and there after he dropped her hand, stopped calling her name as well.

'Hello you there? what happened uncle, why did stop calling her name?' Camilla wailed as she heard silence on the call. 'Camillaaaaa' he cried.

CHAPTER THIRTY

'She's alive, but not responding, what do I do?' he sobbed.

'Okay, hold on I'll call the ambulance.' She decided to make the arrangement as she realised, Alfred wasn't in a condition to work quickly. Alfred sat side legged on the floor, placing her head in his lap, while she lay down unconscious, her eyes closed tight and jaw held firm. The shivering had stopped, but he continued calling her name. His thin quavering voice and breathy noise had started to echo in the house. This was the moment when his heart wanted to believe in the creator, she narrated about. He wanted to hold her feet and apologise, for making her life a living hell, at a very small age. He knew at that point that he wasn't completely responsible for it, but he had the bigger share. And he wanted to repent for all the wrongdoings. Was there a scope for that? He thought weeping, looking up into the sky though there was a barrier of the ceiling. He needed forgiveness and mercy, his daughter needed it too. He felt pity on her. How lifeless body it appeared. He just needed someone to roll a magic stick over her daughter, that her life becomes peaceful and happier. It wasn't possible for an old aged father to look at her daughter in this state. 'OLIVIA!' he shrieked, loudest this time. Wiping the rolling tears, he patted on her cheeks, until she regained consciousness.

Her fingers trembled and eye lashes blinked, with furrowed brows. No she didn't open her eyes yet, but she would. Alfred switched off the stopwatch, it was a duration of twelve minutes and thirty seven seconds. He couldn't believe his eyes, it appeared as though hours had passed. He raised her head, close to his chest, as she loosed unconsciousness, part by part, and kissed her wrist, pressing her hand against his face, weeping overwhelmed by the mixed emotions.

****

Camilla had rushed to her place, unable to avail the ambulance service, leaving Heidi and John at home. Thankfully, by then she had regained her conscious. After having the prescribed tablets, the girls had a conversation, in an attempt to make her feel comfortable after an embarrassing day spent. John called her innumerable times in half an hour, complaining about being unable to pacify Heidi. And hence she left, resisting constantly, as Olivia tried her best to persuade her to have dinner along her before leaving.

****

The next morning, Alfred brought hot coffee from the downstairs, on her wish. She was in the gallery wearing grey oversized t shirt and a black pyjamas and her tangled open hair, sitting on the puffy stool. It was an accompanied sound sleep, Alfred sat all night in her room, while she slept. And of course due to the medications effect, she slept for nine long hours. Taking the mug from the tray, she gestured him to sit along with her. He was sure, that she won't go to the office, this day. He sat placing the tray on the end of floor, looking outside it. The view wasn't that of a beaches, but it was soothing at the moment. Breaking the attraction of positive vibes session from the nature, and the silent conversation between her heart and soul, Alfred interrupted.

'Was there a plan B in your strategy?' he put forward, with stronger thin voice.

She took a moment to join the conversation mentally, ' I never had one, there was just plan A, and if no one is interested in my faith being empowered, than that was my courtesy to invite them all to the call of peace, it's well and good that they are not interested. Their rejection doesn't deviate me from my path.'

'Good to see you determined enough. Don't you think it would be great only if you broaden your perception' He behaved like an intellectual person.

'Perception towards what?' she asked confused, taking first sip of the coffee.

'Towards your initiative'

'It's not an initiative, it's reverting back, a call for the human mankind.'

'It's for the human mankind, right? so take a better platform to reach the world, not just these office folks.' He continued to explain.

'Better platform?'

'The world is your stage, Olly. Your message to the world is a white letter of spirituality. The world doesn't long for such letters anymore. And you've seen this yourself yesterday at the office.'

'Then what?' she asked puzzled. Like a soul starving for feed, just like a daughter lost in the chaos and crowd, longing for a helping hand from her father.

'Why not circulate this white letter in a coloured envelope' he suggested curving a promising smile. This help of his had sparked the long back extinguished love of a father in her heart.

'Then let's get on another mission, till these counted breaths come to an end.' she smiled through sipping coffee.

****

'Check this out, your book has crossed all the records of this publishing house. Can't believe this!' Camilla exclaimed.

'Yeah I checked the sales today morning.' Said Olivia.

'Congratulations, I can't wait to get the success party from you.'

'Anytime, my love, how's Heidi?' She laughed.

'She's great and calls you Olly, when I show her birthday pictures,'

'I just can't wait to hear that!' she smiled heartily as it reminded her of Asher.

'I think she woke up, Ill call you later'

'Take care and bye.'

'Bye' Closing the phone app, she clicked on the text messages, to go through the unread messages. It was Shawn, ' Tonnes of congratulations to you ma'am'

'Who was it Olivia?' Alfred walked in from the his room.

'Camilla! She called to congratulate me' A slight smile took over her face, while praising herself.

'Isabella called me, said she would join us at the lunch.' He informed, sitting on the couch in the living room.

'I'll get the noodles prepared.'

'Tell me if you need some help' he offered assistance.

'Oh no, I'll do it.'

Placing the phone on the counter, she pulled the packet of noodles and got a wok from the drawer. Chose the veggies from the refrigerator to prepare the lunch. Just then the bell rang and Alfred checked the door. It was Isabella, she had lost the case in the court and was banned from the TV screens. She lost her power and eventually got better ties with the family. The reunited members included Bill, James and Clara as well. Many things had changed in the period of past year, which included relations between the daughters and father had improved a lot over the time such that she accepted Alfred's suggestion of inserting the white letter in a coloured envelope before circulating it. Olivia wrote a book named, ' Fate Over Faith: The Feed For Soul'. Again taking help of the library she spent sleepless nights and restless days to complete her debut in writing and thankfully it was an unbeatable success. Heidi turned one year old two months ago, on the day her book was released. However Ryan never turned up to till date.

'Shall I help you with the cup cakes?' Isabella entered into the kitchen.

'It's ok she blended the batter in a jar, after locking the lid and pressing her palm against it, while she ground. After a few moments as she stopped the machine. 'Why did you keep the hand, despite of locking the lid of the jar' Isabella asked.

'That's the amount of trust issue I have.' She replied seriously. Isabella turned back to collect the cutlery.

A while later as they sat on the dining chairs, having lunch, Isabella recalled, 'I still remember, mommy used to prefer the dry saucy noodles and dad, he loved the soupy noodles.'

At which Olivia joined, 'Yeah, earlier I used to love the soupy type too, but later I realised that once the flavoured soup gets over, leftover noodles become tasteless. Isn't it just like life, a concentrated and devoted system makes the life flavoured till the end, but immoral activities makes an unflavoured life.' Just then her phone beeped, it was a new mail.

She clicked it on while eating, 'What's it' Isabella asked.

'An invite from the grey man show' Olivia shrugged her shoulders, taking another spoon.

'No! Please don't!' she exclaimed. 'I mean that's the biggest mistake I made in my career.'

'I think you must go.' Alfred suggested while chewing food.

'Let's see' she nodded.

****

Camilla walked carefully to the ringing bell, as the toys were spread all over the floor. She pulled in the door and john entered, greeting her with a pleasant smile. Before they could engage in a lovey-dovey conversation, Heidi took baby steps towards the superhero of her life. He crouched with opened arms and a heartily smile, as she approached him. Camilla had her lips curved more than the two, witnessing the small and greatest blessings of the life at a time. On the basis of physical characteristics, she was a perfect blend of both her parents, Golden hair and thin lipped like john, dusky complexion and thick brows of Camilla. The couple sat on the chairs having cherries in the lawn, discussing about the hot topics, while Heidi played around them.

'I'm so glad, that things are finally falling in place, for Olly. The thing which satisfies me is no the innumerable number of copies her book sold, it is the mended broken ties with her family, with Mr. Alfred. Its soothes my eyes how she remains happier.'

'I have a guilt to confess' he said with moist eyes.

'What?' she was anxious to know.

'We must not have asked Dad to live at her house, neither when she was away, nor after she returned.' Listening to this she agreed guiltily, 'I know..'

'That time, I was materialistic, now after reading her book, I am looking forward to study spirituality and focus on my deeds, instead of judging others. Who am I to judge anyone? I insist you to read the book, it's indeed a turner of hearts.'

'Yeah sure, this weekend without fail. Thinking of Olivia I suppose, there might still be voids in her heart, of Asher and Ryan. It is clear before her eyes about Asher, but about Ryan, I can bet you that however hard she might be trying to overcome, a part of her would actually await Ryan until her last breath.' John threw some light in the depth.

'No, to be honest I don't think so, she's become stronger then our imagination. I just pray, that nothing breaks her now. And if Ryan's return breaks her, then it's better that he never comes back. After all, he abandoned her in the worst times, there's no meaning of his return now.

'She also got an invitation for interview on the grey man show' she added.

'Oh no, I don't think' he said in disbelief.

'Why would she boast, come on! Her book is really breaking records. But she said she would think about to accept or not. Because Isabella suggested her, not to attend'

'She should go, in my opinion' john suggested.

'Who asked your opinion, Mr!' she teased him. He made a not so offended look, and she laughed, dropping her head on the elbow resting on the chair, staring straight into his eyes and adoring her perfect family.

****

Alfred trudged down the stairs, flowing his arm high all the way, holding a hung dress in the hanger, 'this dress for the interview tomorrow?' While Olivia was busy dusting her study.

'I'll get my dress ready, I think you must rest now' she suggested.

'I missed doing this for you, when you all were children, I got an opportunity to do it now, so let me.' He confessed smiling.

Later at night, Olly broke her sleep to the persistent coughs, yawning like a roar, with eyes lids glued, she walked down, there was he, leaning on the couch, wearing piles of coats and mufflers, with a heavy chest and wheezing breath, he was falling shot of breaths.

'Didn't you take the medicines on time, dad?' she asked while yawning.

He nodded in negativity, unable to speak.

'You must have taken, where is it, shall I get it from the pharmacy?'

'No, it was in the medicines box, but now I can't find it' he said in a louder and quick, falling short of breath. She walked in his room and searched through the shelves, grabbed the medicines box to check, flipping the blisters she couldn't find one. She placed it back, and her sight fell on the a smaller box of medicines lying on the lower shelf. That was the medicine he needed, but below the box was a photograph turned upside down. She made an effort to walk back and pick it up, it was Victoria's photograph in black and white film.

Keeping it just the way it was she walked out handing over the medicine to him. Sat opposite to him on the bean bag, staring upon him. What was it? She thought. She pondered. She focussed. A creature of creator, falling short of every breath. This tiniest observations, made her faith firm and steady.

'I'll pray that you get well soon' she said, standing straight, proceeding towards the staircase. His lips took a formal curve, and he continued using the inhaler. She turned back standing at the stair and continued. 'because, this disease may expiate your sins. if this happens, then how will you be punished on the resurrection day.' She added and marched with her bowed head into her room.

'Your mom, she was this since the day one Olly. Uneducated, uncultured conservative. It's just me who handled her for such a long period.' Alfred narrated stretching his trunk, counting the biggest achievements of life.

'The creator to whom I have submitted myself and before whom I have surrendered myself, asks to respect my parents and that's the reason I am doing that. I remember everything dad, I just can't forget anything.' She stood up and walked towards the Kitchen to keep the empty cup of coffee.

'Who am I to make decisions like the creator on his land. But trust me if I were asked to endanger Alfred as husband or save Alfred as father, I can't promise that my dilemma will come to an end by then.' A tear dropped from her eye and she continued looking at him.'

'I remember how fast you drove to the school on my examination day. I remember the cake you bought on my birthday despite being tired. I remember the pink gown you bought me a night before Christmas, though we had poor financial conditions. I remember how you stole your sight, after I yelled on you. I remember how you carried me in you're arms to the hospital when I fell from a height. I remember how you saved me from mom's scolding when I lost my new lunchbox.' Till now the tear drops had increased and it turned into sobbing

'I can't choose, I can't judge your deeds, I still can't forget mommy crying endlessly over your betrayal, I can't forget the endlessly weeping nights, when I had to console her like a mother consoling her child, I can't forget you abusing her for years, I can't let go of the sight of the strongest lady of the world shattering into million pieces before the tiniest eyes, I can't never forget her hiding the pain in a moment from her eyes before her four children, as she caught you red handed infinite times just because we don't disrespect you. I still remember your screams with which you made her feel powerless. I can't forget your torture dad.'

****

Laying on the bed in the dark room a night before the show with Olivia, Ryan turning and tossing on. He opened the notes app in his phone and started to type. '*Tomorrow is a big day indeed. I am going to meet her after two long years. Had I been truthful to her since the day one, thing wouldn't have ruined midway. How cursed am I, unfortunate to not even touch my child, my son once. For the mistakes of Isabella I punished her, I know how everyday she might have died to live. I lived the same way Olivia. Trust me Olly. I still love you. I avenged Isabella through my show, but the reason for continuing the show is to call you back into my life. I am nothing without you Olly. I am ready to apologise. I need one chance. Hoping to reunite with you.*'

CHAPTER THIRTY-ONE

'What's going on'

'Nothing much, preparing mentally for the interview.'

'I said you should not'

'I don't know why, my heart feels to go'

'All the best, I am sorry I Wont be able to make it tomorrow'

'No probs!'

'Take care'

'Peace be upon you'

These messages were exchanged between the sisters. On Friday midnight. Olivia texted Billy, Clara and James too, an invite for accompanying her, whereas Camilla, John and Alfred had confirmed to join her.

****

This was comparatively a warmer day, in the winter months, Alfred sat on the driving seat silently awaiting Olivia. Among the things that would never change was her taking so long to get ready. She locked the door and rushed dropping the keys in the phone. Olivia was going curious to know that everything between them was ok. Were her words rude? But she was correct, the fire of avenging, the struggle of her mother all life wasn't a small thing to let go. But taunting and teasing wasn't the solution out to it. Who is she to count all his sins? She too was flawed. All the thoughts floated in her mind, until she observed the flyover and she's going to give the interview, thought popped up, splashing all other thoughts. A black overcoat, on a white collared shirt, a bun of brown hair and bright red lipstick. She appeared like an entrepreneur, but the strength she had in herself, the courage to battle several wars, she was a in a pretty delicate thin lipped face. Alfred parked the car in the parking, behind several cars. She walked with least pride and utmost confidence, a true definition of elegance. This was a huge radio station, with some more people than she expected. A man with black hair and large specs welcomed her followed by a handshake. Alfred walked beside her. She was directed to the auditorium. There was a glass cabin with two seats, presently she sat on the chair from the audience. Camilla and John were already there. An impressive surprise was noting the presence of all her office mates seated in the audience. She gulped a clog of nervousness as her palms started to shiver. She exasperated from a pout fidgeting through her fingers, noting which Camilla, rose from her chair and sat beside her. Alfred had taken his place on the other side of her. 'All the best, queen' she threw her arms along, 'Thank you Mérida!' she shrugged. The day she resembled Mérida by all means, her red hair and blue eyes. Her heart raced upon entry of the same specs person and *THE GREY MAN*. He was grey! That too a metallic grey. A jersey costume covering his body, and a robotic metal mask over his head, with windows for his eyes to sneak. The windows were exactly shaped and sizes to his eyes, such that his lashes must have forcibly bended to move out of the window. The man welcomed her to the seat in the glass cabin flooded with mics and speakers. The grey man took his place shaking hand with her. She took her place with a undoubted clearing of throat. After being seated she realised there were water bottles on the table too. The man adjusted the mic near her mouth, while the grey man did for himself. As he did that for him, she saw his eyelids were painted grey, not revealing even the skin complexion.

After making the arrangements, he walked out of the room after instructing her about the live telecast of the show and hence confidence and fluency was encouraged and minute stammering also needed to be avoided.

Switching the several buttons of the mic, he started, 'A warm welcome from your own grey man to the grey man show, I am here fulfilling the promise I made with you all. And now's the time I introduce to our guest at the grey man show, a sensation in the readers and writers club, the writer of book, fate over faith: the feed for soul, in short beauty with brains, welcoming Miss Olivia Whitaker. "*Good morning and a very warm welcome, Miss Olivia Whitaker, on the behalf of the grey man show listeners, I would like to admit, that we are glad to have you on the show. How are you doing today?*"'

'*Peace be upon you, good morning, I am as excited as all of you, it's truly an honour to be a part of this show*' she nodded smiling at the opening statement that was comforting, and she was preparing for the next question.

"*Great. Without wasting anytime, I would love to jump to the Q n A session. So it's as simple as it sounds, we'll enquire about some ideas and you just have to answer it. Beginning with an easier one, what's the significance behind the signature style of your greetings?*"

She smiled needlessly of nervousness, '*Peace, this is the best thing one can wish for everyone. These are the salutations, of a sacred religion. And once you realise that every being in this world is in a long race to achieve one or the other worldly beauty, had they've been told that they actually chase the peace they find after achieving those standards, they would change their directions, their goals. So isn't it so thoughtful to wish a person at first of which they need desperately.'*

'A logical and unrealistic approach, at the same time.'

'Difference in heights of perceiving' she replied not so offended at the comment.

'Moving on to next question, our audience was keen to know, why have you chosen a dry subject for research and studying, this talent of writing could have been used to focus on varied fields.'

Without a moment to think, she started, sitting with crossed legs,' *let's consider that there's some person x, who doesn't have the sleeping times fixed, mindless unhealthy eating, a careless lifestyle, no morals etc. What would you work on, on him getting systematic? Or on the cherry of his cake? Likewise I chose to work on the former as any person with a common sense would do.'*

A moment of silence and he switched on his mic. '*To be honest that was meaningful, the next question awaiting your answer is, what is the religion that you are promoting? Is this created by your own or you are inviting to follow a readymade creed?'* he placed the card on the table on which questions were noted.

'The path of faith which I've chosen after a study of almost two years, has been blamed and Bad named in majority of the world. So this is my attempt to propagate this without mentioning it's name that has been stored in the bad books of many for no absolute reason.' She completed her statement in short, though many explanations created a pressure to speak.

'If you claim to represent a true theology, the ideologies you've mentioned, apparently I can't see you immersed in it, as per your physical appearance. Because a rule book which

directs you about the etiquettes of basic activities, like how to eat, drink and sit, has a description about your wardrobe too.'

She didn't have an answer already in her mind for this, but the explanations popped up, as she chose to justify. *'Consider one more situation, if there's fire in a place, and I realise that the crowd is at risk lives and homes, what do I do? Wear a fireproof costume, get a safe place for myself, find a path to my home. Reach my home and then announce? Or shout and let people know so that everyone becomes safe while I make an escape simultaneously. You think that the producer or the creator of this universe, has invested a sun, moon, stars, land, water, sent down books and also the role models to follow! Just to selfishly acquire knowledge. No. He laid down such a systematic nature, a huge investment for the mankind.'* Her hands stopped waving in the air, as she finished speaking. '*The most important thing'* she added, '*My creator doesn't ask for a 100 percent, he just says good deeds over bad, then who are you and I to pass judgements.'* She shrugged.

'*What does success mean to you?'*

She unfolded the four fingers of the hand, and folded them one by one, '*The exalted lord says, belief, righteous deeds, advice of truth and advice of patience.'*

'Well said, miss Olivia! You've bashed out the stereotypes verbally, impressed with your speech'

'Thank you '

'Moving to the next round of our show "'Rumours, tumours, blames and claims"', are you ready?'

'Ready' she nodded excited about striking the first round successfully.

'There's a rumour about you that you hired your father for housekeeping at your home? Whats this level of disgrace and disrespect?'

Olivia was stunned upon listening this, no, she didn't expect this question. She just wanted to kick herself for doing such a shameful thing. Realising the time being wasted, she denied the pressure on mind, and thought the real reason, why she did that, ' *We had some issues as a family, I have seen a hard time in childhood where I would return home from my work, not sure about mommy would be alive or dead as she was traumatized because of him.*' She gave a short and petite explanation.

'*Rumour no. 2, we heard that you have even tried Killing yourself? How much percent of truth does this thing hold?*' All this time he sat still like a robot, avoiding any body movement. While she crossed her legs, opened, swung, rested elbows on table, dusted her coat, arranged her hair, made partitions in the air.

Her heart stopped pounding upon an easier question being announced. '*it's... 100 percent true*' she announced and decided not to feel guilty about not declining it.

'*Is some gender bias prevalent to you in the journey of success?*'

'*Yes but only up to a extent, that how much beautified may be the guy, he is always referred HANDSOME and however less is a women she's always BEAUTIFUL!*' she stressed on the some of handsome and full of beautiful.

'*Whats the status of your love life?*' This question gave her a creeping sensation and goosebumps. '*No comments*' her smile faded, and she was hoping for a quick change of subject.

'*What if your ex wants to reconcile? Maybe his listening this sitting somewhere in the world.*'

'*No, an absolute no.*' Sheexpressedrigidness.

'A *message for your husband?*' this watered her eyes in an instant, what would she say, taking longer breaths, she wiped the tear with her finger, and pursed her trembling lips. These questions were shaking her confidence, which developed a sense of dislike towards it, she turned her head to look out of the glass cabin, all the people were listening to her, Camilla gestured thumbs up, Alfred threw a fatherly smile and encouraging smile not offended again by him getting exposed on a national radio show. And what? Billy, James and Clara could also be spotted sitting there. James waved a super energetic hi from his place, Clara's fingers and thumb flapped opposite, indicating her to speak, and Billy's watered eyes stared emotionally at her.

'I repeat the question, do you have a message for your husband?'

Clearing the clog in throat, she voiced out quivering with trembling lips.

'Though I left the footprints very old,
there must have been
a sea to your shore,
You are not a deceiver,
I've met your soul'

As she answered, and turned her head back, she could see everyone sitting in the hall raised and clapping hands at the answer.

'Its time that we take a quick break, and I promise you to return back asap, stay tuned, at the grey man show.' He woke up from the chair, and walked out. She turned the card, provided by the director, there was no scheduled break in that. She shrugged and wiped the falling tear. It wasn't a grief, it was just a nervousness of sneaking back into the darkest room in her heart , which she had locked and preserved long ago.

Epilogue

'Thank you for the treat, but a success party is yet to be thrown' Camilla tore the chocolate wrapper for Heidi. The two were sitting on the bench in the garden and Heidi stood by her mother's side. After a long time a peaceful union of the friends took place, post dinner at the nearby park.

'Hey, have you seen this, the abrupt end of show has been making headlines' she proposed while Olivia silently nodded.

'I just hope that prediction doesn't come true. Isabella warned you not to attend the show' she continued.

'Nothing will happen' she looked at the green grass and brown earth beneath, appreciating the perfection of nature in the minute things.

'I wonder why he ended the show, may be he had dysentery' She giggled making fun of the anchor.

'He had to end the show because he had no other choice...' she spoke gazing at her palms and rubbing them together.

'But why?' Camilla wondered.

'Because my answers were sharp enough to pierce through his ego, he never expected that.'

'What? Why would he have expectations from you!' Camilla put forward.

'The day on the radio show, though not an inch of his body sneaked through the costume but I easily figured out who it was.. ' She smiled, with moist eyes.

'Who? ' she pushed her eyes almost out.

'Ryan Wilson it was.'

'How do you know that!' she jumped from the place, almost pushing Heidi.

'His body language while he walked out, His hesitation to speak without auto tune, His persistently asking about my feelings towards husband, the wetting of eyes on my answer, his wish for becoming a journalist, everything had a connection and the moment there was a power cut in the station, his voice echoed all through, there were only a few of them, I could recognise him even in a million people.

Her palms froze again, as she stared at the grass behind, Camilla wrapped her arms around her, 'I wonder how many times your fates destined to prick your heart'

'Until my faith overcomes fate' she smiled, with no tears, no hard cored heart, wrapping her arms around Camilla's. Just a longest hug.

****

Said you, not to attend the show now there are controversies, about the mysterious end of show' Isabella marched pushing in the door of her house.

'A leaf doesn't move against the will of creator, let's see whatever happens by his will' She said sitting on the bean bag, opening her diary, to make an entry after long time.

'How do I explain these astray folks,

The exploration to know the creator, makes me feel armed and unconditionally fearless '

****

'I am proud of you Olly. I m astonished of the fact that the way you concealed my identity, yet you identified me behind the iron masks. You made a right choice. You made a right decision. You don't deserve me. Let all the success be in your way. Wishing you the best life ahead. And if possible please forgive me. Also thank you for understanding me, my heart and my soul. You are right, though you're footprints were engraved on the shore of my heart, the sea waves of ego and revenge, covered them for a moment and yes, I am not a

deceiver' Ryan made a diary entry, sitting at the shore of Klive beach. A place that testimonies their love. Sliding her pictures in the phone, he attempted to forget her but failed as a tear dropped from his left eye. Clearing all the previous grudges and letting go of the misunderstandings from his heart, he sat tucked placing the phone aside, and with his right index finger, he wrote in the sand as her answer echoed in his head, *'I've met your soul'* .

****

'And the employee of the year is, Mrs Olivia, a big round of applause for the dedicated and young employee Johnsons are proud to have worked with, Miss Olivia Whitaker can I please have you on the stage, and to present the award we have Ryan Wilson' Olivia climbed up the stairs with an ear to ear grin reminiscing her hard spent days at the café coffee day and selling flowers to becoming a praised employee at a multi national company. Receiving the award she could feel her beaming smile being stalked by the ever handsome Ryan Wilson, handing over the trophy to her, gaze glued to the prize girl. 'It's an honour to work with a company, that's a dream for many, I'll make sure that I keep doing my best, for the continuity of the Johnson's pride.' She stepped down from the stage holding the trophy and sat on the her seat. Cross stare and stealthily glances on Ryan, blushed her cheeks, looking which he smiled. Trying to look away, she shrugged and turned the head away, but was it that power or attraction of love, that pulled her sight towards Ryan and a treat to his eyes as she twinkled.

The part of her right thumb that he pressed teasingly while presenting the trophy, she pressed it too, below the running water, while taking a shower. She could deny his re entry to her life, but not the memories they had. The first time they met in an award function, she relived the moments which made her heart smile, it was a beautiful phase she thought, applying shampoo on her hair. This is life. You don't get all the doors to success opened at once, but all the doors to failure can be opened at a time, like Olivia had, but with strong will power and faith if she had managed to impress her creator, it was all worth it. This is not the end. She still didn't get the healthy certificate from doctor Brett, she didn't re-join her job, that too a position that was temporarily managed by Camilla, her book made a best seller record but she didn't earn a penny, her bank accounts weren't flooding with money, there was no complete cure to epilepsy, she didn't wipe out Ryan from memories, She could never. She still remembers Asher irrespective of looking or not looking at Heidi. Her head still craved for the affectionate embraces of Ryan, she didn't have grudge against him in her heart. Yes she forgave him. Maybe the day itself when she encountered the heart wrenching betrayal. The scars were still fresh in her heart, when it comes to trust, she had no more courage to throw her heart at the risk of betrayal, after being taught a lesson by life, not once, not twice, innumerable times. Neither did she stop learning, acquiring knowledge. Apart from the standards that society has standardised, she recognised the prime cause of life, and advised it to the world.

****

She got up from the chair in the library, and proceeded towards the book shelf, sneaking from the rim of her specs, she objected, 'Katie, you checked this book just now, and placed it upside down, an effortless task it is, to keep it systematically. Had this carelessness been practiced, we wouldn't have reached the peaks' keeping the book upturned, she picked up her phone and walked out of the library to make a phone call. Meanwhile Mrs Sophie and

Camilla listened silently at her fuming.

'It's no big deal, what's wrong with her?' Katie frowned.

Camilla neared her on tippy toes and whispered, 'She has lost a child because he slept downturned, let it go even if she chants it for lifetime.'

****

For feedback and Queries contact:
ayeshamushtaq_official

www.ingramcontent.com/pod-product-compliance
Ingram Content Group UK Ltd.
Pitfield, Milton Keynes, MK11 3LW, UK
UKHW040005200726
13854UKWH00001B/42

9 798885 916035